RETURN TO STARDUST

by

JOHN KENYON

*In loving memory of my
Sister-in-law Ann,
the youngest of nine children,
who passed away
during the writing of this book.
She was one of the most courageous
And dedicated people I've known, and
she will always be in our thoughts,
our hearts and our memories.*

"Parted by death we say... Yet hand in hand they hold their eternal way."

*Words and Sculpture by Harriet Hosmer, 1953,
Clasped Hands of Robert and Elizabeth Barrett Browning*

CHAPTER 1

Young Jack Moran displayed a devilish grin while he sat in his fifth-grade classroom at the local parochial school he attended in Midlothian, Virginia. Probably no one else in the class noticed his countenance except for one of his best friends sitting in the next row, Roger, who exhibited an eerily similar expression.

The elementary school was run by Franciscan nuns, but their fifth grade English teacher was a gray-haired lay teacher by the name of Mrs. Mulligan. Old, yes, although she seemed ancient to the boys and girls as she stood at the front of the classroom or patrolled the aisles between the desks, scanning the boys. At that age, it was ALWAYS the boys. She peered through her narrow eyeglasses watching for telltale signs of inattentiveness: doodling; being on the wrong page of the lesson; or slipping a just-passed note under their assignment pad or book. The distractions and drive to deviate from the norm could be all too alluring for some students.

Jack had brought a small portable alarm clock from his mother's junk drawer, and had set it to ring at 10:45 a.m. This was precisely the time Mrs. Mulligan was expected to be going through one of the most dreaded of her English grammar lessons—diagramming sentences. Meanwhile, Roger had managed to sneak in an inoperable black tabletop rotary phone he had retrieved from his father's workshop, which was now strategically placed on the floor under his desk.

Perhaps it was divine intervention by the Greek god of satire and mockery, Momus. But at what was undoubtedly the most perfect time—how to diagram a prepositional phrase—the alarm clock went off as if it was part of a July Fourth celebration. Right on cue, Roger snatched the phone from under his desk, lifted the receiver in one swift motion and said, "Hello," in his best receptionist impersonation. He then announced in a loud voice, "It's for you, Mrs. Mulligan."

What made Mrs. Mulligan more flustered—the audacity of the jokers, or the laughter that erupted in the classroom—didn't matter to Jack or Roger. Mrs. Mulligan's first reaction was to march over to the boys and zealously tap them soundly on the head with a thimble she wore on her index finger. (Apparently, she wore it to avoid discomfort when she was writing on the chalkboard). If that were the extent of their reprimand, the boys would have said the joke was a great success and well worth the planning and effort. Unfortunately, they found themselves being marched out of the classroom, and made to stand against the wall in the school corridor as the door closed abruptly behind them.

At that point, the boys quickly fell back on their altar boy training and began to pray to the Virgin Mary that the School Principal, Sister Helen Edward, would not be patrolling the classroom corridors any time before lunch period. But oh, how quickly the gods' favor can turn, if only to amuse themselves. To their horror, a couple moments later, Jack and Roger heard from down the hall and around the corner, the distinct rattle and clank of plastic and metal of what seemed like a thirty-foot strand of rosary beads clinking like Dickens' Ghost of Christmas Past, as the disturbing sound made its way closer and closer to where the stranded juvenile offenders stood. As Sister Edward turned the corner, the boys immediately realized they were trapped in No Man's Land, with the unwelcome classroom door blocking their exit and the German Panzer Division bearing down on the two of them.

Now at that age, before any real growth spurt that would propel them into gangly teenagers, both Jack and Roger were of average height for ten-year-old's—smaller than many girls their own age, and certainly dwarf-like relative to many adults. Meanwhile, the five foot ten, broad-shouldered Sister Helen Edward seemed to them the equivalent of Ray Nitschke, the then warlike linebacker for the Green Bay Packers who terrorized NFL quarterbacks, running backs and receivers alike with a ferocious "take no prisoner" game mentality. The starched white headband under the black habit Sister Helen wore seemed to resemble the headgear of some new team entry into the NFL, without the facemask.

Unfortunately, the lack of a facemask only served to evoke more terror in Jack and Roger, as the Angel of Death's stern, penetrating eyes and red-flushed, demon-like cheeks came to within a couple feet of the two boys. With her arms condemningly folded across her broad chest, the boys were instructed to explain the circumstances that led to their incarceration in the corridor.

As Jack and Roger proceeded to tell her the truth, Jack realized that Sister Edward wasn't going to have them lashed, crucified, or thrown into a den of lions—as a way to demonstrate and instill into their classmates the power and modern relevance of the stories of the Old and New Testament. In fact, for a brief second, Jack was convinced he saw the beginning of a very small smile as she turned to cough—or perhaps to stifle a small laugh.

In the end, their only direct punishment was to stay after school and write on the blackboard one hundred times, "I shall not play practical jokes in the classroom." In addition, they had to explain to their parents why they received a C for "Behaves in Class" on the back of their report card.

In those days of the late 1960s, most Catholic elementary schools listed subject grades on one side, with the "Qualitative" indicators of school performance and behavior on the other—everything from "Penmanship" to "Listens Attentively" to "Obeys Promptly" to "Respect Others." Many child's report card that had a strong grade point average with high marks in Mathematics, English, History, and Geography could be bittersweet and deemed an afterthought if overlooked by the parental reaction to several C's on the qualitative scorecard. Typically, these low marks seemed to be territorial in being applied to the boys only, as girls seemed to be immune to the Franciscan Nun's distaste for what was from their perspective purely a behavioral disorder inherited by the male species.

***

Jack was a regular, cheerful kid, who didn't think of himself as someone particularly special or unique. Not until a number of assorted but distinct men, women and even occasionally children—very real, and exceptionally authentic—started to appear to him. Figures and characters from history both recent and past, sometimes long past. Individuals from all walks of life, some famous, some common folk. Moreover, all of them were deceased.

Or was it all his imagination? But all the characters seemed so real, and even though others couldn't see them, they seemed to have real substance. He could smell them, feel the heat coming off their bodies when they stood or sat next to him. The smells, like the clothes they wore, were what you might expect depending upon the time they roamed the earth or their occupation during their lifetime. The salty, musty, dank smell of the seafaring adventurer. The odor of horse sweat, dirt, and gunpowder from the 19th century war hero. The smell of animal skin and unwashed human flesh from the frontiersman. The smell of powder and perfume on a woman of royal blood from the early 20th century. The smell of ink and parchment paper from a famous author. It all seemed so real. He *couldn't* be dreaming or imagining it.

What also made these people feel so authentic to Jack is they didn't appear as apparitions, specters, or spirits you could see through, like in a mist or fog. They didn't float in the air or appear as only a torso or, heaven forbid, a floating head. They were of real flesh and blood, an arm he felt when someone placed it on his shoulder, or a hand he could shake and feel the grip. Or the delicate hug from a kind, almost motherly woman from long ago.

The visits first started happening to Jack shortly after he had recently turned twelve years old. It was about two months after the tragic event that cruelly transformed his average, everyday family life. An event would haunt Jack for years, and cause him to question life, death, God, and the purpose of his existence.

Before that first appearance, Jack had the typical experiences of a boy growing up in the 1960s and 70s in the suburbs outside Richmond, Virginia in the Town of Midlothian. Despite the alien-sounding name of the town, nothing unexplainable, supernatural, or out-right magical ever seemed to happen there—not that Jack was aware of. He rode his bike one mile to school from his two-story colonial saltbox home, played a mix of sports after school and on weekends at the neighborhood playground, and occasionally got in a little hot water along with his group of neighborhood friends and schoolmates.

Jack was one of the better students in his class, always did his homework, and usually studied for scheduled tests (but sometimes winged it). He was reasonably good at the three main sports – baseball, football and basketball – he and his friends played at the neighborhood playground. Jack was generally well liked, and was considered to be a pretty good-looking kid, with his dark brown hair, hazel-green eyes, "dark Irish" complexion, and cheerful smile. Like many young boys, Jack could be shy and quiet on some occasions, talkative and boisterous on others, depending upon the situation, the company he was in, and his mood. In the right situation, he was thought by some to have a quick wit and a good sense of humor.

Over time, that wit would develop into something that could range from a dry sense of humor, to clever plays on words, to downright silliness. He and his closer pals would often try for the proverbial class prank, even if it risked the potential wrath of Sister Helen Edward.

Despite escaping with their lives after the "alarm clock phone" incident, Sister Helen was not in such a forgiving a mood a few short months later. In violation of strict rules, Jack and a handful of his friends decided to leave school grounds during lunch break to walk down to the local drugstore, which in those days had an old-fashioned soda fountain. Each of the boys put up their thirty-five cents to get a smooth, delicious ice cream soda or a milkshake from Old Doc. Given it was a school day, Doc, a kindly old man who was blind in one eye, gave the boys a quizzical look as they literally leapt onto the fountain's leather bar stools.

Doc suspected that the young troopers were AWOL, but seemed happy to provide them with his velvety, creamy creations. Lost in their all too temporary freedom and exhilaration, it wasn't until Stevie, glancing up at the old copper-plated clock on the far wall, uttered in a panic-stricken voice, "Oh my God, lunch period ended five minutes ago. Sister Helen is going to kill us all!"

A vision flashed in Jack's mind of Sister Helen strangling him to death, as his body writhed in agony and the remains of his vanilla milkshake oozed from his mouth and nose as he took his last breath. They all immediately jumped off their stools and hurried to the door at the front of the store. Allan was slower than the rest to remove his slightly chubby frame from the bar stool, still savoring the last of his dark chocolate milk shake. As Jack heard him say something like, "I'd rather die happy, than not die at all!" Jack wondered if those words would be Allan's last.

The boys proceeded to run through the strip center parking lot, then along the stone wall that fronted the main road, which separated the parish church and school grounds from the commercial strip known locally as the Four Corners. They burst through the side gate and flew up the stone path that wound through the small grotto that led to the parish buildings. The outside grounds where children gathered after lunch for a brief play period were utterly deserted, as the boys slowly and quietly entered the school's side entrance doors. Things were eerily quiet as they inched along the short corridor. A look of dread appeared on their faces as they realized all the classroom doors had already been closed. Class was already in session. The ability somehow to slink back into their seats, like war-hardened veterans crawling along the battlefield floor, seemed no longer to be a viable option.

Jack said to the others, "We have to try and sneak in somehow. Let's peek in the door windowpane and when Mrs. Mulligan's back is turned facing the blackboard, I'll open the door slowly and we'll try to sneak down the first aisle along the left wall on our hands and knees." The others nodded their heads in agreement, but Jack couldn't tell if what he discerned on their ashen faces were looks of determination or panic.

Jack paused as he saw Mrs. Mulligan turn to write something on the board and heard her utter the now foreboding phrase, "dangling preposition." For a brief second, the word dangling conjured up in Jack's mind the bodies of five young boys swinging from the gallows as their classmates gazed up at them with the facial expression that justice had been served.

Jack slowly opened the door, seeing no reaction from his otherwise occupied teacher. Just as he was about to let go of the doorknob and turn toward the side wall, a large white hand extending from a black cloak, not dissimilar to the one worn by Dracula, reached out and grabbed Jack's wrist in a firm grasp. The other boys, who were standing behind him ready to make their move into the classroom, could only see Jack's face and the sudden look of terror as he raised his eyes in horror. They understood why as they heard the part shrill, part husky exclamation come from the yet unseen specter: "Did you boys really think you'd get away with this?"

The boys realized that their amateurish attempts were no match for the experience and skill of Sister Helen

Edward, who had been lurking just inside the door, patiently waiting for her prey like a skillful mountain lion, her fangs dripping with saliva in anticipation of her capture. Yes, capture first, as death would come slowly to her five young victims. As the Sister lined the boys up along the corridor wall outside the classroom, she proceeded to go down the line one by one and give each boy a good slap across the face. Stevie, who was the last in line, wondered if this was a typical defensive move used in the NFL by Ray Nitschke, as Sister Helen slowly approached him. However, that thought was quickly driven from his brain as he felt the sting of what seemed like a hand the size of a catcher's mitt.

After a quick finger-pointing instruction of "*never* do that again," the boys were permitted to enter the classroom and take their seats. Each one lowered their heads and rubbed the side of their faces, one cheek clearly the color of crimson red. Jack wasn't sure if the look on their classmates' faces was one of pity for their suffering, satisfaction for what the boys justly deserved, or pride in what their comrades had accomplished in an albeit foolish mad dash to freedom. Jack did notice a somewhat different look on the face of young Kathy Flynn, as she seemed to smile at Jack in a kind of longing way. He had yet no way of understanding her expression, as he returned her gaze with a kind of quizzical half-smile.

Despite these incidents of typical juvenile unrest and experimentation, Jack was generally liked by his various teachers as someone who was a good student, inquisitive, friendly (although at times a little shy), and generally both responsive and responsible. Jack was also one of the more senior altar boys, and would occasionally be pulled from class to serve a funeral mass for a recently departed parishioner. At Sunday "high masses," he had been elevated to be the senior altar boy or acolyte who would turn the pages of the Testament Book for the priest to read at the appropriate point in the mass, light the accolade candles and incense, and generally help ensure that the other altar boys did what they were supposed to be doing.

Fortunately for Jack and his altar boy compatriots, this was a time long before the later pedophile priest scandals would shake the Church to its very core and hasten the disdain of believers and non-believers alike. Back then, Jack had never had a single experience or suspicion about any sexual provocations by any of the priests in the parish. In fact, he had admired them for their kindness, humility, encouraging words, sense of humor, and joking with the altar boys. One was Father Kelly, who would raise the top of his celebrant robe across his face and do his best imitation of Count Dracula preparing to "drink your blood!" And Father Paul, who seemed generally interested in what the boys' had to say and what was happening in their lives.

It was perhaps because of Jack's admiration for these priests, and his vague inclination of wanting to do something useful with his life, that he did something that caused something of a stir the following year, adding to the delight of many of the religious and lay personnel at the school.

As part of their sixth-grade English final, the students were asked to write a composition on "What You Want to be When You Grow Up." Partly because of his admiration and interaction with some of the parish priests, and partly from a general disposition to be helpful to people, Jack decided to write an essay on why he was considering becoming a priest. Jack had never mentioned this as a possible consideration to his parents, friends or teachers before.

Upon reading his composition, his sixth-grade teacher Mrs. Miller immediately elevated Jack's essay to Sister Helen Edward. Within a couple days, the head of the parish, Monsignor Harvey, was sitting with Jack in the priest's office, trying to get a pulse on Jack's real interest. Convinced he might actually have "the calling," the Monsignor suggested to Jack and his parents that he attend a summer camp in rural Virginia run by the Pallottine Order for young boys who were considering the potential pursuit of a religious life.

So that summer, Jack spent two weeks at the Pallottine Camp, where boys split their time between the usual camp activities of playing baseball, basketball, and swimming in the lake, interspersed with religious programs which included mass (EVERY day!), group talks, and lectures on the life of Christ and the saints.

Jack had a good time at the camp playing sports, swimming, and making new friends. He seemed less interested in the amount of time devoted to praying, Mass, Stations of the Cross, and so on, and decided this was a bit of a lonely and generally dull life to dedicate himself to. So a few weeks after his return, he told an obviously disappointed Monsignor Harvey that he didn't think that he wanted to become a priest after all.

Jack had expressed his early thoughts about the priesthood with honesty and sincerity, and not part of some diabolical plan to win favor. He hoped that the priests, nuns and teachers at his school would not be too disappointed in him, or worse, react harshly or negatively toward him. To Jack's surprise, he found that nearly all the adults treated him with a little more kindness and interest than before. This made Jack feel better and more confident that he had in fact made the right decision not to pursue the religious life. Over the next couple years, this conviction would be reinforced with startling clarity after both seeing the unpleasant fate of the doomed priests in the horror film "The Exorcist," and in getting to first base with Kathy Flynn later in the year behind the grammar school building.

CHAPTER 2

School was out for the summer. Jack and his neighborhood friends were at the playground that stood at the top of their residential neighborhood, and was simply referred to as "The Field." With a reasonably-sized ballfield and paved basketball court slightly elevated beyond left field, the Field was a six-acre refuge for local kids. The customary swings, sandbox and monkey bars were relegated to the northeast corner for daytime use of the younger children, and as a late evening hangout when Jack and his friends were not playing ball. As time went on, it also became a training ground for some of the more curious and more confident boys to stumble and stagger through their early attempts of trying to get to know the opposite sex.

The Field was the boys' oasis, particularly in summer. Chores and other family responsibilities aside, they could generally be found there most mornings, afternoons, and early evenings after supper, enjoying the constant stream of baseball or softball and basketball. Touch football would take precedence in the fall after school commenced again, using the patchy grass field that extended from right field to left center field as the gridiron boundary.

On a typical summer evening, the boys would play games until the sun began its long descent and someone would say, "One more inning," to determine the final winner between the two teams (whose flexible roster of "choosing sides" was typically never the same two days in a row). Following the game, the boys would exit The Field, lugging their bats, balls and mitts down the winding hill that led to their homes. Each boy would drop off the procession of mostly pint-sized athletes, as one by one they would run up the steps of their respective houses, with the usual announcement of, "see you in ten minutes." Because then would begin the evening ritual of "hanging out."

It was on one of these summer evenings as the boys walked home, that a black and white police car passed them going the opposite direction, winding its way up the hill to exit by the two stone pillars separating the neighborhood from the adjoining main road. Jack gave the vehicle a glancing thought, since while it wasn't every day they saw a police car drive through the neighborhood, it was probably a monthly or so occurrence. As Jack split off from his friends to walk the last hundred feet or so to his red-shingled house, he was a little surprised not to see his father's dark blue Buick LaSabre in the driveway, as he typically arrived home not long after Jack and his friends left the house for their evening baseball gathering.

Jack trotted up the concrete and slate stairs framed by a black wrought-iron railing, walked across the narrow wooden attached porch, and tossed his Willie Mays mass-produced baseball glove in the hall corner by the front door. He heard a sigh or moan coming from the living room around the corner from the hall. He turned into the living room to see his mother sitting sedately on the blue sofa with her hands in her lap. As she looked up at Jack, she gave him a painful expression he had never seen on her before.

It was an expression not only of deep sadness; almost fear. But also one of heartfelt empathy for her only son. She had obviously only just stopped crying as evidenced by her flushed cheeks and the handkerchief she held in the lap of her flower-print cotton dress. She said, "Jack, come sit next to me on the couch." As Jack sat down, his feeling of anxiety was obvious to his mother, as she nervously fondled the handkerchief and looked sorrowfully at her boy.

She immediately put Jack's hand in hers, and looked directly into his eyes with love and concern. "Jack, a policeman was just here at the house. He told me another driver hit your father's car on his way home from work, apparently by someone who ran a stop sign, and was probably intoxicated. He told me the car directly impacted your father's driver's side door at a high speed." Her voice faltered and she paused, trying to hold back the tears.

"Your father didn't have a chance, Jack, and he was killed instantly. I'm so sorry Jack. He loved you so much. Just as I do. Somehow we're going to have to try and go on without him." She repeated, "I'm sorry, Jack," as she threw her arms around Jack's shoulders and pulled him close to her. As Jack stared into the sofa's blue cushions with a feeling of sinking into them like quicksand, Jack happened to recall his father's favorite color was blue.

Jack and his mother sat there silently for several minutes just holding on to one another, as tears began to fall gently from his eyes. To Jack, the sofa became a life raft, floating on an empty open ocean, with him and his mother the sole occupants, arms entwined as if huddling from the cold wind and waves that splashed into the empty air around them. That morning Tom Moran had said his usual goodbyes before leaving for work as a manager with a large wholesale distributor. "Bye, Babe," he had said to his wife Patricia, giving her a little peck on the lips. He gave Jack his usual pat on the back saying, "So long, buddy." Now he was gone.

After a few minutes, his mother said she needed to go to the hospital where they had brought his father so she could identify the body, and that she'd like Jack to come with her. Knowing his mother needed him to be with her at this life-changing moment, Jack said, "Sure, Mom." His mother visibly showed the strain and heartbreak creeping over her as she clutched the sofa arm as if necessary to steady herself. She said she wasn't up to driving to the hospital, so she would call a taxi.

Arriving at the hospital some thirty minutes later, Jack and his mother entered the reception lobby. It had a rather sterile appearance and was meagerly furnished with a row of chairs along one wall, decorated with orange plastic seat coverings, and a reception desk manned by an expressionless middle-aged woman. Jack's mother motioned to him to sit and wait in one of the chairs while she went to speak with the woman at the front desk. He couldn't hear what was being said, as the receptionist nodded, picked up the phone, and placed an internal call to the hospital morgue.

Mrs. Moran stood and waited at the front desk for the hospital attendant who would be out momentarily. One minute or so later, a balding man with gray hair who seemed to be in his fifties, appeared in the corridor and made his way to the front desk. He spoke rather softly and calmly to Mrs. Moran, who with a brief wave of her arm pointed to Jack sitting along the wall some twenty feet away. The attendant, who Jack assumed was some kind of doctor given his light blue hospital garb and intelligent look about him—complete with black-rimmed glasses—put his hand lightly on Mrs. Moran's arm as if to offer if not comfort, at least sympathy. The doctor turned out to be the head of the hospital morgue and autopsy department.

At that moment, Mrs. Moran turned away from the doctor and walked over to Jack, her eyes not straying from his face as she approached. She sat down next to him, put her hand on his knee, and gently said, "The doctor thinks it would be best if I just went alone with him to identify Dad. You should just wait here and I'll be back as soon as I can, OK?" Jack nodded while his mother gently squeezed his hand, got up, and walked down the corridor accompanied by the doctor. Jack's eyes followed her seemingly frail frame until she turned the corner and was out of sight.

Jack's mother would tell him a few years later that his father had suffered very serious head and facial injuries as a result of the car crash. In identifying the body—despite the deep head wounds, partially missing scalp and facial lacerations caused by both the other driver's car and Tom's head smashing through the windshield of his car—she was still able to see the rugged good looks of the only man she had ever loved or given herself to. Confronted with such a grizzly appearance, his mother didn't look away in horror as people often do when witnessing just how fragile the human body can be.

Without even so much as a flinch, she gazed down on her husband lying there on the metal table slab with a feeling of love and a sense of farewell to the man whom she thought she'd have a whole life with yet to come. Despite the fullness of the years together, she could not help but feel the pain of emptiness that she knew would now be hers to bear.

Visions of his first comical introduction to her in the local college bar, visions of their first passionate embrace, their feeling of a beautiful new beginning on their sunshine-filled wedding day, their sheer feeling of joy and awe when they shared their first look at their newborn son. Those visions she would now have to keep locked in her heart. While no longer to be shared with any physical presence of Tom, the emotional and spiritual sense of oneness would not be lost in death.

As Jack anxiously waited in the reception area for his mother to reappear, he watched as other people—hospital staff, patients, visitors—continued to parade through the lobby, absorbed in their own thoughts or in shared words with others. In the couple dozen people who happened through the lobby in those twenty minutes or so his mother was absent, Jack witnessed the wide range of human emotions, joys, pains and daily trials that he realized most people will similarly experience some day—some more frequently than others. Jack saw the look of fear, terror— the unknown—as someone would approach the front desk to ask about the status or whereabouts of a loved one just admitted for reasons they weren't always sure of, oftentimes based on vague words that may have been communicated at the time of some fateful occurrence.

He witnessed the smile and laughter of a mother and father wheeling their daughter out to the main entrance— with the required help of an attendant—as their giggling young child experienced the anticipation and thrill of going home to restart where she had left off weeks before her injury. He saw the pained hopeless look of a father and son who had only just left their mother, whose body and will to live was not only failing fast, but also where the combination of fatigue and medication made it difficult for her to communicate with her loved ones, or them with her. Jack saw hospital staff in a variety of contrasting activities, some rushing down the corridor as if on a life-and-death mission, and others idly standing in the hall, joking about the latest episode of their favorite TV show.

So strange, Jack thought, that a place that he considered to be a House of Death, could so emulate the extremes of joy and pain that are part and parcel of the human condition. Jack did not know where these thoughts in his head came from, as he considered himself a "regular guy" who could just be himself around his friends—making jokes, clowning around, playing sports, applying himself in school. But he also thought at times he was perhaps a little different than some of his friends—maybe a little more observant, maybe a little more sensitive or empathetic, maybe even a little smarter or more clever or thoughtful than most of his friends. But these things he generally kept inside himself.

Then again, maybe most people had these same thoughts and feelings but also kept them inside, afraid to share them that they might appear to be too different, or appear to others in their circle as trying to be someone they're not.

When Jack's mother finally emerged in the corridor, her head lowered holding her handkerchief, she walked somewhat slowly, seemingly in a bit of a daze. Jack immediately stood up from his chair, walked over to her, and put his hand in hers, saying, "Come on, Mom. There are a couple taxis outside at the waiting stand. Let's go home." Home. Jack grasped the realization that "home" would never quite be the same place again, when one member of their close-knit trio had been taken away so tragically, so unexpectedly, and seemingly forever.

His mother said little on the way home other than mentioning they would have to bring one of Tom's best suits and a change of clothes to Sheridan's Funeral Home tomorrow morning. Jack had never really experienced death before, except for the family dog, Tipper, who had been hit by a car outside his house. Nevertheless, in the next few days, he would make every effort to be by his mother's side in making the arrangements for the wake, the funeral, the burial—even the headstone. Not only did Jack want to be a help and comfort to his mother, but also somehow, it made him feel like his father was still there beside him, encouraging him as he always did.

Most of the people who came to the wake were relatives or neighbors of the Moran family, many of whom Jack knew well; others were only a passing acquaintance. Then there were a few of Tom's friends from college, and colleagues who had worked with Tom at his last job or a previous one. The wake was scheduled for only a single Thursday night, mainly because Mrs. Moran didn't feel she could struggle through such a sad, painful tragedy for two consecutive days.

She would be forced to listen to and respond to well-meaning compliments and anecdotes about what a good man Tom was, how he cared so much for his family and their well-being. How the funeral home had done such a wonderful job in preparing Tom for his funeral, given the obvious devastation of the car crash. Jack thought that most people said these things because they were expected to say them, or they didn't know what else to say beyond the standard, "I'm sorry for your loss" refrain.

But Jack could also see that people were trying to be comforting and kind, to not only show their respect for Tom, but to show Jack and his mother that they understood the pain they were going through. That they didn't have to go through it alone, that they would go on with the memories of Tom as a husband, a father, a friend. And being an Irish Catholic, with many family gatherings as well as regular mass attendance—not to mention his religious summer camp experience—Jack also understood that much of this tradition was to offer up a celebration of his father's life. That he was "in a better place" of eternal life in the presence of Jesus Christ.

While Jack took some comfort in all that, the pain was still too fresh, the loss too deep. Despite feeling a bit numb, Jack tried to do what he could by putting on a good front for his mother's sake and recognizing the demonstrated sincerity of the well-wishers.

By the time of the funeral, Jack's sadness had worsened. While both the local pastor and Jack's Uncle Charles, Tom's brother, were doing their best to provide meaningful eulogies on Tom's life and his everlasting peace, Jack was barely aware of what they were saying. Instead, his thoughts wandered to his own memories of his father—having a catch and running football plays in the backyard, the family trip to upstate New York where Jack and Tom both stared in awe at the thunderous roar and overwhelming beauty of Niagara Falls, of his father showing Jack how to change the oil on his treasured 1969 LaSabre, of Tom's nod of approval and intimate smile upon seeing Jack's winning shot in the local CYO basketball game. It was these minute events in his life that Jack found to be real and memorable, not mere words from others who did not share these private moments.

By the time of the burial at the Holy Trinity Cemetery, Jack's growing sadness had begun to shift to depression and anger. Anger at the drunk driver responsible for the crash that took his father. Anger at the merciless God who allowed it to happen. Even a little anger at Tom for leaving him fatherless at such a young and vulnerable age.

But Jack kept all these thoughts inside himself, unable or unwilling to share them even with his mother, whom he truly loved. Maybe because he felt a little guilty to be having these self-centered thoughts. Maybe because he knew how much pain she was in, a pain that wrapped around her slight frame like some dark death shroud.

As he turned away from the casket, he gave one last look at the polished cherry wood box that cemetery workers would soon lower into the ground. Would this in fact be the last time he would see or be in the presence of his father? Could the body in the casket even be his father? Or was it just a remnant of a life that had been eviscerated, leaving no physical or even spiritual sense of survival? Jack felt the sudden realization that his life would no longer be the same, that he had entered a new chapter of an uncertain future. He had no way to anticipate or comprehend the manner of the strange events that were soon to overtake him.

CHAPTER 3

In the weeks following the funeral, life for Jack's friends and their families, as well as relatives and friends of the Moran's, pretty much returned to normal. While always trying to be understanding and sensitive to Jack and his mother's loss, people naturally resumed living their lives as before, surrounded by their own family's wants and needs. Life with the ups and downs of careers (or just jobs to some), raising children, trying to maintain a loving (or at least stable) marriage, completing weekend chores, running shopping errands—similar to the routine Jack actively participated in or saw prior to his father's death.

Meanwhile, Mrs. Moran continued to be active with her church, being both a member of the choir and the Rosary Altar Society. She took a job at the same insurance agency she had worked at previously, right up to the time of Jack's birth. Her old boss, Mr. Gray, had always considered Patricia Moran to be a very likeable and competent employee, and happily rehired her at a fair salary relative to what she had earned more than ten years earlier. During that time the agency had grown steadily with population growth of the region, more than doubling its staff to about thirty people since Mrs. Moran last worked there. Bob Gray was indeed very happy to have her back.

A life-long bachelor about ten years older than Mrs. Moran, Bob was a tall, thin, slightly balding man, somewhat plain but not unattractive, who some thought resembled the movie actor Walter Matthau. It would not be a surprise to the other women in the company office that Bob found Mrs. Moran (who he called by her given name, Patricia), quite attractive, even though their behavior toward one another was friendly but always professional. Being a bachelor his whole life, and never behaving as anything but a gentleman around her, Bob never suspected that the nature of his feelings towards Mrs. Moran were apparent to his perceptive employees of the opposite sex.

Meanwhile, Jack somewhat muddled through the remaining weeks of school before summer break. While his general intelligence and strong work ethic enabled him to maintain his grades in most subject areas, it was rather obvious to his teachers that Jack's class participation and academic interest level had significantly waned since Tom's death.

Jack's friends noticed the same attitudinal change in Jack. While he would still join them at the Field to play some baseball or basketball, his spirit seemed a little dampened. While for the most part he still hung out with them roaming the local streets, his spontaneous wit and joking was more subdued, as if his natural internal combustion engine wasn't running on all cylinders. Even one time when his friends suggested they take a bike ride down to Doc's to get an ice cream sundae on a warm July day, Jack excused himself saying he had to help his mother with a few chores around the house.

However, that was just an excuse in order to be alone. After stopping at his house to pick up a can of Coke, Jack instead took a walk by himself to the thirty or so acre woods that extended beyond the local cemetery not too far from Jack's house. He found himself here a couple times a week lately, just sitting alone by a small pond near the center of the wooded tract. He would think about times hanging out with his father, about times with his mom and dad together enjoying a vacation trip or a simple trip to the museum, or just about laughing together at one of their favorite TV shows. Some of those thoughts would bring a slight smile to Jack, but his thoughts would quickly revert to the sense of loss, depression—even anger.

Not only did his anger tend to focus on God and His uncaring nature, but also on the very beliefs he had been raised on. Why did God sit idly by while people suffered tremendous pain and agony? Was Jesus Christ really divine, the Son of God made man? Or was he just a man, albeit a very devout and caring man, who was ahead of his time? Someone with good intentions but whose powers of perception, appeal to the common man, and vision of a different path had angered those in power, thus leading to his ultimate execution. Or was there even really a God after all? Are we on this planet truly alone? Alone as a result of a very complicated Darwinian developmental process, or pure random chance, evolving over billions of years?

At the same time, Jack also wondered, could all the beauty just within his limited view of the pond and its surroundings be derived from pure chance? Didn't there have to be a beginning that had to be created by someone or something to initiate the process of this ever-expanding universe? Someone that started it all, this amazing beauty and diversity of the planet and all its life forms? The stillness of the pond surface, punctuated now and then by the ripple of a small frog making his way. The variety of flowers surrounding the water's edge and extending up the narrow sunlit slopes to the seemingly haphazard rows of oak, pine and maple trees that stood silent watch over the tranquil pond. The small white clouds that moved in procession across the blue sky above, casting reflections of light on the sparking glass-like surface of the pond.

Wrapped in these thoughts that seemed to constantly push and pull him in opposite directions, Jack was suddenly startled to see an elderly man with receding white hair and a long white beard about twenty feet away. The man was sitting on a raised, somewhat flat small boulder just a few feet from the water's edge. He was wearing a dark gray robe tied at the waist with a beaded white cord serving as a belt of sorts.

Jack had neither heard nor seen anyone approaching his place of solitude via one of the two small dirt paths that made their way to his favorite secluded spot. Even more puzzling, Jack had a direct line of sight to the small boulder, and no one had been sitting there just a moment before the old gentleman appeared.

Jack deemed the man's dress to be some sort of monk's outfit. Maybe he was visiting the local parish church, or had business at the cemetery and decided to take a stroll through the woods. Jack immediately sensed a calmness, and gentleness in the man's face and demeanor, so he did not feel the urge to quickly get up and run as if his life depended on it.

Instead, not sure why, Jack felt comfortable enough to be the first to speak, and said, "Hello, my name is Jack. Do you come here often? I've never seen you here before." The old man responded in a soft but confident voice, "No,

I've never been to this spot before. I came here to see you, Jack. My name is Peter."

"To see *me*?" Jack replied with a look of surprise. "Why would you want to see me? I don't even know who you are. And how do you know my *name*?"

"Actually, you do know *of* me Jack, mostly from readings, or stories about my life and times in ancient Judea. And my eventual mission to spread the Truth."

"*Ancient Judea?*" Jack's voice cracked a little as he said it. He felt the urge to leap to his feet and hightail it out of there, but there was something about the man's humility and earnest but intense gaze in his eyes. Jack remained seated, but with a look of puzzlement and skepticism on his face.

Readily seeing Jack's look of concern and bewilderment, the old man said, "Best if I back up a bit, Jack. I'm only here to help you if I can. Mind if I come and sit a little closer so we can talk?"

Jack hesitated a moment thinking to himself that the man didn't appear to be carrying any kind of weapon, given his attire. Since the man appeared to be in his sixties, Jack could quickly take off in a shot if necessary and get far enough out of reach before the old gentleman could even stand up! So Jack tried to sound confident but guardedly said, "Sure, no problem."

Peter lifted his somewhat short but brawny frame and walked over to where Jack sat at the top of a small slope that gently led down to the pond just a few feet away. As Peter sat down, Jack noticed he had rather large, muscular hands, as if he had worked at some kind of physically demanding manual labor, at least in his youth.

Peter began to speak in a soft but reassuring voice. "Jack, my name is Peter, but you are probably more familiar with my full name, Simon Peter. You obviously know me from the scriptures, and from religious studies, as one of the twelve apostles. And whom Our Lord Jesus instructed to spread the Word of God, as His witness."

Peter continued to speak, as Jack sat there with his mouth half open and his eyes popping out of his head. "And, I know what you're thinking Jack. I'm some crazy old man who escaped from the nursing home, and you're trying to decide if you should make a run for it. But I'm not crazy, Jack. And even though only *you* can see me, that doesn't make you crazy either. I'm very real to all your senses—sight, hearing, even touch."

With that, Peter extended his arm and said, "Go ahead. Grasp my arm." Jack cautiously put out his hand and wrapped his fingers around Peter's forearm. It certainly felt real. Peter then extended his right arm and placed it on Jack's shoulder. Jack recalled how his father would put his hand on his shoulder, and he felt the same sense of comfort, of being loved.

"I understand how much you miss your father, Jack," Peter said. "He loves you, and misses you terribly as well, but with the understanding that someday you will see each other again. In the meantime, he hopes that you will stop blaming or hating God, or doubting his existence. Is my sitting here next to you and talking to you not proof of that?"

Jack looked at Peter, wanting to believe, but unsure. With some tenseness in his voice, Jack said: "You say you were with Jesus Christ during his years of preaching, and according to the 'stories' in the New Testament, and as an apostle, a witness to his acts of healing, of miracles, his death, and Resurrection. But so many others believe Jesus was just a prophet, that the miracles were just stories or meant to be parables with some other meaning." Jack sounded doubtful when he said, "It's so hard to believe that he was both human and divine, and that he did in fact rise from the dead. There is no real proof."

Peter spoke with true sincerity in his voice. "Jack, Jesus was human as *well* as divine. He understands the doubt that we all have as human beings. Jesus himself had doubts about going through the painful, excruciating and humiliating death that he foresaw in the Garden of Gethsemane. My brother in Christ, Thomas, doubted me and the other apostles who told him of Jesus's appearance to us after His death and Resurrection. Thomas was haunted for years by Christ's words to him about putting his hands in the wounds Jesus suffered during his execution. Jesus' understanding of normal, even typical, human nature—to doubt what they can't see and touch—were echoed in His words to Thomas, 'Blessed are those who haven't seen or touched and yet believe in Me.' [1]

"Just consider me and my brothers, Andrew and John. We were simple, uneducated fishermen. I myself was a coward during Christ's trial and execution. Do you think I would have had the courage and enlightenment to spread the Word after Christ's death if something tremendous, overwhelming, truly astounding had not happened to me and the others? His very real Resurrection and appearance to us, His instructions to spread His Word, and to witness His Transfiguration to be with His Father, and His promise that He would come again one day.

"I and the other apostles could *never* have risen to carry out His works if we ourselves did not experience something that was truly so powerful, so profound and so unimaginable, that it transfigured each of us to our very core. Moreover, not just *one* of us. All *eleven* of us. Most of us went on to experience our own trials and tribulations of imprisonment and execution in the name of Jesus. And being mostly simple men, we didn't possess the kinds of skills to articulate and to lead in the spread of Jesus's words without being truly inspired and changed. With that power, we were able to spread His Word to many other nations to people of different languages and cultures.

"That is just part of the 'proof' that has been provided to us all." Peter repeated his earlier comment to Jack. "Just as Christ said to the doubting apostle after His appearance following His Resurrection: 'Thomas, because thou hast seen me, thou hast believed: blessed are they that have not seen, and yet have believed.'

Peter could see the emotional impact his words were having on Jack. While Jack said nothing, he could sense Jack's pain in the loss of his father.

"And yes," Peter continued, "the Son of God also understands the pain of loss of a loved one, just as he mourned for Lazarus, and the death of His own earthly father, Joseph. Jesus experienced all of the human emotions, the highs and lows, the joys and sadness, courage and fear, to show us how much he not only loves us, but understands and cares for us."

Listening to Peter, tears had begun to swell in Jack's eyes. Like many people, he had hardened his heart to God because of tragic events in his own life. But as Peter spoke, his feelings of anger began to dissipate. He let the words of Peter, and Jesus, enter his mind and open his heart once more.

"Thank you for helping me to see, Peter. I mean Simon Peter. I mean St. Peter. I mean, I'm sorry, I…"

"It's all good Jack. Just call me Peter. Although, I don't know if I'll be seeing you again. I do not know what God's plan is, but my heart tells me you are a special person, and God has something special planned for you. While I may not see you again, my heart and soul tells me you will be seeing others like me in the times to come.

Hopefully some smarter, or more interesting, or more articulate than me, but be assured they will all have your best interests at heart. Just as your father Tom does."

Jack's head snapped upward at the name of his father. "My father? Will I see my father? Or *when* can I see my father? Doesn't he want to see me?"

"I know your father watches over you Jack," Peter replied. "If and when you can see him while still here on Earth, is not really up to me or him. Even with the understanding that comes with life after death and being in the presence of other loved ones and, most importantly, Jesus Himself, there are a great many things we who have passed on still do not understand. Nor can we predict things to come. Only God knows such things."

Jack felt disappointment not knowing if he would see his father, but tried to understand and accept it, as he lowered his head slightly, gazing at the ground in front of him. When he next looked up, Peter was gone, without a sound or sensation that Jack could discern such as a sudden flash of light or fading image. Nothing.

Could Jack have imagined Peter's appearance and his words of comfort and hope? It all *seemed* so real.

It was then Jack glanced down at the ground between the rock on which Peter had first appeared, and where Jack now sat. Between the two, Jack could clearly see in the soft ground the image of footprints in the form of sandals that made their way toward Jack. Jack saw. And he believed.

CHAPTER 4

It had been over two years since Simon Peter appeared to Jack in the small, secluded woods not far from his home. The experience had indeed had a dramatic effect not only on Jack's innermost thoughts and feelings, but also on his outward behavior and, in turn, the perception of Jack by his friends and family. Jack felt, and others sensed in him, a sense of optimism, a quiet confidence, treating other people with a sense of fairness and equality. Jack had not only taken comfort in Peter's words, but better understood the importance of making the best out of the small fraction of time we're permitted to spend on this Earth.

Of course, as a fifteen-year-old sophomore in high school he was, like everyone else, wrestling with the physical, emotional, and mental changes that go along with adolescence. Like most teenagers, he could at times be overly self-absorbed or self-centered, critical of various adult opinions, and a little cold or even hostile to kids he didn't like (especially bullies, phonies, and people with inflated egos). At times, he also was a bit envious of the guys who excelled in school sports, even though he had made it to second string on the junior varsity basketball team.

In other words, he was human, with the faults and failings that come with it. But all in all, Jack was seen as a generally good natured, easy going, well-liked guy who could get along with most people. (Even though he himself was surprised at being voted "Most Cheerful" by his eighth grade graduating class.)

He gradually returned to being much of his old self with his friends—at least in their perception of him. Doing so, he inevitably got caught up in some of their more questionable behavior. Like the time he and his friends slipped into Kenny's house, with Kenny in the lead, to snatch a much-anticipated sample of liquor from Kenny's parents' fairly well-stocked liquor cabinet. The parents were out to dinner and Kenny's older sister was out on a date.

So as not to be detected, rather than take one or two bottles of some—any type—of alcohol, the raiding party had brought with them a large empty glass jar that had previously contained Folgers instant coffee. Quietly, using hand signals observed watching a couple WWII action pictures of commandos focused on completing their mission, they moved stealthily toward the liquor cabinet. Kenny began to pour samples of various bottles of hooch into the glass jar. Into it went some rye whiskey, gin, a little vermouth, some tequila, a touch of sherry that Kenny's mom liked, and even a little Sambuca. With perhaps only an inch or so of the devil's poison taken from each of the bottles, Kenny's parents were not likely to notice the theft from their adults-only stash.

Slipping out the back door, the *Mission Impossible* squad made their way past the Field, to the nearby two-to-three-acre triangular shaped wooded lot formed by the intersection and separation of the elevated Interstate Highway from the passing railway tracks. This was a frequent and favorite haunt for the boys, which they felt was a secret place where they would be safe from being disturbed by nosy or suspicious adults or older kids.

The small preserve seemed desolate and uninhabited for their clandestine operation. The boys got to their favorite spot, a clearing about twenty feet away from a rock cliff that dropped about thirty feet to the railroad tracks below. Kenny unscrewed the lid to the coffee jar, gulping an impressive slug of the newly discovered, never before conceived mixture. Jack, Charlie, Roger and Tony looked on anxiously in silent anticipation, wondering if Kenny's immediate reaction would be one of disgust.

They were on their toes and ready to jump out of the way should Kenny begin to spurt the hellish liquid from his mouth and nose. Instead, with his own look of apprehension on his face, after savoring the liquid a moment as he swallowed, Kenny blurted out, "Wow, this stuff's really good!"

Immediately, the other boys reached out their hands clamoring for their share of the liquid gold. It all went rather quickly, each one getting perhaps the equivalent of three or four shots of what came to be called "Kenny's Concoction."

Feeling good and perhaps needing to release a little stress, Jack got up from where the boys were sitting in a haphazardly formed circle. Walking over to the edge of the cliff, he turned to his friends and proclaimed loudly, "I can't take it anymore!" Jack then turned, and proceeded to step off the cliff.

The others immediately jumped up and ran to the edge of the cliff crying in horror, "Holy Shit, Jack!" As they looked over the edge of the cliff, there was Jack comfortably sitting on a rock ledge measuring some four feet wide by six feet long that jutted out about four feet below the edge of the precipice. Being a bit of a daredevil, Jack thought it would be a great trick to play on his drinking pals. Jack knew, in their state of slight intoxication that was beginning to take effect, his friends wouldn't immediately recall the existence of the ledge where Jack had stepped off in a perceived suicidal leap to his death.

Jack looked up at his friends standing above him and said with a devilish grin, "Hiya, boys! What's up?" While secretly maybe a little annoyed for a brief moment that Jack had scared the living hell out of them, the friends all laughed with the enthusiasm of one being deceived by a trick well played.

The boys continued to sit there, moderately blitzed, aware they were in no condition to go home. They reminisced with some old stories, including the time about two years earlier at the same wooded hideaway when they stumbled upon Frances Gregory. Frances was a cute ninth grader at the time whose early puberty had garnered much attention from her fellow male students. The boys had discovered her lying under the body of fellow student Stephen Gorman, who was quickly making his way past second base.

After a momentary but necessary pause (for purely educational purposes), the boys had run, not knowing what else to do. Unfortunately, the combination of laughter and noise of rushing through the bushes as they made their escape was undoubtedly heard by the consensual parties involved. This became quite apparent from the shock and embarrassed look on Frances's face the next time Jack and Tony happened to walk past her on the neighborhood street.

This story would be told by the band of brothers for years to come. For the moment at least, the comradery and laughter—not to mention the slight buzz—made Jack feel a little better about the recent changes in his life, thinking to himself that maybe things would get better.

***

One major exception to Jack's increasing sense of ease and flexibility, however, was the increasing close relationship of Jack's mother to her boss, Bob Gray. It had taken Bob about eighteen months after Patricia resumed working for him to finally get up the nerve to ask her out to dinner—an actual date. Bob's attraction to Patricia's soft, pretty features and friendly nature had grown increasingly over the months from friendliness to something much stronger.

Patricia had become increasingly aware of Bob's interest in her, even though he always treated her with respect. He would consciously try and not show any favoritism toward her, other than acknowledging her demonstrated competence and continued growth in her insurance business acumen—deservedly so.

As for herself, Patricia had begun to feel the pangs of loneliness and desire for companionship that often eventually comes to those who have lost a spouse, no matter how cherished that previous relationship had been. Her growing feelings for Bob certainly were not the same as had been her physical and emotional attraction to Tom, her true first love. Rather, she knew Bob to be a good and kind man who treated her well and obviously enjoyed her company. As she increasingly shared his company, her affections began to grow as well.

Jack observed their growing compatibility and ease with each other, and it rubbed him the wrong way. The couple's romantic intentions became increasingly obvious to Jack as they spent more and more time together. Bob frequently would spend some evenings at Jack's home in conversation with his mother in the backyard or sitting on the living room sofa. Occasionally Bob even stayed for dinner.

Slowly, Bob got up the nerve to become more intimate with Patricia. After dinner, Jack might walk in on them sitting on the couch, with Bob holding his mom's hand. They would talk about something funny or weird a client of the firm may have said. They would speak about politics, a book one of them (or both) were reading, or maybe even a bit of celebrity gossip. He could often hear them laughing together about something said, and Jack could see the emotional connection between the two of them getting stronger.

Oftentimes they would even take Jack out to dinner with them, or go see a movie together. While Jack gave them no immediate impression of hostility (he often enjoyed going to some of the good restaurants and catching a newly released flick), the beginnings of the emergence of them being "a family" was slowly burning a hole in Jack's gut.

Certainly, Bob could never replace the love and admiration Jack had for his father. So how could his mother even *think* about being with someone other than Tom? Had she forgotten his memory so soon, how much he loved her and how he made her feel? Sure, like every other married couple, they'd had their differences and spats. (Jack even realized that occasionally he was the focus of some "disagreement"). Nevertheless, Jack knew they loved each other deeply when they were together—the look in their eyes, a knowing glance, holding hands, a simple kiss.

How could his mother seemingly betray all that? Jack's growing distress over the situation began to become more evident to his mother. He didn't seem to talk to her as much when he came home from school, at dinner alone together, or while watching a bit of TV after he'd done his schoolwork. In fact, he seemed to be out of the house more with his friends or doing after school activities, or spent more time in his room on his studies. On a couple occasions, he would barely say a word to Bob when he came over the house.

At first Mrs. Moran thought it was just part of the teenage angst Jack was going through. But with a typical mother's insight and given their closeness over the years, even more so in the period following Tom's death, it wasn't long before Patricia knew very well there was something bothering Jack. She was even fairly certain she knew the nature of the problem. Bob Gray and his relationship with her.

She hesitated confronting Jack about his feelings. She saw that Bob treated Jack with kindness, interest and thoughtfulness, and was trying his best to engage him. In fact, these were some of the qualities about Bob that made her feel more connected to him. She only hoped that, if things continued along this path, even sensing Bob's intentions to try and raise the stakes to something more permanent between the three of them, that Jack would become more accepting. In fact, what Patricia didn't know is that Jack's perspective was also about to be changed for the better. That is, with a little help from a stranger.

CHAPTER 5

It was early October. Saturday night. Earlier that evening Jack had played in a JV basketball game against a rival team a couple town's over. He was feeling good since the coach had put him in late in a close game for his strong defensive skills, hoping to protect their small lead. Jack had come through with a steal with about a minute left in the game, followed by a near perfect pass to his friend Chris on a breakaway to make a final layup and help cement the win.

After the game, his mother had given him a big hug and Bob threw him a high-five with a "Way to go, Jack!" Both his mother and Bob attended nearly all of Jack's weekend games, something that Jack generally appreciated. Later, Jack had gone over to Chris's house with a couple other guys to celebrate with some takeout pizza, while Mr. Gray had taken Mrs. Moran to one of the more expensive romantic Italian restaurants in town.

His mother was still not home when Jack walked from Chris' house to his own at about 9:30. He was pretty beat from the game and postgame activities (including the couple of bottles of beer that he and his friends had pilfered from Chris' parents' basement without them knowing). He got ready for bed, read a chapter from an Isaac Asimov sci-fi novel entitled *The End of Eternity*, and then dozed off to sleep.

He was awakened about two in the morning by a creaking sound coming from the rocking chair he kept in the corner of his ample-sized bedroom. The moonlight peered through the double window facing the rear of the house, and he first thought he was seeing the outline of one of his sport wall posters which included the likes of Michael Jordan, Lawrence Taylor, and (in fond memory of Sister Helen Edward), Ray Nitschke.

In the few seconds it took for his eyes to become more accustomed to the dim light enveloping his room, he was startled when he realized there was an elderly, well-dressed man sitting in his rocking chair. Looking directly at Jack, the man said, "Hello, Jack," as if he and Jack were old acquaintances.

The man appeared to be in his seventies, and had a well-trimmed white beard with thinning white hair and a receding hairline. He was dressed in what no doubt was the high-quality grayish tweed suit of a businessman from the 1920s or 1930s. He was also holding a lighted cigar in his right hand.

It had been some time since Peter had appeared to Jack, so initially Jack had the same sense of questioning if he was imagining this latest visitor. Was he simply still dreaming? Still sleepy, Jack asked the gentleman in a low but audible voice, "Who are *you*?"

The man answered in what sounded to Jack like a German accent from an educated and well-spoken man. "Why, I'm Sigmund Freud! Certainly you've heard of me, Jack, am I right?"

Of course Jack had heard of Sigmund Freud, whether mentioned in some class discussion, or some TV show or movie. He remembered hearing the phrase "a Freudian slip," but wasn't exactly sure what was meant by it. Although he did remember Freud being referred to in some movie by some bully saying to one of his targeted victims about the victim being horny for his own mother. He also knew that Sigmund Freud was long dead.

Jack thought to himself, he certainly hasn't been as dead as long as Simon Peter, so who's to say he isn't real? Somewhat surprising himself with the calmness in his voice, Jack asked the elderly man, "So why are you here? Why are you in my room?" Then perhaps with a little more perturbed tone in his voice, *especially at 2 o'clock in the morning!*" Hesitating for a moment, he then said, "Are you even real, or am I crazy?"

The stranger hesitated a moment and calmly replied. "You know, I once had a man come to my office for an appointment. After he talked to me for about ten minutes, I said to him 'I think you're crazy!' The man got a little upset and indignant and said: '*Crazy?* I'd like a second opinion!' To which I responded, "OK. I think you're *ugly* too!"

Jack shook his head from side to side as if to say to himself, *What did he just say?*, while Sigmund chuckled to himself and leaned back in the rocking chair. The stranger then said in a voice—as if amused with himself— "Sorry, Jack. Just kidding. That's an old Henny Youngman joke. He's one of my fellow Jewish compatriots. I tell you, that guy keeps us in stitches all the time. I think he has enough one-liners to last for all eternity."

Even after his experience with Simon Peter a couple years earlier, Jack still had to wonder if he was losing it. The guy sitting just a few feet away from him seemed to be more like some Jewish comedian from the Catskill Borscht Belt in an era long past than a distinguished psychiatrist of undisputed historical significance.

The man responded, "No Jack, to be a little more serious, you're not crazy. And I should know." He continued to explain. "I'm here for a reason. But a little background first.

"Many of those reported claims of what I professed while active in my life, I repudiated later in life. Some were just misinterpreted. All those theories about the Oedipus complex, and a son's sexual attraction to his mother. That was purely a hysterical reaction to what I was really saying. It has more to do with a son (or husband for that matter) being jealous or envious of a mother's attention to others in her family. What's most important to keep in mind, especially in your case, is that your mother's attention to Bob in no way diminishes her very deep love for you. As your mother, her connection to you is unbreakable and incomparable.

"In fact, part of her relationship with Bob, as sincere as it is, is also for *your* consideration and benefit. In addition to her loneliness for adult companionship, she is also thinking about having a more emotional and financially stable family life for the *both* of you. She realizes you'll be ready and able for college in a couple years, and she knows that Bob is more than willing to help support that dream. In fact, he proposed marriage to her tonight at that romantic Italian restaurant. Besides expressing his real love for your mother, he was hopeful that you could someday accept him as a second father, someone worthy of your love. In fact, being a practical insurance executive, he even mentioned in his proposal how he was in good financial condition, especially after all these years as a bachelor, and knew he could help make a comfortable life for your mother and you. And that included sending you to a good college of your choice."

Sigmund focused his rather intense gaze on Jack and continued. "So, Jack, as in any behavioral science—especially psychology—it is important to find the necessary and correct behavioral response to ease the burdens we place on our psyches. In your case, it's turning that jealousy, and yes selfishness on your part, into one of sincerity for wanting the best for the people we love. For what makes *them* happy. In your mother's case, that means alleviating much of her loneliness. She will always miss your father deeply, more than you can imagine, and there will always be a large hole in her heart in his absence. Nevertheless, she is still relatively young and hopefully has a long life ahead of her, and wants the best for the both of you. And while some people choose to emphasize *sexuality* as being the driving force in my theories of human behavior, what I really believe is that the principal consideration is *love*—love between a man and a woman, love of parents for their children, love of a friend—that really determines our humanity."

Jack had listened attentively to Doctor Freud, and felt he had generally understood what he was saying. Throughout his speech, Jack's gaze had never left the Doctor, who could see the visible change on Jack's face as he listened and he knew Jack had been receptive.

"I guess I was being a little selfish and self-centered. I *do* love my mother very much and want her to be happy. I think I now understand that she needs a life of her own, both now and when the day comes that I move from this house—maybe this town—to a life of my own. Thanks Doc."

"I'm glad you see things a little clearer now, Jack. I knew you would. Both Peter and Tom told me you had some special qualities that will serve you well in life. Even though sometimes those same qualities can make life seem more difficult, whether in the choices we have to make, or in certain relationships with other people."

Jack's eyes brightened at the mention of his father as he eagerly responded: *"So you've met my father in the afterlife?* Peter also mentioned him to me some time ago. Why doesn't he come *see* me?"

Sigmund responded in a compassionate voice, understanding Jack's pain and deep desire to see and speak to Tom. "Yes Jack, we *all* know one another in the afterlife. We are all connected in a way I can't describe. But just like Peter said, it's not something your father can just make happen. There is much we don't understand about God Almighty and how and why he allows some things to happen, while prohibiting others. Just know that your father sees you, surrounds you, and loves you with all his heart.

Jack looked a little disappointed in Doctor Freud's response to if and when he could see his father. So the Doctor thought he'd lighten the mood before his departure.

"But before I go, I'll leave you with one more thought," Sigmund offered. "A doctor friend of mine told me once how a patient had come to him. The doctor told him, 'I have some bad news and some very bad news. The anxious patient said, 'Well might as well tell me the bad news first.' The doctor said, 'The lab called with your test results. They said you have 24 hours to live.' *'24 hours?'* the patient said. 'That's terrible! What could be worse?

What's the very bad news?' The doctor replied, 'I've been trying to reach you since yesterday.'"

Sigmund paused a moment, waiting for a reaction from Jack who looked a little puzzled, then gave a slight chortle. "Sorry, Jack, that's a bad joke. Henny Youngman I'm not. But seriously, my point is death can come to us or any of our loved ones at any time. I hope you'll come to realize death isn't something to fear or obsess over. The point is to make the most of our life while in this world. Live life as if every day will be your last. Because one day, you'll be right!"

With those parting words, Doctor Freud vanished in the blink of an eye, with perhaps just a slight rustling of the window curtain shifting in the soft night breeze to announce his departure.

Before drifting off to sleep again, Jack lay there a few moments, thinking about what the good doctor had said, thinking of his mother and how he could have been more sensitive to her own needs and thoughts, just as she had been so loving to him.

When he awoke the next morning, Jack could smell a slight odor of cigar smoke. He got a can of air freshener out of the bathroom closet and dusted the room with a fine spray to make the smell dissipate. As he was doing so, he also noticed some small specks of cigar ash by the chair where Doctor Freud had sat. Finding the small hand vacuum in the same bathroom closet, he quickly picked up the residue from Sigmund's brief visit, hoping his mother didn't hear the noise, as vacuuming first thing on a Sunday morning wasn't exactly typical of Jack's normal routine.

He made his way down to the kitchen, where his mother was just starting to make some blueberry pancakes, one of Jack's favorite breakfast treats.

"Morning Jack."

"Hi Mom."

They sat in silence for a few minutes, each mulling over their own private thoughts. When the pancakes were done, his mother placed a stack of three in front of him, the golden-brown flapjacks nearly falling over the edge of the plate. "You better cut those up before you put the syrup on them or it'll run off the plate," Mrs. Moran said. "I'm not sure why I made them so large today," she added, as if something had distracted her.

Jack poured the real Vermont maple syrup onto his pancakes. As he began to dig into them, his mother said, "Jack, there's something I want to tell you, that I hope you'll be happy about, or at least okay with."

Jack looked into his mother's inquiring eyes, paused for a moment, and said, "I love you Mom. If marrying Mr. Gray will make you happy, I'm not just okay with it. I'd be happy for you."

Mrs. Moran looked at Jack in stunned silence before her halting reply. "How on earth did you know that Bob proposed to me last night? And that I accepted his proposal?"

Jack looked in her soft hazel eyes, then pointed to her wrist. "Well, I see you're wearing a brand-new bracelet I've never seen before. And you did get home very late last night from that rather fancy Italian restaurant. And I can see how you've grown close to Mr. Gray over the last year or so, and it's obvious how he feels about you. So, I just put two and two together." (Sigmund would be proud of his quick thinking, he thought.)

"Sometimes you just amaze me, Jack Moran," his mother replied in a slightly quivering voice as she kissed his forehead. "I love you so much. And you're growing up to be quite a young man, much like your father. And I want you to know, Jack, my marrying Bob will never change the love and cherished memories I have of your father."

Jack could see the tears in her eyes, glistening in the morning light that streamed onto her face through the kitchen window. "I know that Mom. Like I said, I want you to be happy too. You certainly deserve it. It'll be different, but we'll be a family again. Just one thing." Again he paused a moment. "Can I call Mr. Gray something other than *Mr. Gray*? It will feel really awkward now."

"Of course," she replied. "What would you like to call him?"

"Can I call him Bob? Nothing against Mr. Gray...ouch...I mean Bob. Somehow, I'm just not able to call him Dad. Dad was Dad, and that'll never change."

"I understand, Jack. I'm sure Mr. Gray—sorry, Bob—will be perfectly fine with that. He actually is a very kind and decent man Jack, and he has your best interests at heart, as well as mine."

"I've come to understand that, Mom, so it's all good." Raising his glass of orange juice in a toast, Jack said in a clear, determined voice, "Here's to you and Bob. I wish you all the happiness in the world. Go for it. As a friend of mine recently said, 'You only live once!'"

CHAPTER 6

Jack was driving alone down the Midlothian Turnpike in his six-year-old Ford Thunderbird, not dissimilar to the one his father used to drive before the newer LaSabre, other than being a slate gray color instead of his father's blue one. He was on his way to the Chesterfield Towne Center mall in nearby Richmond, located just five miles from his house. Jack was going there to buy a pair of new shoes and slacks for his upcoming high school graduation in a couple weeks.

It was mid-afternoon about two-thirty, so traffic was moderately light on the two-lane, limited access divided highway. A very light rain had stopped, but the road was still wet and a little slick.

Jack had purchased the used car with some of the money he had made during the last couple of summers, first caddying at a local private golf club for well-off businessmen, doctors, lawyers, dentists, and their families. Once he got his driver's license, despite failing the driver's test the first time for "going too fast" through a yield sign,

Jack had shifted over to parking cars at the club, where he actually made more money in tips than caddying.

His stepfather, Bob, had generously chipped in half of the purchase price for the car. Bob was indeed generous with Jack but also, as a good businessman and now the parent of a teenager, wanted to impress upon Jack the importance of the work ethic and, in his words, "having some skin in the game."

Despite a posted speed limit of fifty-five miles per hour, Jack was doing seventy. He believed the old adage from more experienced drivers that, as long as you didn't go more than fifteen miles per hour over the speed limit, the cops wouldn't pull you over for speeding. Unfortunately, he was tailgating the car in front of him, just as the car in front of him was tailgating the driver two cars ahead of Jack. All going seventy miles per hour on a slick roadway. Obviously, to these drivers, the golden rule of being separated by one car length for every ten miles per hour of speed you were travelling taught in Driver's Ed was something for girls and nerds.

Suddenly the driver two cars ahead of Jack stepped on his brake to make a left turn off the highway onto a dirt road connector between the opposite sides of the turnpike—a connector meant solely for cops and emergency vehicles. (Later Jack would think about the number of illegal traffic infractions going on at one time during the situation and endorse the phrase "the perfect storm.")

The driver in the car ahead of Jack immediately slammed on his brakes, just avoiding slamming into the turning car in front of him. Barreling down on the car in front of him, Jack went through one of those brain-on-steroids moments where he realized—in a split second—there's no way I'm going to stop in time.

Travelling in the left lane, Jack immediately turned the wheel sharply to the right into the vacant lane alongside him, trying to avoid the car in front of him. For one millisecond, Jack saw he was going to be able to avoid hitting the car in front of him, but then realized he was headed for a guard rail jutting out from another small dirt road on the right, and that he was about to hit it dead-on at a ninety-degree angle. Not wearing a seat belt, it probably would mean certain death. (Jack was amazed later how all these thoughts could go through your mind in a few milliseconds, amazed at just how powerful the human brain could really be.)

Making a split-second decision, Jack turned the wheel sharply back to the left to turn away from the guardrail and back onto the highway. While he successfully performed that maneuver, with the combination of speed, the sharp turn of the steering wheel, and the wet road surface, Jack's car began to careen down the highway, making a complete 360-degree revolution as it did. All the while travelling at high speed.

As his car began to make an attempt at a second 360-degree revolution, Jack turned the steering wheel back sharply to the right. The car began to swerve from right to left and back again, as Jack continued to try to straighten out the car and point it in the original direction he was going.

Somehow it worked. He was finally, in a matter of seconds, able to straighten out the car on the two-lane highway, after which he immediately pulled over onto the left-hand shoulder area that was closest to him. Jack put the car in park, leaned back in his seat, and took a deep breath. "Holy Shit!" he said out loud to himself, as it sank into him that he had somehow cheated death. He thought of his father, and how ironic it would have been (not to mention how devastating to his mother), if he had also perished in a car accident. But his death would have been through his own poor judgment, not the same as the innocent, maybe fateful death of his father, who just happened to be at the wrong place at the wrong time.

As Jack sat in his car, half dazed with the blood draining from his now pale face, the driver who had been in the car in front of him pulled up in his late model Chevy Impala behind Jack. He got out of his car and ran up to Jack's window yelling, "Are you okay, man?" He was a tall guy with long blond hair, just a couple years older than Jack.

"*What's wrong with you?*" Jack yelled angrily. "*Why did you do that?*" The young driver, taken aback, anxiously replied, "Hey, I *had* to slam on my brakes or I would have smashed into the guy in front of *me*! He's the idiot for trying to make that left turn where he's not supposed to." Jack got out of his car, and in a calmer voice, realizing the other driver was right, said, "Sorry. But I could have been killed." They both turned to look behind them at the dirt road crossing to see that the other driver who had been at fault had long gone.

The somewhat tall, wiry driver said to Jack, "Man, that was some amazing driving you just did. How the hell were you able to keep the car on the highway?"

"I have no idea," Jack said breathlessly. "Luck, I guess. I just never, ever want to experience that again."

After that incident, Jack couldn't actually be characterized as a "defensive driver," a concept reiterated at almost every Driver's Ed class by the instructor Mr. Burke. Nevertheless, he did improve somewhat on his tailgating habits. Nerd or no nerd. He didn't want to encourage his own death. He felt it wasn't his time yet.

Jack thought to himself, "I'm not sure what it is, but there's a lot I want to do in this life."

While Jack may have impressed himself with his Mario Andretti-like driving skills and quick reactions at the steering wheel, he couldn't help but wonder if he had been in total control—all by himself. Both Simon Peter and Sigmund had said that Tom's father was watching over Jack. Maybe Tom somehow, directly or indirectly, helped control the rapid onslaught of things that happened—that could have gone wrong—in those few seconds that ensured that Jack's life would be saved. That he could go on to do—*to do what?* Jack wondered to himself. Was there anything he could do that would really make a difference to others in this world?

***

Graduation day finally came for Jack and his classmates on a partly sunny Friday afternoon in June. With the weather cooperating over the last couple of days and in the forecast, high school officials were able to hold the ceremony outdoors in the larger of the two local Town parks. Jack was one of the 192 graduates seated in the first four rows of seats divided by a center aisle. Jack's parents, Patricia and Bob, were seated with the other twenty-five rows or so of other student families and friends. Tom's brother and sister, along with their spouses and a few of Jack's cousins, were also in attendance.

Jack had done well in his years at the high school. In addition to finishing seventh in a graduating class of 192, Jack had been awarded the subject medal in History, and had won a one-time scholarship award of $1,000 from the local VFW. Most importantly, he had even been awarded a small partial academic scholarship from his chosen private college, Georgetown University outside Washington, D.C. He would report for Orientation in just a couple of months. Located about two hours from Midlothian, Jack's mom was happy he wouldn't be so far away that he couldn't come home easily enough on holidays and maybe even an occasional weekend.

School officials at the ceremony had politely asked the members of the audience, including the students (perhaps even more so the students) to refrain from clapping or yelling until the last graduate's name was called and he or she stepped off the stage having received their diploma, which were graciously and happily being handed out by the school superintendent, Mr. Westfall. As Jack's name was called and he strode to the stage, Patricia and Bob both beamed with pride and pleasure. Mrs. Moran, now Mrs. Gray, felt a tug of sadness that Tom could not be there to witness Jack's accomplishments. Nonetheless, she felt, even if Tom wasn't watching from beyond, that his spirit was deeply buried in the person that Jack was becoming. At the same time, she put her hand into Bob's, recognizing his own feelings and pride for Jack, having tried to fill the obvious void of Tom in Jack's life in any constructive way he could.

Jack gave Mr. Westfall a firm but appreciative handshake along with his trademark smile. As he was walking away from Mr. Westfall and ahead of the next recipient, Jack was somewhat startled to see an older, somewhat short, gray-bearded man, standing in an open, isolated space just off the stairs to the left that led off the stage. Wearing a black, slightly puffy coat with a raised white collar extending onto his shoulders, the man seemed to be standing with a slight stoop, brought on by age or infirmary.

As Jack passed closest to him some ten feet distant, the somewhat weary looking man gave Jack a confident smile, combined with a thumbs up gesture. With the man's attire being so out of place, and with no one else seeming to be looking at the spot where the peculiar man was standing, Jack realized that it must be another "visitor" from...from wherever they come from. After a parting glance, Jack did his best to avoid any interaction, unsure how he would explain it to anyone else who had absolutely no knowledge of this apparition who was obviously from another time and place in history.

As Jack took his seat again in row three, glancing again over to the spot near the stairway, the man Jack had seen was no longer visible. Jack tried to dismiss the ghostly image as he exchanged hand slaps with some friends sitting next to him and in front of him. Before he knew it, the last graduate's name had been called and was being handed his diploma. The school secretary who had been reading the names stepped aside for Mr. Westfall, who enthusiastically proclaimed into the microphone, "Ladies and Gentlemen, I give you the Midlothian High School graduating class of 1980."

With that cue, the audience rose to their feet in generous applause, as the graduates themselves whooped and yelled as they (or at least most of them) removed their caps and tossed them high into the bright mid-day sky. Except of course for a few of the usual wise guys who decided they were better tossed with the air dynamics of a Frisbee in mind, but thankfully not taking out anyone's eye in the process.

After congratulating their closest friends and classmates, some with delirious laughter, the student's broke ranks to find their families to revel with them and share the moment. Finding his mom and Bob, Jack's mom gave him a big hug, saying, "I'm so proud of you, Jack." Bob extended his hand with a similar look of love and pride and said, "It goes without saying Jack, I'm very proud of you too. I know you worked hard during your four years here, and you deserve a lot of credit for your accomplishments."

Jack released the handshake, took a step closer and put his arms around Bob's shoulders, positioning his head close to Bob's own. "Thanks Dad," Jack said softly. "I appreciate all that you've done, not just for my Mom, but for me as well." As Jack looked into Bob's face, he saw Bob's somewhat reflective expression turn into an emotional and deep one, for this was the first time Jack had ever called Bob "Dad." All Bob could say after some hesitation was a somewhat halting, "Thank you, son." Then, after another brief pause, "I love you." Jack immediately responded with a heartfelt, "I love you too, Dad."

Standing next to Bob just a foot or two away from Jack, his mother had witnessed the sincere and emotional exchange between them and, with water in her still bright hazel-colored eyes, gave Jack a knowing and loving squeeze on his right arm. Jack could almost read his mother's thoughts. She was grateful that Jack had done something slightly noble for both her and Bob's happiness. That going forward, they could now take great comfort in knowing they had taken that next step in becoming a true, loving family. Where before there had been some doubt and unease, perhaps, in each other's minds, now there was none.

CHAPTER 7

After about thirty minutes of people milling around after the graduation ceremony—complete with words of congratulations, hugs, photo-taking, laughter, jokes, and some talk of future plans with the new alumni—Jack said so long to his parents. He made his way to his car, which was parked on the overflow grassy area adjoining the main parking lot. A few dozen fellow graduates would soon be making their way to Kathy Flynn's house to attend a party for her and her friends. While Kathy's parents and a few of her relatives would be hosting the backyard barbeque, they promised to remain indoors and out of the way so as to not interfere. (Unless they suspected or saw any alcohol consumption, which would be strictly prohibited. Well, that was the plan, anyway.)

As most people had already left the ceremony to attend their own planned festivities, by the time Jack got to his car the Thunderbird was somewhat isolated and about fifty feet away from the next nearest parked car. Jack eased into the front seat in a somewhat jubilant mood, not only looking forward to partying with his friends, but feeling good about the exchange he had just moments earlier with Bob, now Dad.

Almost immediately though, he felt a jolt go through him as he glanced in the rear-view mirror to see the old man who had been standing near the stage earlier, calmly sitting in the back seat.

"*Jesus Christ!*" Jack blurted out in a voice one octave higher than his normal one. The old man, keeping his eyes focused on Jack's reflection in the rear-view mirror, sitting quite motionless, serenely replied in a slight Italian accent, "No, I'm not *Him*. Nor would I ever pretend to be. But I can say I do see Him often, and have spoken to Him directly on a number of occasions."

"You scared the *hell* out of me," Jack replied in a somewhat agitated voice.

"Well," the man replied, "that's also more in His line of work than mine, but I get your drift."

Not seeing anyone nearby who might be looking towards his car, Jack turned around slightly in his seat to look directly at the old gentleman. The man had a gray beard that nearly reached his chest, a bit of a ruddy complexion, close-cropped grayish hair, a receding hairline, and somewhat large ears. Jack was again struck by the white collar extending outward some three inches on each side of his neck and slightly above his somewhat stooped shoulders.

"OK, you're obviously not someone even *close* to my time in history, so who exactly are you?" Jack inquired, not quite knowing what to expect. Was this someone of historical significance like his previous visitations, or just a common, everyday person from the distant past?

"Well, I like to think I'm someone of historical significance," the man said, obviously reading Jack's thoughts. "My name is Galileo dei Vincenzo Bonaiuti de' Galelei. But everyone simply refers to me as Galileo."

"*Galileo!*" Jack snapped back. "Why, you *are* famous!" He thought back to his knowledge of history before saying, "Weren't you tried for being a heretic in the eyes of the Church for espousing the belief that the Earth revolved around the Sun, instead of vice versa?"

"Yes, that's right, but just to be clear; I'm not the one who originally proposed the idea. That was my (now) buddy Copernicus. And yes, I was tried and found guilty during the Inquisition period, and was sentenced to spend the last eight years of my life under house arrest as punishment."

There was something about the man that Jack took an instant liking to and found him easy to converse with. Jack shook his head side-to-side saying: "That's so horrible and unfair when you were obviously right in your beliefs and just trying to educate people, but they weren't ready to accept it. It's such a simple premise, and now we know so much more about the workings and mind-boggling vastness of the Universe! How could people be so opposed and angry about your beliefs, when they're so basic to our current understanding?"

"Jack, people are both a product and an ingredient of their own time, place and culture," Galileo explained. "Man was long thought to be the center of the Universe, and that coincided with the Church's teachings and their interpretation of the Bible. Even though the Bible never said it. Rather, their interpretation neatly justified their own roles and powers within the Church, and therefore in society. Both science and religion evolve and change over time, which is just part of the human experience.

"And not to toot my own horn, but I do have a lot of other accomplishments besides being tried as a heretic," Galileo retorted, perhaps in defending his own legacy."

Jack raised his eyebrows inquisitively saying "Likeeee...?"

Galileo countered, "Well, like I was the first one to conceive of a pendulum clock; I vastly improved the newly created telescope to discover not only the rings of Saturn but the four moons of Jupiter; I created a thermoscope, the forerunner of the thermometer; I made advances in both fundamental science (such as motion) as well as applied science (like the strength of materials). I could go on, but suffice it to say my interests were not only in astronomy, but in mechanics, mathematics, even philosophy."[1]

Galileo hesitated a moment, saying, "I'm sorry, I don't mean to make it sound like I'm bragging. The point is I was many other things than what many remember me for, a 'heretic' in the eyes of the Church. Which indirectly relates to why I'm here with you now."

Galileo continued in a part professorial, part friendly, almost fatherly tone. "You see, Jack, it's clear you've been wrestling with what you want to do with your life, what should be your chosen path, so to speak. The reward in this life is taking advantage of your special talents, not to waste them. To do something responsible, not just for yourself but for the sake of others. Not everyone can become a famous inventor, or make a breakthrough medical discovery. To some, their highest attainment may be their role as a good husband or father, wife or mother. It is truly a high calling to unselfishly love someone, to put their needs first, to provide direction and guidance to their life.

"Some of my most rewarding moments on this Earth were the times I spent with my daughter Virginia. Because she was my illegitimate daughter, she had little choice but to enter a convent and devote her life to God. That decision not only made her happy, but also was an achievement in itself, to unselfishly dedicate her life to the praise of God, while at the same time working with many of the downtrodden and ignorant of his flock.

"Jack, I'm just suggesting to you to open your heart and mind, never stop learning and being curious, know that you're here for a purpose, and you will achieve what you hope to achieve."

Galileo continued to counsel Jack. "And just like I encountered many obstacles and people in my life who thought me wrong, misguided, even evil in the minds of some because of my so-called heretical beliefs, you will encounter your own share of liars, scam artists, charlatans and pretenders who are only interested in deceiving you. Who have inflated opinions of themselves, or will try to convince you of their righteousness. But be true to yourself Jack, and those you love. Do what your mind, and heart, and conscience tells you to do, and you will never regret it."

Jack thought aloud. "But there are so many possibilities, and so much I don't know. How will I know what is right?"

"Only God has all the answers, Jack. You wouldn't believe how much you people don't understand. And that doesn't mean just you people on Earth, but all the other inhabitants scattered across the Universe."

"*Wait*," Jack stammered. "So you're telling me that intelligent life *does* in fact exist on other planets?"

"*Of course*," Galileo said with a mentor's grin, somewhat surprised by the question. "There are some 1.5 trillion suns in the Milky Way Galaxy, each with their own set of planets. And there are hundreds of billions of galaxies in the Universe. So, do you think out of those trillions upon trillions of planets, that we humans are the only intelligent life that exists? Besides being incredibly self-centered with an overinflated view of their own importance (much like those who thought the Earth revolved around the Sun), doesn't that seem like an awful waste of real estate? And wouldn't that seem like a huge amount of overkill by the Creator? I mean, not that God doesn't have a sense of humor—He created we humans didn't He—but that would be a huge waste of His energy. And, as best as I can explain it or understand it, it was His Spiritual Energy that He purposely effected to essentially explode that started this whole creation thing in the very beginning."

"Explode? But if God 'exploded' like you say, wouldn't that have utterly destroyed Him?"

"Not explode in the human sense of the word" Galileo responded. "More like He allowed His energy to fully radiate from His Being. And I know what you're going to ask. What was there before the Universe began, what your scientists call the Big Bang. I can only say there was just the spiritual nature of God Almighty. Just because I'm in that spiritual world now, doesn't mean I comprehend it or can explain it. I'm just at total peace and content at being a part of it."

Jack thought about what he had recently heard on his class trip to Washington D.C., including a tour of the Albert Einstein Planetarium at the National Air & Space Museum. There he had watched a fascinating short film about not only the Big Bang Theory, but the point (or was it conjecture) that the Universe continues to expand to this very day, billions of years later.

"Well, as a famous astrologist, can you explain to me if and how or why the Universe continues to expand?"

"Actually, that I do know, or at least part of the answer," Galileo exclaimed. "But only bits and pieces. Your scientists and astrologers tell you that every living thing in the Universe comes from that first Big Bang. So that every living thing is composed of the same particles of what they call "stardust." All the elements that are contained in our bodies essentially come from a star. That's a giant leap from my then-considered heretical proposition that the Earth revolved around the Sun. Quite staggering how far human knowledge has come in just some 500 or so years, right?

"But what no one has yet comprehended—how could they with their focus on physical principles, laws and equations and worldly observations—is that when a living creature possessed of a soul dies, it returns to the stardust from which it came. Moreover, it's that exponential growth of rebirth magnified billions and billions of times throughout the Universe over countless billions of years, that in fact causes the Universe to grow—to *expand outward*! Yes, there is also a spiritual entity within all of God's intelligent creatures that have been infused with a moral consciousness, a soul that allows us to exist simultaneously within the stardust. There, within the realm and presence of God, we are connected to all other creatures blessed with a soul, no matter how distant in the Universe.

"And yes, even to appear to people such as yourself in what was our former physical element, but being seen only by those who are meant to see us. You are one of those chosen people Jack. With all my polymorphic skills and knowledge, I can't explain *how*, I only know it is the truth. And when you're removed from your worldly wants, needs, desires, pride, and arrogance—that is enough."

Galileo, perhaps finding a comfort zone in the pleasure he once took in being a university professor and lecturer, cheerfully continued. "You know, one of my philosophical quotations, you can look it up sometime if you'd like, was 'All truths are easy to understand once they are discovered; the point is to discover them.' So be curious, and confident, in your beliefs, Jack, but not arrogant. You know, even though I was forced to recant my teaching about the Earth revolving around the Sun at my trial, under fear of torture, I did manage some level of satisfaction when I muttered at the conclusion, 'And yet it moves.' So that history would know I had not altered my opinion of the truth just to satisfy my tormentors. Even though it basically cost me much of my freedom for my remaining days."

Jack sat somewhat in awe of Galileo's wide range of knowledge, his powers of persuasion, his obvious interests in so many subject matters, that he felt he could listen to him talk for days on end. In Jack's mind he thought, *so this is what a Renaissance man is.* But Galileo, sensing this in Jack's thoughts and expression, said, "I'd like to stay longer and continue to talk to you Jack, but unfortunately, I have to leave you now."

"Please don't go, Sir. There's so much I could learn from you. I have so many questions. *Please!*"

"Sorry Jack. It's not my decision," Galileo replied, seemingly with some sadness in his voice. "Just keep your eyes and ears open, and your mind at attention, and there are so many paths to learning—and ultimately to discovery.

"With that I have to say goodbye Jack. But, congratulations on your graduation. I wish I had a glass of wine to toast to your future, but alas, no. However, that does remind me of another one of my famous quotes. 'Wine is sunlight, held together by water.'"

And with those final words, Galileo vanished, much like a ray of sunlight reflecting through the car window and then gone, perhaps into stardust.

CHAPTER 8

It was the second week of August, and Jack was only a couple weeks away from heading off to college orientation at Georgetown. He had just walked out of his bedroom after starting to pack some clothes and some favorite personal items. He thought these special treasures would make his transition to dorm life a little easier given the somewhat abrupt break from his comfortable home life and his own space. He had rolled up his favorite Michael Jordan poster, along with a couple of his favorite books which he intended to place between the two bookends he had that were shaped to look like a football cut in half.

As he entered the kitchen to grab a glass of Arnold Palmer made by his mother earlier in the day, he heard a loud creaking thud come from the attached two-car garage. Having moved into a slightly larger and nicer house on a larger lot shortly after the marriage of Bob and Jack's mother, the large two-car garage was a nice feature compared to the narrow one-car garage at the previous house. Furthermore, the house was in a slightly nicer neighborhood, with a little more space and distance between homes.

Jack knew Bob was in the garage making sure Jack's car was up to speed for his approaching departure to Georgetown. Bob, hearing a slight rattle coming from the underside of Jack's car, had seen that a couple bolts holding the muffler were a little loose, so he had jacked up the car while it was in the garage to tighten them and give the underside a more careful visual inspection.

When Jack heard the thud, he immediately rushed through the kitchen door that led into the garage. He gasped in fear when he saw that the car jack had slipped out from under the front bumper, and the car had come down onto Bob's chest. Jack ran to the side of the car and ducked his head under. Bob was unconscious, but breathing and moaning in pain.

"Dad," Jack called out. "Dad, can you hear me? Are you all right?" When Bob didn't respond, Jack's first impulse was to try to pull his body out from under the car, but the chassis was pressed down so hard on Bob's chest that not only couldn't he budge Bob's lanky frame, but Bob seemed to moan even more when Jack tugged on him.

With the garage doors closed and the neighborhood being at a quiet time of day—and no one likely around to help—Jack ran inside to call 911. Jack quickly got a hold of a dispatcher who, after Jack explained what had happened, asked Jack if his father was conscious and breathing. Jack replied no to the first and yes to the second, at which time the dispatcher said he would immediately notify the fire department, followed by the police and an ambulance, but that the fire department should be on the scene in about five minutes.

Jack hung up the phone and rushed back into the garage. He saw that Bob's breathing had become more labored with the tremendous weight of a 3,500-pound car pressing on his chest. He saw that the jack had bent when the car collapsed, so there was no thought of trying to jack the car up again to get Bob free. Jack realized he would lose valuable minutes in trying to round up some neighbors to help him to try to lift the car before the Fire Department arrived.

Acting out of both frustration and fear, Jack, almost instinctively, moved to the side of the car close to the tire where the jack had been placed. With all his might, he hopelessly tried to raise the side of the car to relieve the pressure on Bob's chest. The car didn't budge.

Jack tried again, closing his eyes and muttering out loud, "God, help me, please." Within his next breath, Jack felt the car begin to rise up off the ground. Opening his eyes again, Jack suddenly found himself standing alongside a small group of people helping him to do what he alone could never do.

Without speaking, Jack looked to his right to see two full-grown men who had placed their hands in a similar position to Jack's to help lift the car. Jack's first impression of the men, given a combination of their dress and build, was that one was a soldier from some ancient Roman legion, while of the other was some type of stone mason fresh from helping to construct a new fifteenth century cathedral. To his left stood a rather large, somewhat bulky Germanic-looking woman who seemed to Jack like some eighteenth-century farmer's wife. The first thing that came to Jack's mind when he looked at the other two men on the other side of the farmer's wife were that they had just taken a break from shoveling coal in the furnace of some hundred-year-old luxury steamship.

With what appeared to be little or no strain in their faces, the five strangers and Jack proceeded to lift the car a few inches above Bob's chest. Bob began to inhale and then exhale several large breaths in a labored manner like a fish who had just been tossed onto dry land.

Having raised the car to a sufficient height, the woman next to Jack said in her Germanic or Nordic sounding accent, "Go ahead. Pull him out!" Jack letting go of the car didn't seem to faze the other's ability to keep it steady, as Jack quickly lowered himself on all fours, and began to drag Bob out from beneath the belly of the metallic beast. After he cleared Bob away from the car to safety, Jack grabbed a small bottle of drinking water off one of the garage shelves, poured some on a clean rag, and began to wipe Bobs' face and head, saying "Dad! Dad, are you ok?"

Slowly, Bob opened his eyes, first staring straight ahead with a dazed look on his somewhat reddened face. "What happened?" he said breathlessly. He then seemed to remember the last instant of the jack breaking loose with no time to react as the car fell on his chest. Since then he had been unconscious. Looking up at Jack as he lay on his back on the garage floor, he said, "You pulled me out from under the car? But *how*?"

Jack turned his head to look back at the car to see it was now sitting on all four wheels on the garage floor, and the five muscular helpers were nowhere to be seen.

Jack couldn't think of a better explanation and said, "The jack had slipped out from under the car and it fell on you. So I put the jack back under the front end by the wheel well, jacked it up, and was able to pull you out. And just as I got you clear, the jack collapsed a second time and the car collapsed again."

Bob looked at him questioningly, but then saw the bent jack lying just beside him. "God, I'm glad you were home to save me. Who knows what would have happened to me." As he said this, Bob suddenly became aware of the pain in his chest cavity, and winced. Seeing this, Jack said, "I called 911, and some more people are on their way to help."

"What do you mean by 'more' people?" Bob stammered, gritting his teeth a bit.

Realizing his poor choice of words, Jack said, "I think the dispatcher said he would send the Fire Department, the police and an ambulance."

"Well," Bob replied, wincing in pain, "I guess we don't need the Fire Department or police any more, thanks to your quick thinking. But I think I could use that ambulance." It would turn out Bob not only had a couple broken ribs, but a small fracture to his sternum and bruises to his lungs. But he would be home from the hospital in several days, enough time to see Jack off to college.

Of course, what Jack had in mind when he said, "more help," were the five strangers who had appeared just in the nick of time, then departed again as soon as their work was done. In thinking about the incident later in his bedroom, Jack would ponder the realization that these were not only the first visitors to appear as a group, but that none of them seemed to have any of the historical significance or fame like his earlier visitors, namely Simon Peter, Sigmund Freud and Galileo. Somehow, it made Jack feel a little comforted that these more-or-less average, everyday people from the past, also took an interest in him. That their purpose seemed simply to help him in a time of need, rather than to be some larger-than-life persona there to give him advice, clarity and direction.

It made Jack think to himself, and realize that *everyone* had a purpose in life. *Everyone* had something to offer, from the greatest mathematician at an Ivy League school, to the child with disabilities who he would see on one of those commercials for St. Jude's Hospital. Both were there, in Galileo's words, to "discover" something. In some cases, it was discovery of a new idea or scientific breakthrough. In others, it could simply be to allow someone else to "discover" their most unselfish feelings and heartfelt empathy for another struggling human being.

Jack had read up a little on Galileo in the couple of weeks following his conversation with him—his life, discoveries, beliefs and quotations. Jack thought, maybe that's sort of what Galileo meant when he said, "You cannot teach a man anything; you can only help him find it within himself."

CHAPTER 9

Late August arrived, and Jack had packed his car to the hilt with his belongings. They included necessities, like a rolled-up mattress for the dorm bed frame provided by the school, clothes his mother packed (as if he were going on an around-the-world expedition), to his more personal items that would make him feel more at home in his new accommodations.

Bob was home and recuperating well. He even insisted on helping Jack carry some things out to the car, despite the slightly halting steps he took due to some remaining soreness from his injuries. As Jack stood in the driveway ready to depart, Bob put out his hand to shake Jack's, but as Jack's hand clasped Bob's, Bob pulled him closer with a hug saying, "Good luck Jack. I know you'll do well. There's something *special* about you." (Jack thought to himself, *Boy, if only he knew the truth*).

As Bob gently pried himself apart from Jack, he added, "And thanks again for saving me from that freak accident.

I'm still not sure how you did it, but I'm just thankful you were there and did what you did."

"No problem, Dad. I'm glad I was there at the right time as well. And thanks for everything you've done for me. I couldn't ask for a better father." While even Jack's mother was a little surprised to hear those words from Jack, she nonetheless smiled at Jack's kind words. They certainly had an obvious impact on Bob who, perhaps a little overcome, just nodded his head with a heartfelt acknowledgment.

Like most mothers, Jack's Mom was more visibly emotional. Her thoughts alternated from a visual of Jack laughing as a young boy not very long ago, to his current stature as a young man on the verge of adulthood. But even as he began to resemble his father Tom as a young man more and more, he would always be her baby boy. Such is a mother's fate, whether considered to be a blessing or a curse.

As the now named Mrs. Gray hugged her son, she whispered in a soft voice as her eyes welled up, perhaps also with a thought of Tom. "Please drive safely Jack. Call us when you've gotten settled in the dorm. And let us know if you need anything."

"Sure Mom. I'll be fine. Don't worry."

"I love you, Jack."

"I love you too Mom. I'll be back before you know it. Certainly by Thanksgiving. I'm sure I'll be eager for some of your great home cooking by then. Bye."

Jack waived his hand out the window to his parents as he pulled out of the driveway, noticing how they held each other's hand as they waved goodbye. For a moment, Jack thought back to his initial misgivings about the then Mr. Gray, then Bob, and now Dad. All that had changed from having a more open mind (with a little help from a friend).

How glad he was that he was not leaving his mother alone, but with someone who loved her, and was the right partner and companion for her. Someone she also loved. Someone whom he could now say he loved as a father as well.

***

After driving some two hours from Midlothian to Georgetown using the somewhat confusing directions he had printed out—which required some difficult highway navigating to reach downtown Georgetown. (After all, it was the Washington, D.C. metro area, one of the country's worst traffic nightmares and confounding road systems.) Jack finally made his way onto Prospect Street, some three-tenths of a mile from the University campus. Jack realized he would have to become a quick study on getting around the Georgetown and D.C. area to avoid frustration.

As he drove up Prospect Street toward the campus, he felt a rush of exhilaration, not just from being on the cusp of starting his college experience, but driving past the beautiful (some stunning), array of colonial red brick homes, clapboard houses, and brick-and-stone row houses that lined the neighborhood. What a fascinating historical landscape to take in as he furthered his studies. After all, Georgetown is the oldest Catholic and Jesuit institution of higher learning in the country.

Being not only a history buff but also having an interest in architectural styles and their changes over time, Jack had read up on the development of Georgetown over the summer. While dramatically influenced by the establishment of the nation's capital in 1791 a few miles south along the Potomac River, Georgetown retained its own special character.

Despite several very special pre-Revolutionary buildings, most of the housing stock was developed after 1800, with the majority of that having being constructed after 1870, much of it in the form of row houses reflective of the Victorian period. A variety of styles illustrated larger national trends in architecture with many examples of Georgian mansions and townhouses, Federal and Classical Revival houses, and later developments representing the ante-and-post-bellum periods. [1]

What was hard to believe, especially to first-time visitors and others unfamiliar with its history, was that Georgetown had become one of the metro area's worst slums in the period after WWI, with buildings falling into neglect and disrepair. According to what Jack had read, the area's waterfront, with its prominent C&O Canal, had prospered following the Civil War (becoming a home to many freed slaves) and well into the 1880s, growing into a fashionable quarter. However, a series of floods of the Potomac River beginning in the in the 1880s severely damaged the Canal, causing the company which operated it to go bankrupt.[2] Of course, the C&O Canal Company had also been impacted by an increasing shift to railway transportation as a favored means of transport for its primary cargo, coal from the Allegheny Mountains, ushering in a long period of economic decline.

The downward trend began to finally reverse itself with the New Deal efforts of the 1930s, as owners, landlords, and developers began to take advantage of the solid and architecturally significant building stock of both residential and commercial properties. The trend continued even to today, with former mansions of ship-owners and merchants, as well as older commercial buildings comprised of hotels, taverns, banks, and other commercial properties, being rejuvenated.

Jack could feel the historic vibes as he made his way to the parking lot closest to his assigned dormitory housing, known as Nevils Hall. Instead of beginning to unload his car, he decided to park and take a leisurely stroll around the center of campus to take full advantage of the moment. He had his sights on standing in the Quadrangle, one of the oldest historic sections of the campus, with buildings dating back to the University's founding in 1789.[3]

With his campus map in hand, Jack made his way along one of the paths through Healy's Lawn, passing the statue of Archbishop John Carroll, the founder of GU and the first Catholic bishop in the United States. He proceeded along Old North Way before turning the corner into the Quadrangle, which was an almost completely enclosed courtyard with adjoining buildings connecting on three of its sides.

At the entrance to the Quad, stood the Dahlgren Chapel of the Sacred Heart, a freestanding building flanked by red brick and stone-paved pathways leading to the center of the square. The Chapel, constructed in 1873 in the Gothic Revival architectural style, was actually located in the historic center of the campus, even though it was certainly not the oldest existing structure there.

That honor belonged to the Old North Building, situated directly beyond the Chapel and forming the northernmost side of the U-shaped building envelope that formed the Quad. The Old North Building, lovingly referred to by locals simply as Old North, had been constructed in 1795 in the Georgian style, although it did not officially open until 1797.

It was in that year, on August 7, 1797, that President George Washington gave a speech from the south steps of the building to a group assembled in Dahlgren Quadrangle. Over the next two centuries, numerous presidents would make an address from the same steps, while others attended graduation commencements and still others visited the building. Presidents who engaged in these historic activities included John Quincy Adams, John Taylor, Zachery Taylor, Franklin Pierce, James Buchanan, Andrew Johnson, Ulysses S. Grant, and most recently, Gerald Ford.

One of the most historic moments on the steps was the address Abraham Lincoln gave to the 69th Infantry Regiment of New York in May 1861 to troops temporarily quartered on campus. All-in-all, some one-dozen presidents had either visited Old North or given an address from the same steps that Jack now stood gazing. Accordingly, the name given to the cherished site was, in fact, the President's Steps. Not as old or as famous as the Spanish Steps of Rome, Jack thought, but impressive nonetheless.

Mesmerized by the thought of how many famous people from American history had stood just feet from where he now stood, and wrapped up in the moment, Jack was suddenly surprised by a gentle tap on his left shoulder and a voice saying, "Excuse me?"

In a split second, a list of names raced through Jack's mind, but seemed to center on a single one. Without turning around, Jack simply uttered aloud in an eager yet questioning voice the first and uppermost name on his mind. "George?" Jack said. He slowly turned picturing President Washington in his mind, only to find himself staring into the face of a young man about his own age dressed in jeans and a T-shirt, carrying a dark gray knapsack that seemed heavily laden with books.

"Uuhh....no," said the dark-haired collegiate-looking man wearing black-rimmed eyeglasses. "The name is Kyle. This is my first day here, and I was hoping you could tell me how to get to Ryan Administration Building?"

Jack stood there saying nothing. Half of him was relieved. (How would he be able to strike up a conversation with *the* George Washington with all the other people walking past or otherwise milling around in the Quad?) But the other half of him was disappointed. Who *wouldn't* want to have the opportunity to have a conversation with *the* George Washington?

"Sorry," Jack finally muttered, "this is my first day too. But I have a campus map here." Looking at the map of numbered buildings and index of names, Jack was quickly able to find the Ryan Building and said to Kyle, "Oh, here it is. It looks like you make a right just past the chapel and it's the second building on the right."

"Great, thanks," Kyle responded with a smile. "I gotta get me one of those maps in the bookstore. See you around." With that, Kyle darted off to take care of whatever business he had at Admin.

Jack's heart was still racing a bit from his initial thought and reaction to what if he came face to face to face with George Washington. He shook his head a bit and thought to himself, *maybe I just better go and get settled in my dorm. I've got a lot of unloading and unpacking to do.*

***

Jack unloaded his car, thankful that he had help from assigned upperclassmen given he had more stuff than he thought he originally packed. Everything had to be carried a few hundred feet and up a flight of stairs since the elevator was either too small for larger items or seemed constantly in use.

His unpacking completed, Jack laid back on his newly made-up bed and looked around his room. The two-person standard dorm room was perfectly symmetrical, with a double window on the front wall, with a bed on each side along the adjoining wall, so neither bed location offered a better view than the other. There was a decent-sized desk toward the foot of each bed, followed by a sliding door closet for each occupant, each offering a reasonable number of shelves, storage compartments and a pole for hanging.

Since Jack's roommate hadn't arrived yet, he arbitrarily selected the left side of the room and had already put up a couple of his favorite posters, plus some select knickknacks and books on the double-row wall shelf that hung above his desk. He was looking at his Michael Jordan poster, and thinking about his eagerness to see the nationally ranked Georgetown Hoyas basketball team once the season kicked off in early October.

He recalled the rivalry between Air Jordan and the North Carolina Tar Heels vs. Patrick Ewing and the Georgetown Hoyas, with the final shot by Michael Jordan cementing the win over GU by a score of 63-62 in the NCAA basketball finals just a year ago. While he was certain he would get a little heat for having a poster of the devil incarnate himself who single-handedly destroyed the dreams of the Hoyas, he figured most people would come to agree with him that Jordan was perhaps the best player to ever pick up a basketball.

Students, faculty and alumni took comfort that Georgetown would go on to win its first national title two years later against Houston, with Patrick Ewing winning the Most Outstanding Player award. Under the then and current coach John Thompson, Jack and everyone else with a GU connection looked forward to a continuing track record of "Top 20" teams.

Jack was suddenly shaken out of his sports frame of mind by the sound of something banging against his dorm room door. He moved to the door and opened it to see a tall, blond-haired, athletic-looking young man who was trying to balance a suitcase, a duffle bag, and a lamp while attempting to jar the door open.

"Hi," the young man said. "I guess we're roommates."

"Welcome," Jack replied with a friendly smile. "I just finished setting up myself. My name is Jack Moran."

"Hi Jack. My name is John, John Carroll."

"John Carroll?" Jack said with a grin. "I thought you'd be a lot older and maybe wearing a bishop's purple mitre and carrying a large staff!"

"Funny," John said, with a half-smile, half smirk on his face, but not in an unpleasant manner. "I get a lot of that. But my father, Tom Carroll, is an alumnus and he and my mom thought it would be a clever idea to name me John, after the founder of Georgetown. Seems like the joke's on me."

"Hey, I'm just kidding, man. It's actually a good strong name. Despite the ribbing you'll get, maybe the fringe benefits of a name like that will be more than the small negatives. It could actually be a great pick-up line in meeting girls around here."

"I sure hope so." John said with a little devilish grin. "Maybe it'll give me 'a leg up' if you get my drift."

Jack gave a laugh out loud. "Hey, when you do, don't forget your favorite roommate when you get to the henhouse." John also laughed. "I think we're going to get along just fine, Jack. How about a little help with this stuff?"

"Sure," Jack said as he reached for the lamp.

CHAPTER 10

It was the middle of September, and Jack had been in classes a couple weeks already. Like most freshman, he was still unsure what his major should be, but he had plenty of time to decide. He wasn't even sure which of the specific schools he wanted to enroll in—Business, Foreign Affairs, or the Liberal Arts College. (Jack had no interest in the fourth of the University school branches, the School of Nursing and Health Studies). Nevertheless, since he was required to complete the University Core Curriculum in any event, he also had a full year to decide.

He had enrolled in one of the several required subject areas, including philosophy, writing, history, and theology. Since he thought he might later want to enter the School of Foreign Affairs, he also enrolled in a French language class. Language was a requirement in the Foreign Affairs School and, having taken three years of French in high school, Jack thought that made the most sense.

Jack had already made a few friends in his dorm, including Kyle, the kid he had briefly mistaken for George Washington while he was lost in thought staring at the Presidential Steps that first day. Kyle was certainly no President Washington, a bit nerdy, but a nice guy just the same. Turns out they both shared a love of history.

In fact, as far as American history went, Jack thought he probably could not be in a better place to take advantage of the learning experience that Washington, D.C. had to offer. Just the memorials and museums in and around the Pedestrian Mall alone could keep a history buff like Jack salivating for months, if not years.

Managed and operated by the National Parks Service, the National Mall contained more than a hundred monuments and memorials. As the brochures he picked up during his first weekend as a GU resident said; "Each year, millions of people visit National Mall and Memorial Parks to recreate, to commemorate presidential legacies, to honor our nation's veterans, to make their voices heard, and to celebrate our nation's commitment to freedom and equality."

Jack had already made eagerly awaited visits to some of the Mall's most prominent, well-known museums and monuments. First, the Smithsonian Institute, known as "the nation's attic" with its collection of more than 154 million items of historical significance. Included among those items were the stovepipe hat worn by President Lincoln, the original Teddy Bear named after President Theodore Roosevelt, and the ruby slippers worn by Judy Garland in the 1939 film classic *The Wizard of Oz*.[2]

Next was the Air and Space Museum, with Charles Lindbergh's Spirit of St. Louis plane suspended from the fifty-foot-high ceiling in Flight Hall, along with John Glenn's Friendship Mercury space capsule.

Jack spent an hour sitting on a stone bench just staring at the Washington Monument, a 555-foot marble obelisk towering over D.C., dedicated to the "Father of His Country," who was "First in War, First in Peace, and First in the Hearts of our Countrymen."

Even more impressive to Jack was the Jefferson Memorial, constructed of white marble and designed in a rotunda style reminiscent of Jefferson's own design of his famous home in Charlottesville, Virginia, *Monticello*. On the southern wall were engraved perhaps Jefferson's most famous words from the Declaration of Independence of which he was the principal author:

"We hold these truths to be self-evident, that all men are created equal, that they are endowed by their Creator with certain unalienable rights, that among these are life, liberty, and the pursuit of happiness..." [3]

It had been a very busy day for Jack. He had crowded a ton of touring into seeing the National Mall since the morning hours. But he recalled seeing photos of the Lincoln Memorial lit up at night, and now he could see it slightly over a mile from where he stood at the Jefferson Memorial, at the opposite end of the Mall. It was truly an awe-inspiring site, like some Great Pyramid rising out of the ground to commemorate some divine deity. He just had to see it under the veil of darkness, appearing like some beacon of freedom pulling him toward it. With a fresh burst of energy, he began the thirty-minute walk that would take him to those hallowed steps.

After his long day, Jack was definitely feeling a little tired by the time he arrived at the steps. But just approaching the Lincoln Memorial in the evening hours felt like an almost magical experience, with light emanating out from between the thirty-six fluted Doric columns (one for each state at the time of Lincoln's death). Jack mounted the steps to gaze in awe at the somber yet welcoming solitary figure of Lincoln, nearly twenty feet in height, sitting in contemplation like some ancient god, his hands resting on Roman fasces, a symbol of power and jurisdiction.

Inscribed on opposite walls on either side of Lincoln were perhaps the two greatest speeches ever written, the Gettysburg Address and Lincoln's second inaugural address, the latter given just six weeks before he was to be felled by an assassin's bullet.[4]

Certainly, the first sentence of the Gettysburg Address is ingrained in the minds of most Americans, certainly history buffs and students such as Jack:

Four score and seven years ago our fathers brought forth on this continent, a new nation, conceived in Liberty, and dedicated to the proposition that all men are created equal. [5]

With those thirty words, Lincoln reestablished the just principle of what Jefferson and the other founding fathers had sought to create. In the final sentence of his speech, he reiterated the very framework of what the new democracy, a new experiment, was all about, and what so many thousands had died for in the Civil War conflict:

...that this nation, under God, shall have a new birth of freedom—and that government of the people, by the people, for the people, shall not perish from the earth. [5]

Incredible words, spoken to the common citizen, by an incredible leader. So unfortunate that his life was prematurely forfeited before he could complete his mission and purpose of national unity.

It was at that moment that Jack, standing alone in the Memorial interior in the late evening, noticed a man to his left leaning against one of the interior pilasters. The man was slightly smaller than Jack by a few inches, maybe about five foot eight, with a compact build and jet-black curly hair of medium length, and a dark mustache. He was wearing a dark flannel jacket that seemed reminiscent to Jack of some period piece from around the mid-nineteenth century.

He looked familiar to Jack, like an old photograph he had seen in a schoolbook he had read. Jack glanced back at Lincoln sitting in the chair, and then turned again to the man perhaps fifteen feet away from him.

The man stood up straight and walked toward Jack with the movements of an athlete. He stopped about five feet from Jack and said in a well-spoken, almost theatrical voice, with the hint of a southern accent, "From the look on your face Jack, I gather you recognize me."

Without smiling, but rather with a somewhat strained expression, Jack responded, "I hope I'm wrong, but I think I might."

"Then I shall introduce myself to avoid speculation. I am John Wilkes Booth—actor, son of the Confederacy, and hated assassin."

Jack hesitated a moment, as thoughts of the irony of the situation he found himself in raced through his mind. He felt the anger build inside him, having come face-to-face with such a despicable villain. "Of all the great and famous American heroes, leaders, statesmen I've seen on my walks today, I'm beyond disappointment that I get a visit from *you* of all people. And especially here, where we stand on sacred ground, defiled by your very presence."

"It certainly wasn't my idea Jack. I can't fight the will of you know who," as he pointed an index finger toward the heavens. "You see, it's His idea of poetic justice. Not only for my sin of killing an innocent man whose heart and compassion were as big as his intellect, but also as a reminder to me of my cowardly act—part of my punishment."

"*Punishment?*" Jack nearly shouted. "I would have thought someone like you would be destined to spend eternity in the fires of Hell!"

"Well, Jack, there really aren't any fires, or Hell the way you think of it. For souls deserving of just punishment like me, rather, there is the absence of that 'connection' to all the other souls that have gone before us, or come after us. At least until God decides it is time for us to join with the rest of the spiritual universe. Frankly, I don't know when that time will be, but I have come to understand the utterly despicable nature of the act that I committed, and my just punishment."

Booth continued with a trace of sorrow in his voice. "At the time, I thought of myself as a soldier for the South, and we were still at war. Thousands of my Confederate brothers had been killed or maimed, families and homesteads destroyed, and what we thought of as our cherished way of life…destroyed. I now know that way of life was based on the imposition of a system of human cruelty and injustice. It really was America's Original Sin. And the nation, my countrymen, continue to suffer many of the consequences of that intolerable system.

"And not only did I take a life, I took the life of the one man who would have made things better for my brothers and sisters of the South after the war. Just look at those words on the wall behind me."

Booth tilted his head slightly, motioning to the words from Lincoln's second inaugural address:

With malice toward none, with charity for all, with firmness in the right as God gives us to see the right, let us strive on to finish the work we are in, to bind up the nation's wounds, to care for him who shall have borne the battle and for his widow and his orphan, to do all which may achieve and cherish a just and lasting peace among ourselves and with all nations.[6]

"Does that sound like the words of a vindictive, vengeful man bent on punishing those who had dared to rise up against the Union? Or who would have condoned a system of continued racial segregation, violence and human suffering?" Booth asked. "Of course not. Unfortunately, I never read those words of his prior to the assassination. In firing that bullet into the head of that truly noble man, I doomed the South, my brothers and sisters, to a more difficult and perilous path than if Lincoln had lived.

"I know Lincoln would have embraced the people of the South, his countrymen, much like the father who embraced the return of the prodigal son. He would have helped to rebuild the South, expanded its industries, created laws and institutions that would have helped bind the wounds and create new opportunities for all peoples. That knowledge that I have come to realize, along with my loss of connection to God and my fellow man, is the unbearable punishment I am made to endure, deservedly so.

"But God, in all his great power and wisdom, is also all forgiving. The time will come where I will be able to join in spirit with the rest of my brethren, including my family and friends, which I so, so very much yearn for."

After Booth spoke, Jack almost began to feel sorry for the man, or rather the lost soul that stood before him. But Jack was only human, and he still found it difficult to forgive. Maybe that would have to wait until the afterlife. He looked at Booth with more sadness than anger in his eyes and said, "But why are you here with me now? Why do you visit *me*?"

"The reasons for my appearance to you, Jack, is really two-fold. First, it is part of the pain I am meant to suffer to see someone like you, someone of higher principles and character than I myself demonstrated in my life, standing in admiration of such a great man, and further realizing the harm that I have caused to generations.

"Secondly, Jack, is to perhaps give you some advice, lessons, from the things I have come to understand. Mine was a cowardly act. It was an act more about 'me,' rather than thinking of the consequences to others. So, my message to you is: not only must you think carefully about the consequences of how it might hurt others before you take a certain action, but at the same time, to encourage you that you *should* take action when it is to the undeniable benefit of others. To put it another way, don't take an action that is in fact cowardly. But at the same time, don't be afraid to take an unselfish action, to overcome your fear and to be a hero, rather than a coward, when the moment requires it. When the moment is right, you will know it, and you will find the *strength* to do it."

"I'm not sure I understand," Jack replied.

"You will, Jack. You will. We all face certain moments like that in our lives. For some people, it's as simple as making the conscious decision to not take part in making fun of, or ridiculing somebody who may be simply different than us—whether it's a difference in their culture, their physical appearance, or not being as smart or as privileged as we are. It takes a certain courage to stand up against the bullies, the racists, those who think they are superior or better than others are.

"At the other extreme, it can be the courage of the firefighter to run into a burning building to save the lives of a trapped child, the elderly, or infirmed. Or the courage of the soldier who risks his life to pull a wounded comrade out of the line of fire to safety. That is the courage of heroes."

Still a little confused, Jack replied, "I know I don't always live up to the Christian, well, not just Christians, but the human ideals of justice and benevolence. But I believe I will become, or at least have the opportunity before me to become, a better person. That's one reason I enrolled in a school founded by Jesuits.

"But I may never have the opportunity to be the other kind of hero you mention. I'm really not intending to follow those kinds of paths or livelihoods—a soldier, policeman, fireman, or whatever, which might place me in those kinds of situations."

"Who can say, Jack?" Booth replied. Other than Him, that is," again pointing his finger to the sky. "I think he has some special plans in store for you, or He wouldn't have given you this gift. Do you?"

Jack was still searching for the answer to that question in his own mind, and almost pleadingly asked, "That's what I still don't understand. Why did God choose *me* for this so-called gift? I'm just a regular guy. I'm not that special!"

Booth looked at Jack sympathetically, understanding his doubts. "Jack, throughout history God has often chosen men, women, even children, who didn't possess great wealth, or power, or influence, or other qualities that mankind often looks up to. Rather, to quote the Bible, God spoke to Samuel, saying; 'The Lord does not look at the things man looks at. Man looks at the outward appearance, but the Lord looks at the heart.'

Jack was surprised to hear Booth's words and said, "Kind of ironic to hear words from the Bible spoken by you. I certainly wouldn't consider you to be a religious man based on your history."

"In reality, Jack, having attended both a Quaker-run boarding school and an Episcopalian military school in my youth, I was actually well-versed in the teachings of the Bible." Adding with a slight southern drawl, he continued. "But that doesn't mean I was particularly attentive to practicing those teachings very well during my tenure here on earth."

Jack almost began to feel sorry for the man and wondered what in his upbringing and youth led him to be so misguided and driven by hate. It was clear he was now remorseful for his heinous act, but perhaps only God could truly forgive him and ultimately bring him peace.

Perhaps echoing Jack's thoughts, Booth finally said, "In my own words, Jack, God looks into a person's heart, and their willingness to do good and to trust in Him. Even though you have wavered in that belief in the past, and may waver yet again, God has looked deep into your heart, has seen, and believes in you. Continue to trust in Him."

With that, the troubled assassin—or now to Jack, just a troubled man—known as John Wilkes Booth, vanished in as brief a moment as a flicker of the surrounding lights within the Memorial's main room. Jack looked up at the seated Lincoln and thought how he wished it was old Abe himself that had made his appearance to him, and not Booth. But as he looked into those deep penetrating eyes of Lincoln, Jack felt that maybe he was there in spirit, after all. And maybe we can learn something not just from the good, but from the scoundrels and villains of the world as well.

CHAPTER 11

O ver the next couple of months, Jack was getting increasingly comfortable with university life. Beyond life in classrooms and lecture halls—listening to the various professors and teaching assistants with their wide variety of personalities and mannerisms—he was beginning to understand hot buttons and oftentimes liberal vs. conservative leanings of these subject matter experts.

His gradual acclimation also extended to the pluses and minuses of dormitory life. The minuses were many, whether it be loss of privacy, disruptions from noise or interruptions, limitations of space or, with no fridge in the room, the inability to grab that cold soft drink or some ice cream in the late evenings that was so easily available (and underappreciated) while living at home.

On the plus side, he had made a fair number of friends already, both in his dorm and in some of his classes. Despite the distractions, it was also fun, or at least less boring, to almost always have some level of activity, people, and spontaneous conversations that were part of dorm life and campus life in general.

Jack was also becoming more knowledgeable of the surrounding Georgetown neighborhood. His level of interest and excitement in the history and architecture of the area had grown. That included some of the many college bars in the area. While there were some two dozen bars in Georgetown proper, many of the more upscale ones could not be considered your typical college bar, and students didn't frequent those (unless they were on a hot date and trying to impress a hoped-for girlfriend).

He would have loved to visit what was the last remaining Federal-period tavern in the area, City Tavern, one of its oldest buildings, dating back to 1796. Unfortunately, it had long been a private club under the City Tavern Association that was founded in 1959 to restore the building. In its early days, the tavern had been frequented by many of the country's founding fathers, including George Washington, Thomas Jefferson and John Adams.[1]

Cool stuff, Jack thought to himself. Jack imagined how great it would be to share a beer with GW, Tom J and Mr. A. But despite the visitations and very real manifestations he had experienced so far, he figured this was just a pie in the sky fantasy that would never materialize. And he was probably right. There seemed to be more meaning behind his meetings with his otherworldly compatriots than simply an excuse to belt down a few beers.

Jack's attitude was like many students. He worked hard at his studies, but also liked to party on weekends with his friends as long as he kept up with getting good grades. And given the distractions of dormitory life, and sometimes the difficulty of concentrating sitting at his tiny desk in his room writing a difficult essay or composition, he often found himself sitting in the large hall of the University's Lauinger Library—or occasionally one of its many study rooms.

One such day sitting in the main Hall of the library, he noticed a girl from one of his lecture halls seated about twenty feet away on the opposite side of the long oak table. As part of the core curriculum requiring two social science courses, she had also selected the one Introduction to General Psychology. Jack had selected the course because he thought it would be interesting—that he might learn more about what makes people tick and behave the way they do, giving him a better idea on how to understand, respond, and communicate with them. Perhaps.

He had noticed the girl in his large class of about 200 students, but didn't know her name. She certainly was cute—very cute—with her slightly wavy blond hair that came down about six inches past her shoulders. He had never gotten close enough to her to notice much in the way of her other features, but he thought that maybe this was his chance.

He tried to think of something clever to say, maybe related to some concept or behavior principle picked up from their psychology class that he could turn into a humorous introduction.

He thought about asking her if he could borrow a pen from her, that he had forgotten his. Then, as she handed the pen to him, to say something about one of the five psychological functions they had learned in class being "motivation,"... that he really had a pen of his own but was using that excuse as motivation to introduce himself to her. But Jack thought that might be a little weird or awkward, so he let the thought pass.

Instead, being a pretty straight shooter and not one to play games, Jack decided the direct approach was the simplest and most honest. He simply walked up to the table where she was sitting, sat down opposite her, and said, "Hi, my name is Jack. Jack Moran. You're in Professor Temple's Psych class, right?"

She looked up at him, and Jack was immediately struck by her beautiful blue eyes. At first, she seemed to offer no hint of expression as to what she was thinking, but then said, "Yes, hi. I recognize you too. My name is Sarah. Sarah Mack."

"Nice to meet you, Sarah. Hope I'm not interrupting you or anything."

"No, no problem.... Jack." She smiled a little when she said his name, which was a little encouraging to Jack. She leaned over and whispered, so as not to disturb anyone nearby, saying "In fact, I'm working on that essay assignment Professor Temple gave us and, sorry to say, I'm struggling with it a little bit."

"Oh yeah," Jack replied matter of fact. "We were discussing *Thinking and Intelligence* in class and "what makes smarts." The assignment is to describe three smart people and what contributes to their intelligence. I know it's not due until the end of the month, but I already finished writing mine."

"Really?" Sarah replied a little sheepishly.

Jack realized this may have come off a little cocky, and tried to reel it back in a bit by saying: "I had a couple other papers due around the same time and just decided to knock off what I thought was the easiest one first."

"The easiest one?" Sarah replied quizzically.

Jack felt the hole he was digging for himself getting deeper, and again tried to retreat. "You see, I had read some interesting historical biography stuff over the summer and so it was fresh on my mind. Otherwise, I'm sure it would have been difficult for me."

Sarah seemed to accept that response, to his relief. "So, what three people did you write about?"

"Well, I wrote my essay on Sigmund Freud, Galileo, and Abraham Lincoln."

"Well, that's a little bit of an odd, but interesting trio," Sarah replied.

Jack felt at least he had her attention. "Well, just prior to talking about *Thinking and Intelligence* in class, we also talked about the concept of Perception. I think perception is a key attribute of intelligence, and I happen to know all three of those guys were very perceptive, so I decided to write about them."

"What do you mean 'you happen to know' they were very perceptive?"

Jack mumbled something unintelligible, telling himself not to panic, as he tried to think of something to say.

"Well, from what they said or did, and the insights they made as documented in history, they obviously were very perceptive, and intelligent, individuals. That's all."

"Oh, I see." Sarah smiled. "I think you've given me some insight yourself, Jack, as to how to approach this assignment. Thanks."

"Glad I could help, Sarah." Jack thought maybe he better not overstay his welcome, since Sarah obviously had some work to do.

"I'll let you get back to your assignment. I have some studying to do myself for the history course I'm taking. Our professor, Wilcox, loves to call on people in class to see if they've actually done the reading assignments, and comprehended it. He reminds me a little of the very imposing Professor Kingsfield in the movie *Paper Chase*. I don't want to be embarrassed like one of the law students Kingsfield liked to humiliate in his class through his Socratic teaching style when they were not up to speed."

"Oh, I *love* that movie," Sarah said with some delight. "I think that's one professor that I'll try to avoid. Thanks for the warning. That's two helpful pieces of advice you've given me tonight, Jack." She smiled warmly, but somewhat shyly. "How can I repay your kindness?"

Jack hesitated a brief moment, but he quickly recovered, thinking about needing an excuse to come up to her the next time he saw her in class. He smiled and said, "Do you have an extra pen I can borrow?"

CHAPTER 12

That weekend, Jack attended the Hoyas Friday night basketball game at their home court, US Air Arena located in Landover, Maryland, a suburb east of D.C. It was another dominant win, this time over Seton Hall, led by sophomore Allen Iverson. Jack and a few of his friends had traveled the ten miles from campus to the arena by means of one of the free buses provided to students by the University.

Jack was hoping he might see Sarah there, but had no idea if she had any interest whatsoever in basketball. Not seeing her on his particular bus, or lined up to get on one of the other buses, he had scanned the student seating areas upon arrival at the arena to try and find her, but to no avail.

After the game, he went to a couple of the local college bars off campus, also hoping to catch a glimpse of Sarah, but again, without success. Maybe, he thought to himself, that was a good thing, rather than find her at the bar with another student rival. *Rival?* Jack thought to himself. *I haven't' even been out on a single date, or been with her among a group of friends for crying out loud. How can I consider myself a possible 'rival' to some other guy?*

But there was no doubt about it; there was something about Sarah that he liked. Jack wasn't shy. Rather, he was one of those people who found it easy to talk to some people almost from the get go, while others took him a long time to warm up to and feel comfortable enough to converse with minus the usual inhibitions. For some yet unclear reason, Sarah was definitely in the first category. While totally a premature assessment on his part, he thought Sarah might feel the same way, having observed her somewhat solitary behavior in Psych class. That was certainly not unusual among many, perhaps most students, especially freshman.

Jack walked from his dorm to attend Tuesday afternoon's lecture by Professor Temple with more eagerness than usual. He knew, unless she was sick or something, that Sarah would be in Psyche class. He arrived a few minutes early, hoping that not only would she be there but also that he might find an empty seat next to her.

He was in luck. He spotted her sitting in the fifth row left of the center aisle, the third seat in. Both chairs on either side of her were empty. He shuffled into the aisle where she sat and said, "I'm always good at returning things, so here's your pen back. And thanks."

Sarah smiled. "No problem, Jack. Like I said, I owe you."

Gesturing to the empty seat to her right, Jack said, "Mind if I sit here?"

She gestured, "Not at all." As Jack sat down, he couldn't help but notice how she filled out the front of her cotton pullover sweater rather nicely. While a little hard to tell sitting down, he imagined she had a very attractive figure.

Jack turned toward her. "So how did you make out on that essay for Psych class?"

"Thanks to your insight and suggestion, it's done. I thought about some of the most perceptive women I know, either personally or from history. So, I chose Abigail Adams, Margaret Thatcher, and, last but not least, my grandmother. You obviously know your history, so I don't need to tell you about the first two. As for my grandmother, she actually was the principal of our local high school for many years, and she's one of the most perceptive and smartest people I know. She only retired a couple years ago."

"That's great!" Jack exclaimed. "Where's your high school? Where are you from?"

"I'm from Lebanon, Pennsylvania. That's where my grandmother was principal of Lebanon High School."

"Lebanon, where exactly is that?"

"Oh, it's about twenty-five miles east of Harrisburg, or about a ninety-minute drive west of Philly."

"OK, I know about where it is then."

As Jack uttered those words, Professor Temple entered the door at the front of the lecture hall, and conversations among the students quickly quieted down.

The Professor began his lecture by saying, "Good afternoon class. Today we're going to discuss one of the five major domains of psychology, namely biological."

Jack glanced sideways at Sarah, who was becoming increasingly attractive to him. As he sat close to her, he could smell a whiff of the fragrant shampoo from her blond hair. He thought to himself, *I'd better pay close attention. This could prove to be not only interesting, but also very educational.*

***

After class ended, Jack asked Sarah if she had any more classes scheduled today.

"Yes, I have a core theology course in an hour in this same building," she said, as she fumbled with her books a bit. Jack said he also had a history class an hour from now in a nearby building.

"Rather than go back to our dorms, would you like to grab a cup of coffee and hang out for a while before our next class?" Jack asked with a hopeful look in his eyes.

Sarah played with the end of her hair, smiled and said, "Sure." Jack not only thought Sarah had a very nice smile, but he was struck again by those amazing bluish-gray eyes.

As they walked to Healy Student Center for coffee, Jack finally had a chance to see Sarah in other than a sitting position. She was probably a shade under five foot seven or about five inches shorter than he was. Her slightly wavy blond hair framed her face, which Jack began to think was more than just very cute, but some might consider to be beautiful. Her figure he would probably describe as curvy yet sleek. With her high cheekbones, and hint of rosy cheeks on a somewhat pale complexion, Jack thought she really had the makings of a model. But he doubted, with her somewhat shy, introverted personality, that she would be interested in something like that.

After picking up their coffee, which he insisted on paying for, Jack suggested they sit outside on one of the benches in front of the Lauinger Library. Having introduced himself to Sarah inside the library, Jack thought that maybe it would be a lucky sanctuary for him.

As they sat on a stone bench outside the imposing stone building, Jack tried to get to know Sarah better by asking about all the typical things you might want to know about a new acquaintance, especially one of the opposite sex. How did she like GU so far? Any idea what she wanted to major in or have in the way of a career? What was it like growing up in Lebanon? Did she have any brothers or sisters?

As Sarah talked, he found himself increasingly interested in her life, her background, her beliefs, what she had to say—in other words—what kind of person she was. In doing so, she in turn seemed less reserved and more comfortable than he thought she might be in talking to him.

Unlike Jack, she came from a large family of three sisters and two brothers, with Sarah being the second oldest behind her sister Kate. Her brothers, Brian and Stephen, followed her, with her sister Ellie being the baby of the family. Her siblings were generally about two years apart, which she said made for a fun, sometimes riotous, upbringing, but undoubtedly stressful at times for her parents. With her father being a teacher, and her mother a nurse, she considered herself strictly middle class. But, with five mouths to feed, clothe, educate and entertain, their family certainly didn't live "high on the hog," in her words.

As Jack questioned her, Sarah said she was thinking of getting a liberal arts degree, with perhaps a major in English/writing/literature, or along those lines, and actually get her accreditation to become a teacher, like her father. Unlike her father, who taught high school mathematics, her focus was on becoming an elementary school teacher. "I don't quite possess the confidence and speaking abilities of my father, and I think I might have a tough time with teenagers, who can be a little aggressive at times. But I love young kids, especially the lower grades, and I think not only would I love teaching them, but I think I could be good at it."

Meanwhile, Jack sat listening attentively, absorbing it all—not only her soft features, but the gentle melody of her voice and sincerity of her expression. Her demeanor and tone were certainly more friendly rather than serious or self-absorbed.

Sarah stopped talking for a moment and glanced at her watch. "Wow, the time went really fast! We only have ten minutes to get to our next classes, so I guess we had better go. And I never got to ask you some of the same questions you asked me, to tell me about yourself, Jack."

"Well," Jack said with a smile, "that was part of the plan. To keep you in suspense so I could have things to talk to you about next time we meet."

Sarah smiled as she brushed her hair back from her forehead. "I look forward to that Jack. You know, I don't usually open up to people as easily as I seem to be able to talk to you."

Jack gave his best wry, jokester smile. "It's my gift."

Sarah laughed at his words and expression, saying, "I guess so. We'll have to do it again soon."

"How about this Friday night? We can catch whatever movie is playing at the auditorium and then maybe grab a beer at Bulldog Tavern. What do you say, as long as it's yes?"

Sarah smiled back at Jack, but at the same time seemed a little unsure, or apprehensive. After a brief pause, she said, "Sure, I'd like that, Jack."

"Great," Jack smiled. "Those movies typically start at eight o'clock Fridays, so suppose I meet you in front of your dorm at 7:30? What dorm are you in anyway?"

"That time works. I'm in Reynolds Hall, just before the Athletics Center building."

"OK. I'll see you then."

With that, Sarah got up from the bench, gave a little short wave, and said, "OK. Bye Jack."

As Sarah walked off to her next class, Jack realized he should have offered to walk back toward the lecture hall with her, as he was going in that general direction anyway. Maybe she felt a little surprised or apprehensive Jack had asked her out so quickly. But she seemed genuinely interested in talking to him, and seeing him again. Maybe it was just nerves on her part.

As Jack walked toward his next class, he had to pass by the Student Center again, so he quickly looked at the schedule on the bulletin board in the lobby to verify the show time and see what movie was playing. His eyes nearly bugged out of his head, and his heart seemed to flutter a bit when he saw the movie playing Friday evening was *The Paper Chase,* starring Timothy Bottoms and John Houseman. *What incredible luck,* he thought to himself. *It must be a good omen.* Then he remembered one of the expressions uttered by the Franklin Ford III character in the movie as he thought to himself, *'Damn Good.'*

CHAPTER 13

Friday evening arrived and Jack took the stroll from Nevils Hall to Reynolds Hall. With Daylight Savings time only a couple weeks old, it was already well after sunset, but it was a clear evening with just a slight breeze. The temperature was in the mid-60's, so Jack was wearing jeans and a long sleeve Eddie Bauer casual shirt. As he ambled along Library Walk on his way to meet Sarah, despite his slight nervousness of his date with her, he felt comforted by his surroundings. Lights emanated from the paned glass windows on the row of brick buildings while the vintage lampposts cast a subtle light on the patterned cement walkway. Jack felt lucky to be here. He was hoping his luck would hold out on his date with Sarah.

He reached Sarah's dorm building a few minutes early, so as not to make a bad first impression by being late. A few students made their way in or out of the entrance double doors while Jack watched with anticipation. He was eagerly looking forward to his date with Sarah.

Sarah walked through the doors about five minutes late, and strolled up to Jack. She smiled as she said, "Sorry I'm a little late. I was just talking to my mom."

Jack gave her a big smile in return and responded, "It was worth the wait!"

Sarah's eyes seem to light up, combined with just a hint of blushing. But Jack meant it. She looked great with her blond hair flowing down onto a light purple cotton sweater, which fell just below the top of her black slacks. Jack didn't know it then, but Sarah was also really looking forward to her date with Jack, and a bit nervous as well.

"Did you see what movie is playing tonight?" Jack asked.

"I *did!*" Sarah exclaimed. "That's quite a coincidence. You couldn't have had anything to do with that, could you?"

"I wish I could say yes, but it's just a coincidence. Maybe it's a good omen. Or it could be a bad omen, like that we're doomed to be burdened with prickly professors like Professor Kingsfield."

Sarah laughed, "Oh God, I hope not."

Arriving at the auditorium, Jack and Sarah grabbed two seats along the aisle of the fifth row of the hall. They both agreed it was very interesting how many students were in attendance to watch a movie about academic pressures at an elite law school, considering they found themselves under a less severe but nonetheless challenging and at times difficult environment of their own at Georgetown University. At the same time, there were probably few if any students attending the showing who would voluntarily decide to chuck their pursuit of an undergraduate degree from Georgetown the way the lead character of the film, Harvard law student James Hart, does at the end of the film—contemptuously making a paper airplane out of the unopened letter containing his final grades and tossing it sailing into the ocean waves.

***

After the movie, Jack and Sarah made their way to Bulldog Tavern located in the Healy Student Center. It was relatively crowded, but they were fortunate to grab a high-top table for two just as another couple was leaving.

The Tavern was a campus favorite, as it was designed to reflect both the historical and cultural favoritism of all things Georgetown. The pub included a beautiful walnut slab top bar, as well as original and restored campus light fixtures. In addition to the standing area at the bar and an adjoining wall of high tops, there were a half dozen large wood booths, along with several standalone tables in the middle of the floor. It was a favorite place for couples, with the larger single crowd perhaps preferring the somewhat more basic (grungier?) joints off campus where guys in particular could be a little louder and—as the night wore on—a little rowdier.

Jack ordered a Sierra Nevada Pale Ale draft while Sarah asked for a Miller Lite. (Two years later the ability of underclassmen to do so would be curtailed when the legal drinking age would be raised to 21). They also decided they were in the mood for a snack, so they ordered a plate of nachos with all the toppings, including chili.

Jack and Sarah talked a little about the movie they had just seen. Both had viewed it a couple times before, and both especially agreed how great John Houseman was in his role as Professor Kingsfield, for which he won an Oscar. They both recognized that the ending of the movie was meant to portray the leading character, James Hart, as perhaps noble and rebellious. But they also felt it was a little reckless or arrogant on his part.

Sarah decided to change the subject. "So, Jack, when we spoke the other day, you got me to tell you a lot about my growing up, my family and my life in Pennsylvania, and some of my aspirations. So now it's time for *you* to tell *me* more about yourself!"

Jack found it easy to talk to Sarah. He didn't mind at all chatting about his history and background, even many personal things he normally kept to himself, like the death of his father. He talked about growing up with his friends in the neighborhood, a couple stories about Sister Helen Edward, and the infamous Kenny's Concoction cocktail mix.

Jack was a little hesitant at first to tell Sarah about his brief but sincere interest of becoming a priest at one time. He didn't want her to think he was a little nerdy or pious or something. But Sarah seemed to consider his "premature" vocation as an affirmation of her growing opinion that Jack was a kind person, someone who was willing to be more of a help than a hindrance or turn a blind eye to people in need.

Perhaps to offset any delusions of himself as a do-gooder, Jack also told Sarah about a couple of the less admirable things he and his friends did while still in grammar school, thinking it was amusing at the time. Like when they would steal a loaf of Italian bread on their way home from Sunday mass as it lay sitting in a box of baked goods left by the local bakery in the alcove of a nearby Italian restaurant prior to its daily opening. Or lying hidden on the slanted roof of the Main Street bus shelter and shooting hard peas from their newly acquired slingshots at the local gas station across the street—to the confusion and dismay of station customers. Sarah laughed at many of

Jack's stories, at the same time playfully shaking her finger at him as if to say "bad boy."

Jack mentioned how he had played on his high school basketball team as a second stringer, and found out that Sarah had been a member of her high school volleyball squad. Sarah seemed impressed when he told her he had received a small partial academic scholarship to Georgetown, but hoped she didn't think he was bragging when Sarah admitted she had received admission only after being placed on the waiting list.

When Jack told her the story of his father's car accident, how painful it had been for his mother and himself, Sarah could see some of the pain Jack still felt with the loss of his father. He was sincere, however, when he told of his happiness for his mother having fallen in love and married again, and how he couldn't have asked for a nicer stepfather, someone he also loved.

Not only did Jack find it very easy to talk to Sarah about these things, but perhaps deep down or subconsciously he really wanted Sarah to know about him, to understand his thoughts and feelings as a way of getting closer to her. The more time he spent with her, the more he wanted to get close to her. Being a normal college freshman (well, normal other than the extremely unusual appearances of his "visitors" from the afterlife), Jack was undeniably attracted to Sarah's physical appearance. The more he looked at her, the more he was struck by the beauty of her face, made all the more incredible by her sparkling eyes and soft, shiny blond hair. He also could imagine she had a body to die for under those clothes.

Jack had known other attractive girls. But there was something about Sarah he felt attracted to like no one ever before. The expressions on her face when she smiled or laughed, the interest she seemed to take in listening to him.

She seemed both smart, kind, and unpretentious—like she didn't believe in having any false airs like some other girls he had known. She didn't impress Jack as some budding intellectual only interested in what she had to say, but rather she was a young woman who possessed a lot of common sense and decency.

After spending a couple hours at the Tavern, Jack walked Sarah back to her dorm. While he wanted to hold her hand as they walked, he didn't have the nerve to do so, thinking she might think it much too presumptuous on his part, and maybe expecting something more in the way of a sexual climax to the evening. He stood with her outside Reynolds Hall, not quite knowing what to say. He said the typical or perhaps most expected things young people usually say under similar circumstances, whether they were sincere or not. But he was sincere. "I had a really nice time tonight Sarah."

"So did I, Jack. Really."

He wondered what to do next. Should he bend over to give her a kiss good night? Would that be too forward? What if she reacted, well, with no reaction, or worse, recoiled in horror?

Before he could decide what to do, Sarah leaned into Jack slightly and gave him a short but sweet kiss on the lips. While not long and passionate, Jack thought, *hey, at least it's a promising start. I hope.*

"Good night, Jack. See you in Psych class."

"Sure thing. Save me a seat," Jack said in earnest.

"Absolutely," Sarah replied with a sweet grin.

As Sarah walked into her building alone, Jack lips curled in a broad smile and his eyes brightened. *Wow* Jack said to himself. *I think she actually likes me!*

***

Over the next several weeks, Jack and Sarah began to spend an increasing amount of time together. Besides seeing each other in Psych class, they would often agree to meet each other in the library to study or work on other course assignments. Frequently they would meet for a meal and sit together in the dining hall, sometimes with a few of Jack's friends and other times with a group of Sarah's friends, usually consisting of a fluid coed mix.

Virtually every week, on one or two weekend evenings Jack and Sarah would see a movie, catch a Hoyas home basketball game, or attend the occasional University music concert. Like most college students, they would frequent some of the nearby campus bars on weekends.

Neither one would get shit-faced like some of their friends, with no discrimination among the sexes on that front. (Although it always took fewer beers for the girls to get a little tipsy). Jack always found it interesting to see the girls' reaction to too much alcohol consumption and the resulting intoxication. Some would get more rambunctious, seemingly trying to keep up with the guys. Some would get a little playful, even a little seductive to a guy they were very interested in.

Jack was well aware that some people would end up hooking up and suddenly disappear from the bar to go back to someone's dorm room for a little amorous activity and hormonal adventure. Nothing wrong with that, Jack thought. College is a time of experimentation, exploration and learning the ropes, so to speak—for both sexes. It would be a long time before many of his friends and acquaintances would be ready to settle down, or really discover what it means to love someone.

But Jack felt differently about Sarah. Of course, his feelings of sexual attraction to Sarah were nothing short of intense. After all—she was hot! But all they had done so far was some pretty heavy make outs. Jack wasn't new to sex. He had done the dastardly deed with a few girls from high school in his senior year and the summer leading up to it. And while he'd liked those girls to some extent, none of those relationships had lasted very long. (One of them was a simple one-and-done stemming from both he and his companion having too much to drink at a summer house party bash).

But Sarah was special. He had no idea if she was a virgin, not that it mattered to him. He certainly knew her well enough to know she certainly wasn't the promiscuous type. But he was trying to go slow. Sarah was undoubtedly hot in the eyes of most guys—that is anyone who wasn't blind. He didn't want to pressure her, or scare her off.

He could tell she liked him from all the time they were spending together. The way they talked with each other, enjoyed each other's company and conversation. Or just the times lying on the grassy lawn and not talking, just being together. One Sunday Jack and Sarah even took a day trip to visit some of the memorials and exhibits along or near the National Mall. There was still a lot that he hadn't seen on his earlier visits, like the National Gallery of Art, Einstein Planetarium, the National Museum of American History, and the newly added Vietnam Veterans Memorial. Sarah enjoyed a love of history similar to Jack, especially American history.

That day along the Mall, Jack had been a little nervous that one of his former or a new "visitor" would appear to him and create a difficult, if not impossible, situation for him. How could he ever explain to Sarah about the implausible gift that had been given to him? Or, maybe it wasn't a gift, but actually a curse, if it prevented him from ever being able to share or explain it to someone with whom he might want to spend his whole life? Would anyone ever be able to love him enough to believe him?

As if college academic life at a highly ranked institution wasn't stressful enough, Jack had been thinking more and more about all these feelings and questions coming at him all at once. When and what should he tell Sarah about his strong feelings for her? How strong were her feelings for him? Were his feelings reciprocated? He seemed ready to burst and wanted to take Sarah in his arms and make love to her, but was it too soon for her? Was she ready for that? Did she even think about Jack in that way? Even in his most wishful thinking, if all the planets were aligned and he and Sarah were meant to be together, how the hell could he ever hope to explain his "gift" to her without her thinking he was a nut job, delusional, or just some kind of jerk who wanted to impress her, or take advantage of her?

Such were the thoughts going through Jack's head one such Saturday evening when he was walking Sarah back to her dorm after a night out with some friends. Sarah noticed how the usually talkative Jack had gotten rather quiet on the walk back, perhaps even a little melancholy.

"What's the matter, Jack? Are you OK? You seem very quiet, or a little tense. Is everything alright?"

"Oh, yeah. I'm fine. I just have some things on my mind about school. And my step-dad told me my mom wasn't feeling great lately. But he said not to worry, she probably just caught some kind of virus or bug."

Sarah looked at Jack as they stopped in front of her residence hall, looking at him with those piercing blue eyes that seemed to see directly into his soul. "You know you can talk to me about anything, right Jack? At least I hope you feel you can."

"Of course, I know that. We're simpatico, right?" Jack said, trying to lighten the mood a little bit.

"Yes, I think so!" Sarah said sincerely and smiled. With that, she leaned into Jack, put her arms around him and gave him a long intense kiss that seemed to have no end. He felt the passion and intensity ripple through his body like a wave washing over him.

"Wow," Jack almost gasped. "If that's what I can get from being in a somewhat crappy mood, perhaps I should be in a crappy mood more often."

"Well, not *too* often, Jack. I'd rather you be your normal, cheerful self."

"Don't worry, I will. It's nothing. Meet you in the dining hall lobby at ten tomorrow morning for breakfast?"

Sarah placed her hand on his cheek. "It's a date! Good night, Jack." As she began to walk away she turned to look over her shoulder and said with a grin, "And breakfast will be my treat,"—knowing full well the cost of breakfast was already fully covered under the school's mandatory meal plan.

Jack flashed a thumbs up in acknowledgment of her little tease. He stood there a moment watching her walk into the building and disappear. He thought to himself, *maybe I'm kidding myself, but Sarah must have some strong feelings for me after the time we've spent together over the last several weeks. And after that kiss! I've never been kissed like that before. She must care about me.*

"Of course she cares about you, Jack. Why shouldn't she?" a voice announced from behind him.

Jack turned to see a pleasant looking middle-aged woman with wavy black hair cascading down to her shoulders. She was wearing a heavy satin black dress with buttons down the center topped by a white lace collar. Her dress appeared to be like something from around the Victorian period.

But she was not alone. In fact, she was accompanied by not just one, but two other women, both wearing outfits from different time periods in history. One was an older, somewhat plain but gentle looking woman with gray hair topped by a cotton knit cap, in a costume evoking the post American Revolution period. The third person was by far the most elegantly dressed in a richly embroidered gown, wearing a pearl necklace and a jeweled tiara. She not only looked like royalty from a different time and place, but had a classic beauty and poise about her.

Since it was only about eleven thirty on a Saturday evening, there were still a fair number of students out and about. Jack didn't see how he could manage to have a conversation with these three strangers, who were visible only to him, without immediately drawing unwanted attention to himself. So he whispered in a low voice, barely opening his mouth to speak in his best attempt at being a ventriloquist. "I don't know who you are, or what this is about. But there's a small garden area around the corner of the building where I think we can talk undisturbed, so if you'll please just follow me...."

"Certainly, Jack. Please lead the way," replied the dark-haired woman.

As Jack walked in front of the three strangers, he wondered who they were, since he didn't definitively recognize any of them from his history books.

They reached the garden area, where a few large bushes secluded them from view.

Perhaps Jack felt a little impressed with himself at first that not one—but three—women would appear to him at the same time. Feeling a little self-indulgent, he somewhat brazenly said, "Gee, I must really rate to have all three of you appear to me at once. I'm guessing this must be pretty important!"

The woman who had first spoken to Jack was the first to speak. "I think you'll agree, it's extremely important."

That certainly got Jack's attention, as he tried to act a little more humbly. "Please, go ahead. What's this all about?"

"Now, before we tell you *why* we're here to visit you, Jack, we should introduce ourselves. I am Elizabeth Barrett Browning. Hopefully you know of me from some of my poems?"

Jack nodded in the affirmative, certainly recognizing her name and reputation as a great poetess, but withheld admitting that he had never knowingly actually read any of her poems. It wasn't until later that he discovered she had written the famous poem *"How Do I Love Thee?"* with its opening phrase, "How do I love thee? Let me count the ways."

"And I am Abigail Adams, wife to one of our founding fathers and second President of the United States, John Adams." Again, Jack nodded respectfully in recognition, although he also didn't really know much about Mrs. Adams other than the depiction of her in another of his favorite musical drama films, the adaption from the book and play *1776*.

Lastly, the aristocratic woman with her fair complexion and brown-reddish hair, placed in a braided bun under her tiara, spoke in a confident voice. With a foreign accent Jack didn't readily discern she said, "I am Tsarina Alexandra Feodorovna, wife of Tsar Nicholas II of Russia, the last ruler of the Russian Empire." As she spoke, Jack thought she spoke perhaps with more of a German than Russian accent, not yet knowing her historical background and early life.

"It's very nice to meet all three of you," Jack ventured. Meanwhile, he was thinking to himself, *these are three pretty remarkable women from the past. I wonder what they want to say to me?*

Elizabeth was the first to speak again. "Well, it may seem a little premature, maybe even a little bold on our part, but I'll tell you what we wanted to share with you, Jack." With those words, Jack finally realized that his visitors were actually capable of reading his thoughts, something he would keep in mind next time they appeared to him when other people were around. So if necessary and possible, he might have a conversation with them "in his head", so to speak, without looking like he was talking out loud to himself and garnering the attention of others in his vicinity.

Elizabeth continued. "Jack, the three of us know you have very strong feelings for Sarah. We also know you're wondering if she has similar feelings for you. And despite your sincere feelings, having never really been in love before, you're thinking maybe it's just an infatuation on your part, because it all seems to be happening so quickly."

Jack thought to himself. *How do they know this stuff?*

Elizabeth continued. "Of course you're physically and sexually attracted to Sarah! She's a beautiful girl. That's normal. But beyond what you worry may be the infatuation, you've found so many qualities of Sarah that attract her to you: the ease with which you can talk with her, and she with you; her kindness; she's unpretentious but fun-loving; and she shares many of the same interests, like history. Yet she has her own independent views, likes and dislikes, and she demonstrates both level-headedness and common sense. Sarah will be a loving, supportive partner to the person with whom she chooses to spend and share the rest of her life, assuming that person feels the same way.

"And you know, I think if you tell her how you feel, you'd be surprised that she would tell you the same about how she feels about you! You're both so young. If you're in love with one another, there's no rush to get married. That will come in time. I assure you, if you're right for each other, and I—I should say, all three of us, think you are—that period of time together will be a time to only grow closer and more assured of one another.

"You know, Jack. You're probably wondering…these three women…in many ways they appear to be so different. What do they have in common?"

Well," Jack said. "You *can* read my mind!"

Elizabeth took a step toward Jack, smiled softly, and spoke to Jack in an earnest voice. "Let me try to explain, Jack. You see, in each of our own individual ways, each of us was very much in love with our husbands, and each of us was in some way, a romantic. Also, each of us fell in love with our husbands within a very, very short time of our first meeting. In many, if not most ways, introductions, conversations, and communications in an attempt to connect were much more formal in our days than they are today. But we were perhaps a little ahead of our time in our desire and ability to express our love to our loved one in our private lives, and as you'll see, in our words."

Abigail, her hands nestled in front of her, stepped forward and finally spoke. Jack could sense the strength and wisdom in her face. "Jack, I met my future husband, John, when I was just fifteen years old. We married when I was 20. We were married for 54 years prior to my passing.[1] As you know from being a student of American history, my husband was a very opinionated man, somewhat stubborn, and argumentative with his fellow Revolutionary and political associates. However, the two of us had a deep respect for one another, and a strong emotional and intellectual connection. History has handed down the many letters of our correspondence over the years, as he was away from home so often given his heavy responsibilities. These words, however, I think best show the depth of my love for John:

...should I draw you the picture of my heart it would be what I hope you would still love though it contained nothing new. The early possession you obtained there, and the absolute power you have obtained over it, leaves not the smallest space unoccupied. [2]

As Abigail spoke these words, somehow the written pages appeared in Jack's mind as if supernaturally placed into his consciousness. He could read the words from her letter on the cotton rag paper as she had originally written them in her stylistic script.

Alexandra was the next to speak. Her appearance was elegant and regal, but her expression seemed, to Jack, to be one of kindness and empathy. "Jack, I met my future husband, Nicholas, when I was but twelve years old, and he was 16, at the wedding of his uncle and my sister." Despite her royal appearance, she spoke in a very friendly, almost cheerful manner. "After rejecting other marriage proposals, some which came with pressure from my beloved grandmother, Queen Victoria, Nicholas and I were finally wed when I was twenty-two and he was twenty-six.[3] Despite the very tumultuous and difficult times, including having to deal with misunderstandings and distortions about our degree of care for the Russian people, Nicholas and I loved each other with all our hearts for the twenty-four years we were married. Even up to the time of the tragic death of our entire family at the hands of cowardly murderers during the Russian Revolution of 1917.

"I remember one letter I wrote to Nicholas when his duties required him to travel again far from our home. Once again, a handwritten letter on a high-quality linen paper appeared clearly in Jack's mind, almost as if he was holding it up before his eyes. Alexandra read the words on the paper:

Off you go again alone and it's with a very heavy heart I part from you. No more kisses and tender caresses for ever so long — I want to bury myself in you, hold you tight in my arms, make you feel the intense love of mine.

You are my very life Sweetheart, and every separation gives such endless heartache...Goodbye my Angel, Husband of my heart. I envy my flowers that will accompany you. I press you tightly to my breast, kiss every sweet place with tender love...[4]

"But now, Nicholas and I and our children are together, forever in eternity. No more sorrow. No more pain. Just the love for each other, basking in God's love for us all."

Jack continued to stand there silently, mesmerized by these three incredible women.

Finally, Elizabeth began to speak, in her soft but confident tone, her own written words from long past. At first, Jack thought she was directing her words to him. But, with Elizabeth's gaze directed more to the heavens, and by the tone and expression of that gentle voice, Jack realized these were words she had written to her dear husband, poet Robert Browning,

And now listen to me in turn. You have touched me more profoundly than I thought even you could have touched me—my heart was full when you came here today. Henceforward I am yours for everything....[5]

Elizabeth paused after her words, before saying, "I did not meet my husband Robert until I was nearly forty years old. Perhaps because of bouts with various illnesses, I had never married up until that time. Even though Robert was six years my junior, we almost immediately felt like kindred spirits, and knew we were meant to be together. Despite my age of forty three at the time, we would be blessed by a son in the third year of our marriage.[6] My illnesses would finally overcome me after fifteen years of our cherished life together."

At that moment, a Frisbee came flying over some bushes and fell to the ground just a couple feet in front of Jack. A student came jogging around the bushes to reclaim the Frisbee, when he saw Jack standing there by himself. Jack could see the strange look the student gave Jack as he stood there all alone behind the bushes, so he said, "I think I may have lost my watch around here when the clasp broke, so I'm just searching for it."

The student gave Jack an ambivalent, "Okay. Good luck, man."

Jack turned to the ladies after the student left saying, "Sorry about that. I'm glad the Frisbee didn't hit one of you."

"Not to worry, Jack," Elizabeth smiled. "But in my day, I'd much prefer the game of crochet, to whatever that game is."

Jack returned the smile with a little chuckle saying, "Well, I'm afraid crochet is a little out of my league."

Jack said pleasantly, "Before we were so rudely interrupted," then continued in a more serious tone. "Those are all beautiful words ladies—expressions of love—to each of your cherished husbands. But I don't think I could ever speak in the same manner. I'm not that...," Jack paused, trying to think of the correct word, before saying, "*poetic!*"

Elizabeth spoke. "It's not the words themselves that we're saying are important, Jack. It's having the conviction to say what's truly in your heart to Sarah, to tell her how you feel about her."

After those words, Elizabeth lifted her hands to show she was holding a sculpture of two hands—nothing more— obviously the hands of a man and a woman in each other's gentle grasp. As she held the sculpture up, she looked at Jack.

"I don't know if you've ever seen this sculpture. It's well known, at least in certain circles of both art and literature. It's called *Clasped Hands of Robert and Elizabeth Barrett Browning*. It is a replica of a sculpture by Harriett Hosmer that was done when she visited us in Rome about midway through our marriage."[7]

Jack gazed at the fine textural quality of the sculpture that seemed to emote the sensitive oneness of the two lovers. While her hand is cradled inside his larger hand, hers is facing front and more visible, as if to show the sense of equality and partnership between the two.

"You see, Jack. This is what you and Sarah could have, to enjoy that unique intimacy that only two people truly in love can share. Don't be afraid of telling Sarah how you feel. Life is an adventure, and no one knows what day may be our last. Live it like today could be the final day, and love those closest to you."

With those final words of encouragement, the women vanished as quickly as they had appeared. But Jack felt refreshed, even inspired by what these three very different women had to say. How their words touched him and what they could teach him.

Jack emerged from the garden alone, with a sense of anticipation. He pictured Sarah in his mind, her beautiful eyes peering up into his. He would lay awake much of the night thinking of her, eagerly waiting to talk with her the next day.

He had something very important he wanted to say to her, and to her alone.

CHAPTER 14

The next day Jack arrived at the dining hall just after ten o'clock to find Sarah already sitting in the lobby. As he sat down next to her, he squeezed her gently on her shoulder, smiled broadly, and said cheerfully, "Hi Sarah, how's it going?"

She offered Jack her bright smile. "Hi Jack. I'm doing fine. You seem to be a little more cheerful today than you were last night!"

"Yes, I am. In fact, there's something I want to talk to you about, or to tell you".

The dining hall was its usual noisy, bustling place, with students chatting at tables, dishes clattering—quite a lot of activity. It wasn't the atmosphere Jack wanted to talk to Sarah about concerning what was on his mind.

"Listen," Jack suggested. "Instead of having breakfast here, how about we hop in my car and drive to the National Arboretum? It's only about twenty minutes away, and it's going to be a nice sunny day. We can grab some food just outside the Arboretum and sit down in the park to eat."

"Sure Jack, that sounds nice." She looked at him quizzically. "This isn't just an excuse to go for a ride in the car you keep on campus that you hardly ever seem to use, is it?"

"No, I just thought it would be a nice spot to talk, being outside and roaming through all the gardens and collections they have there. I was looking at a brochure in the Student Center one day and it looks pretty cool. And private."

"Private, aye." Sarah squinted. "You're not going to tell me something bad, are you?"

"No, not at all. But then, that partly depends on your reaction."

Sarah looked a little perplexed. Or perhaps concerned. Nevertheless, Jack seemed intent on his plan for the day, so she told herself to be patient and just let Jack say what he wanted to say at the right time and place. "OK, Jack. But you *are* being a little mysterious. I'll just run back to my dorm and grab a warmer jacket in case the weather changes. I'll meet you back here in ten minutes."

***

After parking in a lot off New York Avenue outside the entrance to the Arboretum, Jack and Sarah bought a couple toasted bagels with cream cheese and coffees and walked across the street to enter the park along Springhouse Road.

Neither had ever been there before, but it was actually a very impressive place. In Jack's mind, the photos in the brochure, with its landscaped walkways, beautiful gardens and variety of tree grottos, made it seem like a nice romantic spot. After all, after last night's visitation, wasn't he a student of romance? Well, at least he wanted to be.

They immediately spotted a small pond adjoining a grove of trees and decided to sit down on the grass to eat their bagels. As they ate and chatted, Jack still gave no hint of what he wanted to talk to Sarah about. He seemed to be waiting for the right moment.

He had spotted a direction sign on the way in which pointed to one of the Arboretum's favorite attractions, the Friendship Garden.[1] He mentioned it to Sarah, saying why don't we take a walk to the Garden where we could sit and talk? In hindsight, Jack realized this was probably not the best choice in terms of the garden's name. Sarah's first thought, she later told him, was she was afraid Jack was going to tell her how he really liked her, but just as a friend, that maybe it was time to move on to other people.

Jack and Sarah walked side by side along the walkway leading to the garden. It was a beautiful sunny day, a little cool, but barely a whisper of a breeze. They were fortunate no one else was sitting on one of the few benches in the garden, as most visitors seemed to be more interested in strolling along the many trails of the 412-acre park to get a sampling of the many collections and exhibits.

The garden they sat in, with broad stretches of grasses, perennials and ferns, was designed to evoke the spirit of a wild meadow and a natural aesthetic. Jack was certainly hoping that the calmness of the surroundings would spill over into his own self for what he wished to say to Sarah, and that she would be equally receptive.

Jack began, nervously, to speak the words that had been circling in his brain for weeks, but only began to formulate into some coherent expression as he lay awake last night in his bed. He put his two hands on top of

Sarah's, while a fleeting image of *Clasping Hands* popped into his head.

"Sarah, I know we've only known each other a short time. But in that short time, I think I've come to know you so very well. We've spent a lot of time together, and we seem to enjoy each other's company so much. I think you're beautiful, but so much more than that. The way we so easily talk to one another, your smile, your likes and dislikes, your sense of kindness and being so down to earth. I know it may seem like it's too soon to be saying this, but it's not infatuation. I know it's not just that.

"What I'm trying to say, Sarah, is I love you. I certainly don't want to scare you off by saying this, but I'd be the happiest and luckiest guy in the world if I thought we could spend the rest of our lives together. I realize we have to get through school and graduate, find jobs—all that stuff. But if I thought you felt the same way, the wait wouldn't seem like forever. That you wanted to share your life with me as well. I....I...."

Jack felt he was starting to ramble when Sarah placed her index finger across his lips, and then cradled his face in her two hands.

"You don't have to say any more Jack. Because I love you too." She paused for one moment and smiled. "I'm not one to make quick decisions and jump headfirst into the unknown, but I think I've felt this way after just spending the first few times with you. I love you, Jack. You make me so happy to know that you feel the same way. I wasn't sure you did. Now I know, and we can stop any pretensions or wondering. I'm yours, Jack. Forever."

For a brief moment, Jack thought he heard the voice of Elizabeth, Abigail and Alexandra exclaiming in unison, "*We told you so, Jack!*" But this time he realized it really *was* just his imagination. He leaned forward, as Sarah did the same. They kissed in a long, slow passionate embrace. For the two of them, it felt simultaneously both exhilarating and a release of pent-up doubts and anxiety.

Jack and Sarah spent the next couple hours walking hand-in-hand through parts of the arboretum. They walked through the National Grove of States, where displays of trees representing the fifty states (and the District of Columbia, of course) are arrayed over some thirty acres. Each of the plots displays a grouping of a state's official tree species, including magnolias, dogwoods, spruces, oaks, pines, maples and buckeyes just to name a few.

After resting in the grove on one of the furnished picnic benches, they took a leisurely stroll through portions of what is called the Asian Collection. Sloping down toward the Anacostia River, the Asian Collections area afforded dramatic views of the surroundings, especially from the Chinese pagoda-style gazebo. Here the couple stopped to breathe in the beauty that they could now share together.

Perhaps it was the calmness and serenity they both felt in this moment, that Sarah was the first to raise the inevitable question of what was perhaps the next logical question. "I love you, Jack. I know maybe we're both a little shy and nervous about this, and you might feel like you don't want to press me so soon. Now that I know what I had hoped for, I want us to be together in every sense. I want to give myself to you and you to me. You're the only one for me, Jack."

"You really are amazing, girl," Jack replied, almost flabbergasted. "It's only natural, but I didn't want to press you. I've obviously thought about it, like maybe only every day, and anticipated it for some time, but was unsure how you felt—until today."

Jack tried to look serious. "So, this is a beautiful spot. How about right here, now?"

"*What?*" Sarah said in surprise. "I do love you Jack. But, *here? Now?*" She stammered a bit saying, "I just *couldn't*...I mean..."

Jack grinned and grabbed her around the waist. "I'm just kidding you, Sarah. I didn't mean to shock you. I certainly would never put you in that position. I wouldn't be any more comfortable here than you would."

"Well, that's a relief! You had me worried for a moment."

"Sorry. Bad joke I guess. I have a better idea, if you're up for it. Right by the bagel place we stopped at earlier, I noticed what looked like a cute bed and breakfast kind of place. We could book a room for one night next weekend, and then visit the arboretum again the next day. I really find this place pretty cool and serene. It'll always have a special meaning for me—for both of us, I mean."

"I like that idea, Jack. I think I'd be a lot more comfortable away from campus and the dorms anyway. I like my privacy, and I would find doing anything on campus kind of nerve wracking."

"Me too. So are you ready for this…for the two of us?"

"Nervous. But ready." She looked into Jack's eyes. "I'm sure I want to spend my life with you, Jack."

"And I with you, Sarah. I've never been more sure of anything. I know we'll have to wait quite a while, but how does the future Mrs. Moran sound to you?"

"Just perfect. Mr. Moran." They kissed, and took in the unimpeded views, a perfect reflection on the start of something new and beautiful in their own lives.

CHAPTER 15

Later that evening, Jack made a reservation for the following Saturday at the Quincy House, the B&B he had spotted by the arboretum. Jack made the reservation in the name of Mr. and Mrs. Dan Jones. This was at least a step above his initial thought of Mr. and Mrs. John Smith when he was first asked by the hotel receptionist but, on afterthought, a pretty unsophisticated choice just the same. But what the hell, he was new at this, and admittedly a little nervous.

Initially his nervousness stemmed from two seemingly contradictory thoughts, part complete joy and part fear. His yin and yang of dark and bright. On the one hand, he felt overjoyed that in just a few days he would be in the loving arms of his beautiful Sarah. On the other hand, he was also rather nervous. What if things went badly? She might not feel the same intensity for him she thought she did—that he felt for her.

As he lay there in his bed, a more palpable concern began to invade his thoughts. He hadn't really thought about it much before, as he was first so focused on telling Sarah how he felt about her, and then overjoyed that she felt the same way about him. But now he had a bigger dilemma. *How am I going to tell the woman I love and want to spend my life with...how am I going to tell her...my secret?*

Again, Jack wondered whether his gift was actually a curse. A curse that would never allow him to be with Sarah. If he tried to hide it from her, he would feel dishonest. It would be more like a betrayal. She deserved to know everything about him. He was afraid if he told her, she would probably think he was deranged or delusional.

How could she accept the fact that dead people from throughout history not only appear to him, but also impart valuable life advice—*and sometimes crack jokes?* And only *he* can see them. How they'd helped him, given him some insight into this life—and the afterlife— and even aided him in helping others in unusual situations, like his step-dad's accident. *She'll think I'm bonkers,* Jack thought to himself. *Or worse, think I only pretended to have these incredible feelings for her just to get her in the sack.*

But I love her so much, and I know she loves me, he thought to himself. *I can see it in her eyes, her words, her mannerisms—everything about her. Maybe I'll just have to trust that. Trust her. But it's an awful lot to ask.*

***

Saturday finally arrived and Jack and Sarah drove to the northwest corner of D.C. in his Thunderbird. They both had a decent amount of schoolwork to complete to free up the remainder of the weekend for themselves, so they didn't arrive at the B&B until about six o'clock. When Jack checked in at the front desk as Mr. and Mrs. Dan Jones, he could swear he saw the hotel clerk flash a slight grin at seeing the young, attractive couple with their overnight suitcases in tow.

As they entered their room, Jack and Sarah smiled at each other, pleased with the cozy atmosphere the room offered, complete with a queen-sized bed and private bath. Jack had specifically picked this Deluxe room, which was described on its web site as "ideal for couples planning a romantic getaway, this room has a warm, charming ambiance with wood paneling and scenic garden views at the back of the house."

The couple tossed their bags on a small loveseat, and then quickly freshened up before heading out for a bite to eat. As they walked along the main drag, they spotted an enticing tavern with a colonial style ambience. They could see through the glass window several other mostly younger and middle-aged couples inside, so they decided to give it a try.

The hostess showed them to a booth Jack pointed to, and they immediately ordered a couple beers to break the ice and calm their nerves. They toasted their newfound love, delighting in the moment with small talk and some laughter. Jack ordered the Tavern Angus Burger Special, while Sarah ordered a plate of two generous portions of Maryland crab cakes. Neither completely finished their meals, perhaps fearing getting indigestion or something that might ruin their planned activities back at the hotel.

When they got into their room, Jack pulled Sarah to him, held her tight, and gave her a long, deep kiss. Sarah looked up at Jack with those bright blue eyes saying, "Okay, I guess we've come too far to back out now."

"Back out?" Even though Sarah's words took him by surprise, Jack sounded sincere and understanding when he replied, "It's okay if you're not quite ready Sarah. I love you and want you to feel right about this."

"I was just joking, you idiot." Sarah smiled with a big grin. "Of course I want to. I've been thinking about you all week."

Jack gave a forced laugh, since the last thing he really wanted to do was to back out now. "Very funny, girl. Don't toy with my heart."

"I'm sorry. Maybe I was teasing you to get back for the gazebo incident the other day in the park. You know, where you made me think you wanted to make love right there...on the grass...outside? I promise I won't ever toy with your heart again." She looked up at Jack with those penetrating blue eyes. "You fill every inch of my heart, Jack."

Her words resonated with those that Abigail Adams had spoken to Jack just a week ago.

Sarah was very happy, but naturally a little nervous nonetheless. She glanced at the bed, then said in a voice somehow confident yet timid at the same time, "I'm going to get a couple things out of my overnight bag and go into the bathroom to put on something, as they say in the movies, a little more comfortable." She turned to look over her shoulder as she walked into the bathroom. "And why don't you get ready for bed at the same time, handsome."

After Sarah closed the bathroom door, Jack pulled the covers down on the bed, stripped down to his boxer shorts, and waited. He then thought to dim the lights, thinking Sarah might be more comfortable that way.

After about five minutes, Sarah opened the door to the bath, closed the light, and stepped into the room. Jack was sitting on the edge of the bed less than 10 feet away. Sarah was wearing what he later understood was called a pale blue see-through teddy that came down to the middle of her thighs.

"I hope you're not disappointed," she said a little nervously.

"Are you kidding? You look *incredible*," Jack said with both love and assurance in his heart and voice. He stood up, walked over to Sarah, took her by the hand, and maneuvered her toward the full-length mirror that hung on the wall outside the bathroom. He turned her to face the reflection as he stood behind her, lightly pressing up against her back.

She wondered what he was doing, as he lowered the fine satin straps on her shoulder and let her teddy fall to the ground. Jack looked at her beautiful curves, the roundness of her full breasts, and her soft, almost glowing skin, before focusing on her sparkling eyes reflected by the light. "You're even more beautiful than I ever imagined, Sarah. I'm incredibly lucky that you love me the same way I love you."

Sarah turned smiling, but perhaps holding back a tear of happiness. Jack took her by the hand and led her to the bed. He took off his boxers as they crawled under the bedsheet. As he touched her warm skin and she touched his, he whispered, "I love you, Sarah." Sarah immediately responded with "I love you too, Jack." She held him more tightly, and they felt their bodies meld into each other to become one for the very first time, like two streams flowing into one another, being absorbed to become a single, gently rushing river.

***

When he awoke the next morning at about seven o'clock, Sarah was still sleeping soundly on her side facing away from Jack. He leaned over to look at her gentle face framed by her blond hair draped over her cheek. He didn't want to wake her unnecessarily, but couldn't resist putting his arms across her shoulders and pulling himself up close to her. She made a slight moaning sound but remained asleep.

As he lay there cradling Sarah in his arms, Jack felt like this was the happiest he had ever felt in his life. He recalled what Doctor Freud had said to him about the connection we all feel to one another in the afterlife. Jack thought maybe it's something like how I feel now, this incredibly strong connection I feel with Sarah, as if they were the only two souls in the universe. He thought maybe that's what people meant by what he had previously thought of as a rather trite expression, "Heaven on Earth."

But knowing he felt this extraordinary love for Sarah, and knowing he cared for her more than anything in this world, how could he not tell her his secret? How might she change toward him once he made his startling revelation? But he knew he would have too. Later today. The arboretum would be the place he would tell her.

***

After eating their complimentary B&B breakfast of assorted pastries, fruit, coffee and juice, Jack and Sarah checked out of the hotel, threw their bags in Jack's car, and walked into the arboretum for the second time in a week.

They walked hand-in-hand down the trails of Fern Valley with its array of woodland wildflowers and yellow witch-hazel blossoms. Strolled past the stunning holly and magnolia collections. Finally, they reached the Dogwood Collection and stopped to sit on a stone bench, offering spectacular views of the Anacostia River. While the dogwoods were naturally at their most beautiful in early spring, the autumn leaves, having turned to coral and burgundy colors, offered a quiet, restful setting.

Sarah turned to Jack with a smile and said, "I'm so glad we made love last night, Jack. Promise me we'll always be this happy."

At first Jack smiled back, but then his face took on a more serious expression. "There's nothing I want more in the world, Sarah. But I have to tell you something, something about myself. I love you too much to keep any secrets from you, but I'm afraid. Afraid what you might think of me."

Almost immediately, Sarah's skin began to turn a little cold. "What do you mean, Jack?" she said with obvious concern in her voice, but also trying to elevate his mood. "Nothing you could do, short to being a mass murderer or rapist or something, could make me change the way I feel about you. Don't you know that?"

"I certainly hope so. But it's nothing like that. It's not something I did, or some fault I have. It's...well...it's something that happens to me."

She looked at Jack with love in her eyes. "Tell me, Jack. Maybe I can help."

"No. It's not like that. You see..." Jack was finding this extremely difficult. "I know this will sound crazy, but ever since shortly after my father died, I've been getting visits. Visits from people ...from the afterlife. *Dead* people. Some famous. Some not. I'm not sure *why* they appear to me. They offer advice, help, direction, tell me there's something special about me. Exactly what that is, I don't know. But it keeps happening." Jack stopped talking as his mood became increasingly sad as he watched the expression on Sarah's face turn from doubt to concern. And then what he thought was fear.

"Please say something, Sarah. Anything."

As she held his hands even tighter in her grasp, Sarah stared directly into Jack's eyes, and he could almost feel her heart reaching outside her body to wrap itself in his. "I'm not sure what to say Jack, other than I love you. And if you're having these delusions, I'll be at your side to talk to the best doctors, go through whatever counseling you need to help rid yourself of these hallucinations. Anything. I promise I'll be with you every step of the way, Jack."

Jack fully understood how difficult it would be for Sarah to comprehend the truth. "But that's just it, Sarah. I'm not crazy or suffering from a mental illness. Have I ever given you any indication, until now, that I was psychotic in any way? What I'm trying to tell you is, this is real. It *really* happens to me."

Suddenly Sarah, still looking distraught, seemed to peer over Jack's shoulder, as if seeing something almost as disturbing as what she just heard.

"Jack, I want to understand you completely. I love you. There's obviously much more to this—whatever it is—that we need to talk about." Sarah paused, as Jack could see something else was distracting her. She continued, "But before we do, I'm very uneasy about that man who's leaning against that dogwood tree about thirty feet behind you. He seems to be staring at us. I didn't see him walk up to that tree. He just suddenly appeared there!"

Jack turned around and saw a relatively young, middle-aged man dressed in jeans, a white cotton shirt and a casual black leather jacket, leaning against the tree. As Sarah had said, he *was* staring directly at them.

"Oh my God," Jack blurted in almost a whisper. "It's my father. My father, Tom."

CHAPTER 16

Jack stared back at his father in disbelief for a few seconds, before turning toward Sarah. To say that Sarah looked confused and apprehensive was an understatement. It didn't give her a lot of comfort that Jack himself looked somewhat shocked and shaken.

Jack didn't quite know what was more astounding: that his father had actually, finally appeared to him, after all the longing Jack had felt for years; or the fact that Sarah could actually see his father as well as *he* could. This had never happened before.

Sarah clutched Jack by the arm. She asked innocently, "What do you mean it's your father? Do you mean your step-father?"

"No," Jack responded without hesitation. "I mean my real father, Tom, who died from a car accident many years ago. But how is it you can see him too? I'm the only one who has been able to see these people from the afterlife, at least up until now. I'm not sure how or why you can see him now as well."

Jack started to stand up. "We have to go talk to him. Are you able to do that with me, Sarah?" He took both her hands in his, knowing quite well how Sarah would respond.

"Yes Jack. Of course. Just hold my hand. I still don't understand what's happening here."

Jack and Sarah walked slowly toward Tom. Normally, Jack might run at a gallop toward him and lunge into his arms, but he had Sarah to think about now. This phenomenon—his "gift," which he had just begun to try and explain to her—was obviously new and startling to Sarah, and she would naturally be a little fragile at the moment.

As they came within a couple feet of Tom, Jack let go of Sarah's hand and, with tears in his eyes, nearly leapt forward and embraced his father. "Oh, Dad," he said softly. "I'm so glad to see you. I've been hoping for this for a long time. I miss you so much."

Tom hugged his son and spoke in the comforting voice Jack had been used to hearing growing up. "And I can't tell you how happy I am to see you, Jack. To be able to hug you. I never got a final chance to do that the day of my accident. Just to hug you and tell you one more time how much I love you."

They embraced for a moment before Tom motioned toward Sarah. "Well, Jack, aren't you going to introduce me?"

"Oh God. I'm sorry, Sarah" as he wiped tears from his eyes. "I'm a bit overwhelmed at the moment."

"That makes two of us Jack," Sarah replied, trying to sound a little normal, despite the very strange circumstances.

Jack smiled, saying to himself, *No wonder I love this woman."*

"Dad, this is Sarah. Sarah, I'd like to introduce you to my father, Tom."

"It's a pleasure to meet you, Sarah. Although I wish the circumstances could be a little more...conventional!" he said with an engaging smile.

Sarah smiled, sensing a bit of the same personality traits and sense of humor in Tom as she saw in Jack. She could see the very strong resemblance between Jack and Tom. With his dark brown hair, and slightly more broad shoulders, Tom looked how she expected Jack might look like in about 15 years. Except for the eyes, which in Tom's case were a dark blue.

Jack had shown her a photo of his father once when she visited him in his dorm room—Tom posing proudly beside his old prized Buick LaSabre. There was no mistaking this was Jack's father. If the striking resemblance wasn't convincing enough, the obvious rapport and love between the two men would remove any doubt she might have.

Still though, she was obviously confused and in somewhat of a state of shock. She first thought about extending her hand to shake Tom's. Instead, she took a couple short steps forward, placed her right hand on Tom's left arm, leaned in and gave him a gentle kiss on his cheek.

Tom looked at Sarah, acknowledging her warmth and, under the circumstances, perhaps courageous gesture. He shifted his eyes toward Jack and said, "You've done exceptionally well, Jack!"

Sarah, without looking away, looked into Tom's eyes. "I don' understand how this is possible, Mr...."

"Please, just call me Tom, Sarah."

"It's so nice to meet you—to see you. Jack has told me a lot about you and growing up in Virginia." Sarah paused, then continued in a flustered tone, "Wait a minute. I'm speaking to you, Jack's dead father Tom, like this is some kind of everyday occurrence? Am I the delusional one? I mean, I just don't understand. How—how is this possible?"

Jack could see Sarah was a little disconcerted. Not surprising under the circumstances. He turned to look at his father, with an expression imploring him for help.

Tom looked lovingly at Sarah. "Well, you see, Sarah. It was necessary to see how the relationship between the two of you developed before I got, well, 'permission' for lack of a better word, to make a visit to both Jack *and* you. I've been watching, from afar, but I can see the love the two of you have for each other, and that you have every intention of spending the rest of your lives together.

"So for me—and others—it is very important that you believe in the very special gift that Jack has been given. Jack wants—and needs—you to believe in him. I could see the fear that appeared in your eyes as Jack, to his credit, tried to begin to explain to you what has happened to him. He loves you, and respects you, in a way that would make hiding it from you or lying to you about it, impossible for him.

"We didn't want you to think Jack was crazy. Or delusional. Instead, we thought the best way to convince you, and eliminate any possibility of doubt, was to show you how real it actually *is*. That Jack is telling you the truth!"

As Tom spoke, Sarah could feel her doubts slowly melting away. Despite the strange, if not impossible, circumstances, this kind man's calmness and sincerity were enough to convince her. She was a practical woman, but she couldn't doubt her own senses. Or her love for Jack.

Her total assurance that Jack felt the same way about her. And she believed.

Sarah smiled with a knowing expression of acceptance, upon which Tom remarked, "Thank you for believing Sarah. You've made Jack, and this old man, very happy!"

Sarah acknowledged Tom's heartfelt reply. "Well, Jack knows me to be a pretty practical, common sense kind of person, and I certainly can't deny my own senses." As she was saying this, Sarah thought to herself, *I can't believe I'm so calmly talking to Jack's dead father. But there is something so peaceful—almost heavenly—about him.*

Accepting this sense of ease Sarah felt in Tom's presence, she continued in a composed voice, looking into Tom's benevolent face. "Just as I understand and love Jack in a way that I know he wouldn't lie to me, or intentionally try to hurt or deceive me in any way." Turning to Jack, she said with conviction, "So yes, Jack, I do believe in what you were trying, so desperately and so thoughtfully, to tell me earlier. I mean, I can't doubt what I can see and touch."

"See Dad, I really *have* done exceptionally well—in finding and falling in love with Sarah, that is."

"Yes, you have son, just as I was exceptionally lucky to fall in love with your mother. Those were the happiest years of my life."

Jack understood, and turned to give Sarah a loving hug and brief kiss.

At which point his head seemed to jerk up as he said, "Hey, wait a minute Dad. What exactly did you mean by '*we* thought'"?

"Well, by 'we', I mean not only your friends that you've met already, like Simon Peter, Doctor Freud, Galileo, and most recently, Elizabeth, Abigail and Alexandra, and others, but"—Tom extended his arms to a raised position over his head and brought them down by his sides in a broad sweeping motion—"all of us in the universal afterlife that are now connected. As others have told you, that's hard for even us to fully comprehend or explain. We just somehow sense it and know it to be the truth."

"Wait a minute", Sarah interjected. "Jack, you mean to tell me you've met St. Peter, Galileo, and all those others! Boy, have you and I got a lot to catch up on!" she exclaimed, pausing. Feeling comfortable and at ease despite the extremely strange circumstances, she turned to Jack's father, "But first, Tom. Now that I have you here, I want to hear all about Jack's early years with you growing up in Midlothian."

Jack winced a little, knowing his father would be more than happy to tell an embarrassing story or two about Jack as a young boy. But what the heck. The three of them were together now, probably for a very short while, and who knows if they were ever going to be together again—at least in this life.

"Okay, okay," Jack said somewhat begrudgingly. "But just remember Dad, I'm not eight years old anymore!"

"Don't worry, Jack. I promise to tell the truth, the whole truth, and nothing but the truth, so help me God."

"Yeah." Jack grimaced. "That's what I'm afraid of."

For the next hour or so, Jack, Sarah and Tom sat on the lawn overlooking the Anacostia River, while Tom regaled Sarah with some funny, some poignant, and some commendable stories of Jack as a young boy. The three of them laughed as Tom reminisced about some previously told stories regarding Sister Helen Edward. Including some of the antics Jack and his friends thought they could get away with. Tom told about Jack imitating some of his relatives (with striking clarity and unbeknownst to them) when they came for a visit. Like his imitation of the very proper Aunt May and the jocular laugh of his Uncle Ed.

A few other couples or families who happened to walk by could only see Jack and Sarah sitting off by themselves and laughing, with no idea of the extraordinary nature of their conversation.

As Tom spoke, Sarah saw not only the similarities in their cadence, mannerisms, and sense of humor, but also the influence Tom had in Jack growing up to be a kind, sincere person.

Finally, Tom stood up and took one more glance at the lovely surroundings. "It certainly is a beautiful view. I'm sorry to have to leave you two, but I must."

Jack's head snapped upward, with a somewhat pained look on his face. "Can't you stay longer Dad? There's still so much to talk about."

"Sorry Jack, it's not really in my control. Of course I loved seeing you, and want you to know that I always have and always will love you. You were the greatest gift your mother and I could ever ask for. But actually, my visit today was more about Sarah than you. Sarah may never see any of the other visitors from beyond the grave that have yet to appear to you. My appearance to her today was, well, an exception. As exceptional as she is, and that your love for one another is. But she had to know the truth about you, so she believes in sharing that truth with you as you go through your lives together."

Jack's shoulders slackened as if dejected that his father was leaving so soon. He had longed to see him for so many years, the short time they had together this afternoon didn't seem near enough.

Sarah could see the dejection in Jack's face, and tried to make the best of something neither could change. She looked at Tom with those bright blue eyes with a heartfelt expression. "Thank you, Tom. It might sound a little corny, but I feel like I just got a little taste of heaven talking with you. And I promise I will never doubt Jack." She flashed Jack a playful wide-eyed look. "No matter what extraordinary tales he tells me." She said smiling. "Because I know the kind of person he is, and I know he would only tell me the truth. I love him with all my heart, and want to share my life with him."

"I know you will, Sarah. And some day, when you hold your and Jack's baby in your arms, you can think of me as the grandfather who wished he could be there."

As Sarah seemed to blush slightly, Jack blurted, "Wow! Dad! Grandfather? Aren't you getting a little ahead of yourself?"

"Of course. I know you both have a long way to go until that happens. But just allow an old man to get his jollies. An old, departed man."

"Yeah, Jack. Give your dad a break. Or should I say grandpa!" Sarah replied with a slight laugh.

Tom nodded approvingly. "She's a keeper, Jack!" he said with some gusto. He paused, as if contemplating some private thought. "I love you both. You may not see me again, but I'll be keeping my eyes on you. Live your life for each other. That's a bond that no one will ever be able to sever. Good-bye."

At that moment, the sun that had been blocked by the tree branches extending out and over their heads found a temporary tiny break in the leaves, which caused the sun to shine through with a quick blinding light. And in that instance, Tom disappeared.

Jack, at first looking toward the spot his father was just standing, turned to Sarah. "I'm so sorry to see him go." He paused briefly. "But I'm so glad you got to meet him. He was a very special guy."

Sarah smiled and as she held his hand tightly and said, "So are you, Jack. So are you."

CHAPTER 17

It had been an extraordinary 24 hours for Sarah and Jack. They had made love to each other for the first time, had promised themselves to each other for the rest of their lives, and had met and spent time with Jack's deceased father, Tom. Furthermore, Sarah had come to know and understand the secret he'd been so worried about trying to explain to her. Yes, Jack had a gift. But so did Sarah. Only a special person like Sarah could accept Jack's secret and love him unconditionally—no matter what.

The next couple of weeks were fairly uneventful. Both Jack and Sarah continued to work hard at their studies, but spent even more time together in the library or other study halls on campus. Rather than being distracted from their dedication to their academic pursuits, their new found love seemed to motivate them even more to do well in school.

They talked about doing well so they could graduate with high marks, get good jobs, and so be better able to start a new life together as husband and wife shortly after graduation. While they knew marriage was a long way off, clearly that is what they both wanted. They talked about giving each other promise rings, even though marriage was quite distant. Instead, they decided not to in order to avoid the constant questioning from relatives and friends that might cause. They had promised each other in their hearts, and that's all that mattered to them.

When Thanksgiving came, both Sarah and Jack went back to their hometowns and their parents to celebrate the annual family tradition. While home during the holiday break, Jack participated in a midnight run for the homeless, distributing donated clothes, candy bars, and the like. Meanwhile, Sarah and her family put in a half-day at their local church preparing and serving lower income families, seniors, and others with a traditional Thanksgiving dinner with all the fixings.

While wanting to downplay it a bit, they both decided to tell their parents that they'd met someone at Georgetown that they really liked. Jack's mom perked up as he tried to casually mention it Thanksgiving morning while she was preparing dinner for the half-dozen relatives that would be coming over later that day to celebrate.

Knowing how Jack really wasn't one to talk much about his girlfriends, his mom immediately picked up on her son's level of interest. Obviously very curious, as any mother would be, she asked in an almost matter-of-fact tone, trying not to be too intrusive, "So tell me about her, Jack."

Jack told his mother her name was Sarah, she was very pretty and smart yet down to earth, and she lived in Lebanon, Pennsylvania. Jack pulled out a photo of Sarah and himself taken by a buddy of his at a college function. Mrs. Gray studied it with the eyes of a police detective searching for clues. "Why she's beautiful, Jack!"

"I certainly think so. But she's also incredibly nice, and kind. I know Dad would have really liked her." He immediately realized that might have sounded a bit strange to say, so quickly said, "And I'm sure Bob will too!"

Something in the way Jack had said it, with such conviction and ease, made Mrs. Gray remark jokingly, "The way you say it, it's like you actually introduced her to him."

Jack hesitated and took a deep gulp. "I wish I could, but you know what I mean. Just as I'm sure you'll like her. And Bob too!"

"You're a good judge of character, Jack. If you like her, I'm sure we will too. Now how about helping me peel some of those apples for the apple pie I'm making for our Thanksgiving feast?"

Meanwhile, Sarah was going through a similar baptism of fire with her mother at her home in Lebanon. "He sounds very nice, Sarah. And handsome too, from the photo. Maybe he can come visit you here during the semester break after Christmas and stay a couple days. Your brother is going to be off on some kind of road trip down South with a couple of his buddies, so his room will be free much of the time. I'll check on the dates he'll be gone and let you know. How does that sound?"

"That sounds great, Mom! I'm sure you'll like him." From the tone in Sarah's voice, Mrs. Mack knew that this was no casual interest on Sarah's part. Like most mothers, when it comes to their children, they have an uncanny sixth sense.

***

Back at Georgetown, Sarah and Jack were thrilled to see each other after being apart for the Thanksgiving break, even though it had been less than a week. Sarah wasn't sure how Jack would react to her mother's invitation to visit them in Pennsylvania after Christmas. Somewhat to her surprise, Jack was actually thrilled. He hated the idea of being away from Sarah for nearly a month, so a visit to the Keystone State sounded perfect.

Following Thanksgiving, students would have only two more weeks of classes before "study days," which would be followed by final exams. With only one weekend in between, Jack and Sarah decided to take another trip to the National Mall in D.C. Besides sharing a keen interest in American history, Jack was eager to tell Sarah about his experience at the Lincoln Memorial with John Wilkes Booth—now that he didn't have to fear her running away from him screaming for protection from the local D.C. police.

It was a Saturday, and while Congress was not in session, neither had ever been to the U.S. Capitol Building, so they decided that would be a good place to start the day's activities. As they approached the iconic structure, located at the eastern end of the Mall, Sarah and Jack were both impressed by its classical architectural beauty and enormous size. The Capitol is the seat of the legislative branch of the federal government, and—like the principal buildings of the executive and judicial branches (namely the White House and Supreme Court Building)—it is built in a neoclassical style with a white exterior.[1]

While the original building was constructed in 1800, it was severely damaged in the burning of Washington, D.C by the British during the War of 1812. Since that time, it had been extensively renovated and expanded on several occasions, with the addition of the House and Senate wings in the 1850s, and the addition of its huge dome in the 1860s. The last major expansion came in 1958 with the expansion of the East Portico and the replacement of the original sandstone Corinthian columns with marble. (Those original columns were now an outdoor display at the National Arboretum.)

The building was declared a National Historic Landmark in 1960, not surprising in that its design draws heavily on notable churches and landmarks in Europe, including St. Peter's Basilica in the Vatican and St. Paul's Cathedral in London.

The interior of the Capitol is replete with countless works of arts: sculptures, paintings, carvings and whole sections that depict either symbolic or actual events of the American story, the story of democracy and man's quest for freedom. These included, among many others: the murals on the walls of the first floor depicting Benjamin Franklin, Robert Fulton, and more recently added, the Moon Landing and the Space Shuttle Challenger crew; the National Statuary Hall Collection, containing statues of two famous people from each State; the Crypt, originally intended for the internment of George Washington (whose last will requested he be buried at Mount Vernon instead), but now displaying a massive Abraham Lincoln bust; the Old Supreme Court Chamber; plus the separated and distinctive House and Senate Chambers.

Despite these amazing features, for Jack and Sarah, their undisputed highlight of the Capitol was the Rotunda. Included on the east and west walls are eight large paintings. The four paintings on the east wall depict the founding of America, including *The Embarkation of the Pilgrims* by Robert Weir. The four paintings on the west side are the work of John Trumbull, and include the signing of the *Declaration of Independence,* and the *Surrender of Lord Cornwallis* at Yorktown.

Within the Rotunda, Jack and Sarah's favorite was Brumidi's fresco, suspended 180 feet above the Rotunda floor beneath the top of the dome. It depicted not only *The Apotheosis of Washington*, but also the equally spectacular and famous, *Frieze of American History*. *The Apotheosis* represents Washington sitting in the heavens with the goddesses of victory and liberty to his right and left. Along the perimeter are various renderings, some of which symbolize war, science, commerce and agriculture.

The *Frieze of American History*, while actually a painting, resembles a stone carving by use of a frieze technique that creates the appearance of three dimensions. The frieze consists of a circular band that illustrates nineteen scenes from American history, including *The Landing of Columbus, Captain Smith and Pocahontas, the Battle of Lexington, Peace at the End of the Civil War,* and the *Birth of Aviation.*

Jack and Sarah were in awe and certainly inspired by the atmosphere created by the marvelous and beautiful surroundings, the history it encapsulated, and the implied sacrifices of the many men and women depicted or symbolized in creating the American story. They could have spent hours touring the interior of the Capitol, but something in Jack sensed that it was time to make a visit to the Senate Chamber.

The floor of the Senate Chamber was empty, as the members of Congress were not in session, and access to the main floor by the general public was not permitted. However, Jack and Sarah made their way to the balcony seating area above the main floor, where they joined about twenty or so other visitors. They sat off to one side somewhat by themselves, and gazed upon the semi-circular tiered platform where the one hundred Senators sat facing a raised rostrum. The two lovers exchanged words with one another about some of the great leaders and momentous events which had taken place in this chamber, from presidential pronouncements, to long arduous debates.

Jack was sitting in the front row of the visitor's balcony, or gallery as it was called, with Sarah seated to his immediate left. As Jack was in mid-sentence talking about some historical event, his eyes widened like that of the Cheshire Cat and he became suddenly silent. Sarah noticed immediately and said, "What's the matter, Jack?"

"Don't you see who's sitting in the chair right next to you? I'm looking straight at him."

Sarah turned and said, "I don't see anything but an empty chair Jack." She paused briefly but then remembered that her "gift" of being given the opportunity to see and speak with Jack's father Tom came with a cautionary caveat that it might be a solitary event in her case. Having totally accepted Jack's own gift, she in no way doubted Jack that someone, not visible to her, was sitting next to her at this very moment.

"Well, I'm sorry Jack, but you know what your father said. It might just be one and done for me!"

"I'm very sorry to hear that, Sarah. Undoubtedly you'd be very impressed." With that, Jack looked in Sarah's direction, but was actually looking just past her to the seemingly empty seat. "It's an honor to meet you, Mr. Churchill. I know you can't see or hear him Sarah, but he can hear you. Please say hello to Sir Winston Churchill."

Sarah choked a bit on her words as she said, "Are you kidding me? I'm actually missing *Churchill?*"

Seated as they were, Jack appeared to any other tourists in the gallery to be talking to Sarah all the while having a conversation with Sir Winston. The former Prime Minister looked exactly like photos that Jack had seen of him as an elder statesman. Even sitting down, Jack could tell Sir Winston was of only moderate height and overweight. He was quite bald, and below his broad face, his sagging jowls were quite evident.

Sarah, meanwhile, looked a little flustered after her last exclamation and was wondering what to do. She turned her head ever so slightly in the direction of the empty chair and said, "I'm very pleased to meet you Mr. Churchill. I wish I could shake your hand or something, but I guess that's not possible either."

With that, Sarah decided to extend her hand slightly and put it on the armrest on the chair to her left. However, she felt nothing but space as her hand settled on the armrest. Except perhaps some vague feeling that her hand had passed through a kind of shadow of some sort. But Jack could clearly see that for Sarah, there would be nothing to see, feel, hear, touch, or smell of their esteemed guest.

That privilege was to be for Jack alone, who could see that Sir Winston's arm stood resting exactly where Sarah had placed her hand. Somehow, both appendages were visible and appeared whole to him, but they seemed to be in a different spatial plane or dimension of sorts.

Sir Winston, alternating his eyes to Jack, then to Sarah, and back to Jack again finally spoke. "It's a pleasure to meet you as well, Jack. And your bonnie lass Sarah. Your father told me she was quite lovely, and he didn't exaggerate."

Jack nodded graciously. "Thank you, Mr. Churchill. I'll tell Sarah what you said about her later."

"Wait...What? Tell me what Jack" Sarah interrupted. "This isn't quite fair or easy to be in my position you know," she protested. Jack figured she was just pretending to be a little miffed, but could understand her feeling a little left out or awkward.

Jack hoped to calm any hurt feelings she might have. "Sir Winston just told me you were a beautiful, bonnie lass!"

Sarah blushed slightly, saying, "Well, tell Mr. Churchill I said that's very kind and sweet of him. UUHHH, I mean, sorry, he can hear me, so I guess you don't need to tell him. This is all a bit too confusing for me, being half in the dark, so why don't the two of you have your conversation, and I'll just sit here quietly and listen to what you say, Jack. You can fill in the blanks for me later. Okay, gentlemen?"

Sir Winston responded, "Not only very attractive, but also very smart and practical as well, hey Jack?"

"Yes, she is all of those things." Jack said with a smile, as Sarah looked at Jack while squinting her face in mocked irritation.

"Okay, Okay, sorry Sarah. I get it." Looking across Sarah to Sir Winston again, Jack asked the great man, "So what brings you here, Sir, eerr, Mr....I'm sorry, I'm not sure how to address you properly."

"No need to be formal, Jack. Just call me Winston. It's certainly better than "Copperknob,"[2] as he grimaced, referring to a rather cruel nickname he was called by his childhood classmates because of his mop of red hair, made all the more cruel because of a stutter and slight lisp he had as a youth.

"Sure, thank you...Winston," he said. Sarah gave a look of surprise at Jack's sudden familiarity with one of history's greatest leaders and war heroes.

"So, what brings you here of all places, the U.S. Senate chamber, to see *me*?"

As Sir Winston began to speak, Sarah could see the enthralled look on Jack's face as he listened to the rhythm and cadence in the British Bulldog's speech. It was difficult to believe that someone who had been plagued by a stutter and a lisp when young could develop into such a great orator who spoke with an almost musical quality.

"Actually Jack, not only did I travel to America on a number of occasions over the years, usually at the request or invitation of one of your Presidents, but I actually spoke to a joint session of Congress in this very chamber many decades ago." He had Jack's full attention.

"Yes, Jack, it was December 26, 1941,[3] less than three weeks after Japan's unprovoked attack on Pearl Harbor. As I'm sure you know your history, much of the general public in your country (including many prominent citizens such as Charles Lindbergh), were reluctant to enter the War before that day, that horrible day that my friend, FDR, rightfully called 'a date that will live in infamy.' Being the day after Christmas, the holidays had thinned the ranks of many of your legislative leaders, so the joint session was held here instead of the House Chamber. Despite that, there was a full house on the floor and in the gallery, consisting of members of Congress, Supreme Court justices, cabinet members, and many of their wives.

"As you know, in the couple of years leading up to the United States declaring war on Japan, your country had been a supporter to the Allied forces through their Lend Lease Program, providing vast amounts of food, oil and munitions to fight the dreaded Nazi war machine. Immediately after declaring war against Japan, Germany declared war on the U.S. being an Axis power aligned with Japan. So just three days after announcing their declaration of war against Japan, the U.S declared war on Germany. I immediately made my way across the Atlantic to meet with FDR and other military and political leaders to plan and coordinate strategy.

"Having already declared war, the purpose of my speech was really, as the British Prime Minister, to get the United States to win support from your leaders for *my* concept of the war. Thankfully, we did that, including the sharing of military intelligence and military bases. We even created a joint military command called the Combined Chiefs of Staff. The most successful of those coordinated operations was obviously the landing at Normandy in June 1944."

Jack sat, enthralled as Sir Winston continued.

"In my speech that day, some thought I was being overly conservative when I predicted, even with the tremendous might of the U.S. now fully committed to the effort, it would take at least 18 months to turn the tide of the war. I said it would take time to mobilize and develop our resources, and that would mean some ground would be lost and it would only be regained at a great cost. That the forces aligned against us were enormous; they were bitter; they were ruthless. In actuality, it would be nearly three and a half years of bloodshed, countless deaths and massive destruction before we would be able to declare Victory in Europe in May 1945. It took another two months before we could similarly declare Victory over Japan. And the latter only coming after the tragic, fateful, but unfortunately necessary decision by your leaders to drop the atomic bombs on Hiroshima and Nagasaki."

Jack interrupted. "No disrespect, Winston—gee I really feel kind of weird calling you that—this is all very interesting history. But I'm still not sure what it has to do with me. And while I'm incredibly flattered that you're here visiting me, I'm still not sure exactly *why*!"

"Well, Jack, there are a few lines from that speech of mine, that I hope you take to heart. That you internalize them in some way, because at some future time and place they might give you the strength, direction and courage you might need."

"What words are those?" Jack inquired.

Winston then quoted a few lines from his speech:

"That the task which has been set for us is not above our strength. That its pangs and toils are not beyond our endurance. As long as we have faith in our cause, and an unconquerable willpower, salvation will not be denied us." [4]

Sir Winston paused a brief moment, and then continued with more words from his speech:

"He must indeed have a blind soul who cannot see that some great purpose and design is being worked out here below of which we have the honor to be the faithful servants. It is not given to us to peer into the mysteries of the future...In the words of the Psalmist: "He shall not be afraid of evil tidings. His heart is fixed, trusting in the Lord."

Jack gazed at Sir Winston and humbly replied, "Those are certainly great words to live by, but I'm just a college student from Virginia! I'm not sure what *I* can do." In his own mind, Jack still didn't understand why these people had selected him to appear. Where was it all leading? If anywhere.

Winston thoughtfully looked at Jack, speaking to him as his own father might were he still alive.

"All of us are called upon to do unexpected things in our lives. Some require kindness. Some require forgiveness. Some require courage. And it often confronts you without warning. The only advice I can give to you, Jack, is to be strong and be prepared."

"I'll certainly think hard about what you've said," Jack replied respectfully. "About what all my special visitors have said. And pray I have the courage to do the right thing."

"That's all anyone can do, Jack. As one of my more famous quotes go, 'Success is not final; failure is not fatal. It is the courage to continue that counts.'

"But I have one more story to tell you before I go Jack. Some people think it's true, others think it's just a persistent legend. The story goes like this:

"One day, a poor Scottish farmer named Fleming heard a cry for help coming from a nearby bog. He dropped his tools and ran to the bog to find a terrified boy mired in black muck, screaming and struggling to free himself. Farmer Fleming saved the boy from what would have been a slow and terrifying death.

"The next day, a fancy carriage pulled up to the farmer's sparse cottage. Out stepped an elegantly dressed nobleman who introduced himself as the father of the boy the farmer had saved.

'I want to repay you for saving my son's life,' said the nobleman.

'No,' the Scottish farmer replied, 'I can't accept payment for what I did.' At that moment, the farmer's own son came to the door of the family hovel.

Seeing the boy, the nobleman said, 'I'll make you a deal. Let me take him and give him a good education. If the lad is anything like his father, he'll grow to be a man you can be proud of.'

"And that he did. In time, Farmer Fleming's son graduated from St. Mary's Hospital Medical School in London, and went on to become known throughout the world as the noted Sir Alexander Fleming, the discoverer of Penicillin. Years afterward, in 1943 to be exact, the nobleman's son was stricken with pneumonia. What saved him? Penicillin.

"The name of the nobleman, Jack, was Lord Randolph Churchill. His son's name. Sir Winston Churchill."[5]

"Is the story true?" Jack wondered aloud. Sir Winston responded, "Maybe it is, and maybe it's just a charming story. Nevertheless, the point it makes is a profound one, Jack. Nobody knows what the future will hold for him or her. Everyone has something to offer. And doing something kind, or even courageous, that may help the life of someone who may go on to do something wonderful, is at the root of our faith in both God and man, and a reward in and of itself."

With those parting words, Sir Winston gave Jack the "V for Victory" sign that he was so famous for as the British Bulldog of WWII, and said, "Goodbye Jack. And hold on tight to that girl of yours. She's special too!" He smiled, and disappeared.

"Jack started to lean forward saying, "No, please don't go yet. I..." But Winston was gone.

Sarah could immediately tell from Jack's words and body language that Sir Winston had indeed departed, although she thought that might not be the right word for someone who was *already* dead. "Is he gone, Jack?"

"Yes, I'm afraid so. There's more I wanted to talk to him about, but...he did give me some good advice though."

"Like what?" Sarah asked.

"Well, like hold tight onto that girl of yours. Which, my love, I fully intend to do. Always and forever." Jack leaned over and gave Sarah a long but tender kiss.

CHAPTER 18

It was three days after Christmas, and Jack was eagerly packing a suitcase in anticipation of visiting Sarah at her home in Lebanon. They had spent very little time together after the Churchill incident, between studying and taking final exams, completing required course papers, and then travelling to their respective homes to spend Christmas with their families.

Jack was certainly happy to see his parents and spend some time with family and friends back home. Yes, maybe Christmas had gotten overly commercialized, but he still loved the sights, sounds and smells of the holiday season. From the vibrant smell of the balsam tree his mother painstakingly decorated in the living room, to the fresh garland over the fireplace, to the Santa Claus collection of figurines his father Tom had started that was now his, and to which he tried to add a new figure every couple of years. He enjoyed walking through the neighborhood and driving down his city streets taking in the colorful lights, wreaths and lawn decorations, even when some of the exterior displays were overdone, whimsical, or just plain tacky.

Even after two weeks of his mom playing traditional Christmas music at home, or listening to Christmas rock songs on the radio, he continued to enjoy the sounds of the festive season. After nearly four months of campus dining, he particularly enjoyed the Christmas dinner his mom had made, with several contributions of desserts from the relatives who had come to their house to celebrate December the 25th. He also definitely appreciated the Christmas gifts his mother and father had given him, not just some new clothes, but especially the envelope of cash that would come in handy for his occasional romantic getaways with Sarah.

In his heart though, he knew very well that something was missing. That was his almost aching desire to share the seasonal joys with Sarah. He knew she shared a similar passion for most things Christmas, and knew she was enjoying the same things several hours away with her own family and friends. His thoughts were never far from Sarah—holding her hand, her touch, the smell of her hair, her laughter, a private conversation. All those special and intimate things. Thankfully, he would be driving up to Pennsylvania to see her in just two days on the 29th, to spend nearly a week at her family's house. And that, he thought, was the best Christmas present he could wish for.

The next day, he checked out his Thunderbird for the 260-mile drive to Lebanon. Air pressure in his snow ties - check. Engine oil on full—check. Antifreeze level safely reading to thirty-four degrees below zero—check. Transmission fluid—check. Spare tire good—check.

After breakfast the next morning—his mother made him his favorite blueberry pancakes—he said his goodbyes to his mother and father, and smiled to himself as he hopped in his car. He knew he'd be holding Sarah in his arms and giving her a hello kiss in about four hours' time, with the welcome forecast of chilly but sunny weather for the drive north.

***

Jack arrived at Sarah's home on Spring Street early that afternoon. The Mack family split-level ranch house was quite similar to every other split-level ranch home in the neighborhood, having been developed as a new suburban subdivision in the 1960s. It appeared to Jack to be a solid middle-working class neighborhood, probably with its fair share of teachers, nurses, police officers, firefighters, retail service workers, and employees of the nearby Bayer pharmaceutical plant.

Sarah had obviously been on the lookout for him, so immediately after Jack pulled into the driveway, he was barely out of his car seat before Sarah hurried up to him to give him a big kiss hello. "God, it's good to see you, Jack. I missed you."

Jack teased, "Well, the only time I really missed you was when I was thinking about you. Which was just about every waking moment. You look great, Sarah. Merry Christmas by the way."

"And Merry Christmas to you, Jack Moran. Come inside and meet my parents. And don't be nervous. They don't bite."

"Don't I get a last meal or cigarette or something before I meet them?"

"Oh, stop" as Sarah gave him a little love punch on his upper arm. "I'm sure they'll love you just the way I do. Well, not *exactly* the way I do." She winked.

"Stop toying with me, wench" as Jack tried to look serious, but he couldn't keep up the pretense, smiled, and took the liberty of another kiss.

Jack grabbed his suitcase as Sarah led him up the front steps. He said, "Okay, ready as I'll ever be," as he approached the front door. He gave her a last quick glance, pretending to look horrified, which she rightfully acknowledged with a well-deserved smirk.

Jack cautiously entered the Examination Room of House Mack. Sarah's mom and dad seemed to be waiting for him as they peered down from the main floor landing as Jack entered the foyer. He gave a short wave and said hello, as Sarah dragged him up the half flight of stairs.

Sarah's parents, who appeared to be in their mid to late forties, gave a friendly smile as they greeted Jack. As he got to the top of the landing, Sarah's mom leaned in and gave him a slight welcoming peck on the cheek. She had light brown hair, an attractive face, and was someone who obviously had successfully tried to maintain her nice figure. Jack could see immediately where Sarah had gotten her good looks from, as well as perhaps her friendly manner.

Not that her father was a sinister looking troll of some kind. He was nearly six feet tall, had a slightly receding hairline, and looked to Jack like someone who might have been a good athlete in his youth. And while he seemed to greet Jack warmly, there was something in his eyes that made Jack feel like he was sizing him up a bit. Something any father would naturally do to a new boyfriend of his daughter, especially a boyfriend she seemed so keen on. At the same time, Jack was sizing up Sarah's father, saying to himself, *I guess this is where Sarah gets her common sense, practical side.*

Mrs. Mack smiled. "Welcome Jack," she said. "Sarah's told us a lot about you." Obviously not *everything*, Jack thought to himself, or you'd probably have a patrol car out front blocking me from getting within a hundred feet of your daughter.

"It's very nice to meet both of you," Jack replied. "Thank you so much for letting me stay here. I'm really looking forward to my visit."

Sarah showed Jack to her brother's room where he would be sleeping (much to the disappointment of both of them). After Mrs. Mack made a late lunch for the four of them, and after some small talk about Jack's home, family and Georgetown, Sarah told her parents she was going to show Jack around town, and would be back before dinner. (They were both looking forward to some time when they could be alone together.)

The happy couple made their way to the downtown area, parked Jack's car, and began to walk around the small city center. The downtown district comprised about a fifteen square block area of a few hundred buildings. Most of the buildings were constructed from about the 1920s to the 1950s and made of brick or stone, although there were several older attractive wood frame commercial buildings, as well as a handful of more modern structures—all generally ranging from two or three to five stories in height.

The area included some interesting and attractive historical architectural gems like the Lebanon Farmers Market building (originally the County Jail building constructed in 1892), the Samler Building (with its distinctive conical roof, built around 1900), and the gothic St. Luke's Episcopal Church (constructed in 1880).[1]

Sarah made a point to show Jack the place downtown where many residents would gather not only to ring in the

New Year in a few days, but where they would repeat the local tradition of lowering a twelve foot long, 150-pound Lebanon bologna at midnight. It would be encased in a metal frame, already in place (presently without the bologna), to be suspended and lowered from a fire department truck. The bologna, donated by the owners of Weaver's Famous Lebanon Bologna, would then in turn be donated to a local rescue mission after the celebration.

Jack, visualizing a twelve-foot bologna as some sort of oversized phallic symbol, said something to Sarah about what appeared to be an obvious sexual preoccupation on the minds of Lebanon residents. Sarah laughed after giving him a not too gentle slug on his arm and said, "Well, Jack Moran, we certainly know what's on your mind."

"Can you blame me? I'm with my girl for the Christmas and New Year holidays, I love you, you look fantastic, and we haven't been alone since our very first night together."

"Yes, I know. Hopefully we can figure something out while you're here. By the way, speaking of New Years, one of my best friends in town is having a New Year's Eve party at her house and you and I are invited. Is that okay with you?"

"Of course, I'd be happy anywhere, as long as I can hold you in my arms and give you a long kiss at the stroke of midnight."

Sarah gave Jack her best seductive look, combined with a smile and a wink, and replied, "You can count on it."

***

The following day was Thursday, and with the New Year's Eve party not until Friday night, Jack and Sarah spent most of the day doing a little shopping, stopping for lunch at a local pub, and taking an afternoon hike. After dinner at the Mack residence, at Sarah's suggestion, they decided to take the twenty-minute drive to visit Hershey, Pennsylvania.

Hershey had been founded as a company town in 1903 by Milton Hershey, candy magnate and philanthropist and founder of the Hershey Company.[2] It was home to Hershey Park, originally created by Mr. Hershey in 1906 as a leisure park for Hershey employees, but which opened to the general public a few years later. Over the years, it had been expanded greatly to include various themed areas, a zoo, and a large number of roller coasters. Just outside the Park was the famous Hershey Chocolate Factory, where millions of pounds of chocolate delights were produced every year—from Hershey chocolate bars, to Kisses, to Kit Kats, to Reese's, and many other blissful treats.

Jack had never been to Hershey, but Sarah knew he certainly had a sweet tooth for chocolate. She thought it would be a fun evening. Sarah, who had made many, many trips to Hershey over the years with her parents and friends, even flaunted a little of her knowledge about the history of Hershey. She told Jack the interesting fact that during WWII the plant was turned over to the war effort to produce a Hershey creation named Field Ration D. It consisted of a four-ounce bar that provided six hundred calories, would not melt, and helped to sustain soldiers when other food was scarce. "In fact," Sarah proclaimed while reciting her history on the drive to Hershey, "the plant produced 500,000 bars a day for our fighting soldiers."

"I'm impressed. You sure know your Hershey chocolate, don't you," Jack teased. "Well, I've got something that I think will make that chocolate taste even better."

With that, Jack reached into his coat pocket and pulled out a narrow joint. "A friend down the hall in my dorm gave me this just before semester break as a kind of Christmas present. Have you ever smoked a joint before?" Jack asked with curiosity.

"Only once at a party the summer before Georgetown," Sarah replied a little apprehensively. "What about you?"

"Not much. A few times. The college-age brother of a girl I dated briefly in senior year of high school gave me my first joint. Want to smoke this before we get to the park? It'll be good for some laughs."

"Okay, Jack," Sarah replied a little apprehensively. "If you want me too."

"Sure, what's the harm?"

Before they pulled into the Hershey Park parking lot, Jack drove around the less developed area east of the park while he and Sarah shared a joint. They only smoked about half of it before turning into the parking lot.

They had come primarily to see *Hersheypark Christmas Candylane*, where more than five million twinkling lights were on display as you walked through the park. They both were a little high, but pretty well under control. The lights seemed to sparkle and dance as if they were almost alive. The variety of displays and what seemed like hundreds of different colors and shapes had Jack and Sarah in a holiday high. They came upon the *Noel* light show, and watched and listened to some 250,000 lights dancing to the music of traditional holiday tunes.

They stopped to pause at the iconic *Kissmas Tree*, which allowed Jack to demand, "You may not be chocolate, but how about a sweet kiss nonetheless from my favorite piece of candy?" Sarah pretended to cringe and shake her head at Jack's corny joke, but then burst into a big smile followed by a hug and a big kiss.

Jack, feeling both happy and a little stoned, and emboldened by her kiss, then proceeded to walk over to one of the several Hershey costumed characters walking around. Sarah gave a loud, somewhat embarrassed laugh as Jack tried to put his arms around the Hershey Kiss character, but couldn't quite get his arms around the costumed person's unusual shape and wide girth.

After a couple hours of enjoying the sights and sounds, they sat down to eat what tasted like—with both of them having the munchies—the best chocolate ice cream they had ever tasted. The two lovebirds then walked back to the car to make the drive back to Lebanon. They both seemed deliriously happy to have found one other and to be sharing and enjoying each other's company.

As they pulled out of the lot, Jack retrieved the remaining half of the joint and suggested they have a few last hits. Sarah wondered out loud if Jack should drive after smoking, but he assured her he'd be fine. Jack turned down Cocoa Avenue, then onto Chocolate Avenue. They each had a few hits as Jack pulled onto I-78 eastbound.

Jack thought he was being funny when he said to Sarah: "Hey, let's see how fast this old Thunderbird can go."

While there were few cars on the road, Sarah looked at Jack with an expression of concern, thinking this was probably not a good idea at the moment. Meanwhile, Jack accelerated up to sixty miles per hour. He gripped the wheel tighter, sat up straight in his seat, and began to say out loud—"seventy…seventy five...eighty!"

Sarah was getting nervous, and a little upset, and said in a serious tone, "Jack, please slow down." But Jack continued to trumpet, "eighty-five…ninety miles per hour!"

All this time, without pressing his foot down lower on the accelerator.

Sarah didn't have a direct line of sight with the speedometer. If she had leaned over a bit to look, she would have realized what Jack was doing. At this point, instead, Sarah shouted almost hysterically at Jack, "JACK. PLEASE SLOW DOWN!"

Jack immediately began to laugh. "Sarah, all this time I've been driving in the right-hand lane at the same sixty miles per hour," he said. "I was just pulling your leg because you're a little stoned."

While Jack thought he was being both clever and funny, he nearly swallowed his tongue seeing the look on Sarah's face, as she folded her arms across her chest and looked straight ahead.

"That wasn't at all funny Jack. You nearly scared me half to death."

Jack saw readily that what may have been funny to him, could be terrifying to someone else who might be having a little bout of paranoia from smoking. He reached over and put his hand on the leg of her jeans and said apologetically, "I'm really sorry, Sarah. I guess I wasn't thinking how you might react. I'll never do something stupid like that at your expense again. I never want to see that look of displeasure or disappointment on your face ever again. I love you too much."

"I love you too, Jack." She turned to look at him in the eyes and said, "Is that a promise?"

He tried to give her his most winning, humble smile. "May I never be allowed to eat another piece of chocolate if I break my promise to you, okay?"

"Okay, Jack," Sarah replied, perhaps still pouting a bit.

Jack pleaded, "How about a make-up kiss after our first disagreement"?

With those words spoken, Sarah inched over closer to him, smiled, and gave him a soft peck on the cheek. "I can't ever stay mad at you, Jack." Then somewhat dryly added, "I think."

Jack's eyes brightened a bit. "Hey, how about we find a nice deserted place for a little passionate atonement? It will be our first make-up session!"

"Well, if you weren't so irresistible and charming, I'd say no, but I guess I can't help myself. But where could we go?"

"This looks like a pretty deserted section along this stretch of the highway. I bet if we get off the next exit, we can find a private spot to park. OK?"

OK, I guess I'm game if you are. As long as it's private. And safe."

"I'm sure I can find a spot."

With that, Jack pulled off the next exit onto a two-lane local country road. The area seemed to be absent of all but an occasional house, and was mostly characterized by gently rolling fields punctuated by reasonably dense wooded surroundings.

Jack noticed a small dirt road without a mailbox or anything else on the main road that would make it appear to be a residence of any kind. He pulled in and after some fifty feet found a small open area behind some trees, where he figured he could park safely without anyone being the wiser.

He turned off the headlights as he parked in a small opening between rows of tall pine trees. Being late December, it was only about forty degrees outside. Jack decided to leave the car running with the heat on low, making sure to crack the two front windows to avoid an embarrassing death from carbon monoxide poisoning.

Although, Jack thought to himself, there could be worse ways to die than dying in the arms of his precious Sarah.

Jack had a large blanket in the back trunk, and he grabbed it as he and Sarah piled into the back seat of the Thunderbird. They began to kiss and touch each other and then started removing most of each other's clothes. The warmth of their skin got hotter and hotter as they embraced and caressed each other. Finally, Sarah got on top of Jack, and as she moved rhythmically back and forth, Sarah whispered, "I love you, Jack." Jack responded almost breathlessly, "I love you too Sarah, with all my heart."

They didn't know how long they had made love, as time seemed to be suspended in their own little world of just the two of them. They had fallen asleep afterward, still covered by the blanket, with Sarah laying half on top of Jack and half against the back seat upright. Suddenly there was a loud knock on the glass of the side door window, with a blaring flashlight being directed at the two of them.

Jack covered his eyes and looked up to see a man in a police uniform standing outside the car, who almost immediately said in a loud, but not hostile voice, "You kids shouldn't be here. Get you stuff together and get out of here. Pronto!" The tone of his voice was almost fatherly, as maybe he had kids of his own about their age. He was professional enough, and kind enough, not to gawk at the nearly naked young couple, but instead immediately walked back to his police cruiser, which had pulled up behind Jack's Thunderbird. Nonetheless, Jack was embarrassed and upset to say the least, but not nearly as much as Sarah, who seemed to be totally mortified. All she could manage to say was, "Oh shit!" As the cop got back in his car and waited for the two lovebirds to hustle out of there.

Jack and Sarah both quickly dressed while still in the back seat, slumped down, and climbed back into the front seat. As Jack turned his lights on to put the car in gear, the cop car backed into a side opening to allow the two desperados to pass and make their getaway.

"God Jack, that was awful! I'm still shaking. Something really bad could have happened to us. Thank God that police officer was nice enough to just give us a warning and let us leave."

Jack felt bad. "I'm sorry I put you in that situation, Sarah. Jack wondered aloud, "How on earth did he even know we were there?" The only thing he could think of was the headlights from the cop's car might have reflected off the exhaust rising from Jack's car as the police car was driving past.

Jack could see Sarah was visibly upset, rightfully so. He could see she not only looked distressed, but a little fearful about what could have actually happened. He promised himself he would need to be more considerate and protective of her, no matter how much he wanted to be alone with her. "I guess we better go straight home to your parents. I hope you're not mad at me? I just wanted to be alone with you. I'm Sorry."

"I'm not mad at you Jack," she said, although still visibly upset. "I want to be alone with you too, but we have to figure out a better way, and be more careful. That was too close for comfort. And yes, I think we should go straight home. Between the 'simulated highway speeding' incident and the police shining a light at us laying naked in the back seat, I think I've had quite enough excitement for one night."

Sarah thought her words may have sounded more critical than she intended. She put her hand on Jack's leg as he pulled onto the highway—as Jack made sure to stay in the right lane and go less than sixty miles per hour. Sarah smiled, saying, "One thing for sure, Jack Moran. Life with you certainly isn't dull!"

Jack returned the smile and thought to himself what a lucky guy he was. *Sarah sure is one hell of a woman,* he thought. He realized he had been a bit of a jerk and selfish putting her in those situations. He knew in his heart and in his head that there was certainly a lot more to their relationship than just joking around, enjoying each other's company, and having sex. He promised himself, from now on, he would always put her well-being and feelings first. He thought, *Isn't that what loving someone really means? I guess I still have some growing up to do to become the man she deserves.*

Jack thought about his conversation with Elizabeth, Abigail and Alexandra. He imagined that the love those three women expressed for their husbands was equally felt by their husbands for them—not only loving them—but respecting and caring for them as individuals whom they would always put first and foremost in their lives.

Jack glanced at Sarah and squeezed her hand briefly before returning both hands to the steering wheel. She returned the gesture with her loving smile. All was good between the two of them, as Jack's car exited the highway at the sign marked Lebanon.

***

The next day, New Year's Eve, was fairly uneventful for Sarah and Jack. They both wanted just to relax under the radar after last night's excitement. They hung out at Sarah's parents' house, talking, reading, and watching a couple college football games. Sarah's mom made a light dinner for them, as she knew they'd have lots of food at

Sarah's friend Cathy's New Year's Eve party later that evening.

The invitees were told to dress "respectably," since Cathy's parents would be home (but nearly invisible), and after all, it was the holidays. Jack put on a wool tweed jacket to go with his gray slacks and white, open neck dress shirt. Sarah had on a white cotton, high neck dress that showed off her great figure. Jack tried to do his best Billy Crystal interpretation of the Saturday Night Live show when he voiced in his best Latin accent, "You look marvelous!" And she did!

Cathy's father was a doctor, and they lived in an attractive traditional center hall colonial on Mead Street. The party was being held in their large finished basement that included a wet bar, a working jukebox, and an above ground patio outside two sliding glass doors. It was a great setup for a party, and everyone was looking forward to having a great time.

There were probably about two dozen people attending the party, mostly couples, but several single guys and girls as well. In addition to soda, beer and wine was available, but folks were instructed to "keep it tame" given that Cathy's parents were there, and revelers had to drive home sometime well after midnight.

Sarah introduced Jack to all her friends, most of whom seemed to be nice, genial people like herself. Jack didn't know if this was natural selection on Sarah's part of whom she picked as friends, or if it was something broader having to do with growing up in a down to earth place like Lebanon.

Everyone was having a good time talking, reminiscing about high school and college life, and listening to a lot of great records on the jukebox, from 1960s oldies to Allman

Brothers, the Band, the Grateful Dead, the Beatles, the Rolling Stones, and a few more "fresh" artists.

About 11:45, Cathy turned on the television along the large side wall so people could watch the traditional "Dick Clark's New Year's Rockin' Eve" from Times Square broadcast on ABC with coverage of the annual ball drop. The ball sat atop the roof of 1 Times Square, consisting of a geodesic sphere measuring twelve feet in diameter, and weighing in at nearly twelve thousand pounds.[3]

People were gathered in a large group in front of the TV at 11:59 when the ball began its slow descent. The estimated one million spectators in Times Square began to yell louder and louder in anticipation. At twenty seconds until midnight, the TV hosts were joined by the people in Cathy's basement, including Sarah and Jack, in counting down the final seconds. They all yelled in unison, "5...4...3...2...1....Happy New Year!" The Times Square crowd frenzy crested as people screamed, hugged and kissed, and as 3,000 pounds of confetti in the form of thirty million pieces of colored paper blasted over the euphoric, massive assembly.

While a mini version of Times Square was taking place in Cathy's basement, Jack and Sarah had embraced in a long, simmering kiss that felt like it went on for minutes. They were of like mind, body and soul, happy and appreciative that they had found each other and fallen in love. They could look forward not only to the New Year together, but also to a life together.

Finally, knowing no one would hear them amidst all the commotion, or were really paying attention to them, Jack whispered to Sarah, "I love you Sarah, so very much. I think we're perfect for each other. I know we talked about this, but I don't think I ever actually gave you an official

John Kenyon

proposal. Will you promise me you'll spend the rest of your life with me, as my wife someday?"

Sarah gazed into Jack's loving, hopeful eyes. "Of course I will Jack. There's nothing I want more. And yes, you're perfect for me, too. I just wish we didn't have to wait so long. But I know it has to be that way. But when?"

"I guess in nearly four years, soon after we graduate. I know it seems like forever, but we'll have a lifetime together. We can get through anything by each other's sides, with your hand in mine. Okay?"

"Okay, Jack." They kissed again. Neither had ever been happier. What Jack couldn't possibly know is he would soon be faced with a different fateful decision—not in 4 years, but in less than four days.

CHAPTER 19

It was a few days after New Year's, and it was time for Jack to head back to Virginia. He had some things he had to help his dad with around the house, Sarah's brother would be returning in a couple days and want his room back, and they would both be heading back to Georgetown in about a week.

Jack decided to take Sarah out to a quaint little romantic Italian restaurant in town before his drive to Virginia. They would have an early dinner and he would drop her off before departing for the four-hour trip. He expected to be home in Midlothian around midnight.

Late afternoon Tuesday, he packed his car, said his goodbyes to Sarah's parents and thanked them for their hospitality. Sarah was glad that Jack seemed to have made a good impression on her parents, especially when Sarah's mom kissed him goodbye and remarked what a nice couple the two made. Even Sarah's father gave Jack a fatherly pat on the back as he said goodbye.

Sarah and Jack enjoyed their homemade pasta and eggplant parmigiana dinners by candlelight, along with a couple glasses of cabernet. Just one each, as Jack had a long drive ahead of him. After dinner, Jack drove Sarah back to her house, walked her to the front door, and they said their goodbyes. Sarah put her arms around the back of Jack's neck, pulled him close and gave him a long kiss. "HHMMM." Jack grinned. "I'm glad it will only be a week until I see you again."

Jack smiled, but could see the water forming in Sarah's beautiful blue eyes. "Hey, don't be sad. It'll only be a week."

"That's just part of the reason. I'm really just very happy Jack. You know?"

"I know. Me too." With that, Jack gave her one last kiss and waved goodbye as he got into his car.

***

Jack had been driving for over two hours, and was travelling south on I-495, the Capital Beltway, some fifteen miles west of D.C. It was about 10:30 on a Tuesday night and hardly anyone was on the road. He was listening to one of his favorite albums on his cassette player, the Allman Brother's Eat a Peach. Jack was thinking about the last several days with Sarah—Hershey Park, the close call with the police in the back seat of the Thunderbird, the New Year's Eve party (and that long, lingering kiss), and their romantic dinner earlier that evening.

He was approaching the bridge that traverses the Potomac River near the border of Maryland and Virginia when he suddenly heard a voice in his head telling him to get off the next exit once he crossed the bridge. The voice sounded much like his father Tom's voice, and seemed so clear that he turned his head around to take a quick look in the back seat to see if Tom was in fact sitting there. But there was nobody.

A few seconds later, he heard the voice again. It sounded so real and seemingly recognizable that Jack didn't question following the instructions. Upon crossing the bridge, he got off the next exit just across the river. The sign read Scott's Run Nature Preserve. Jack knew the area, as he and a few of his high school friends had been up there a couple times during the summer. They would hike some of the many trails and sit by the picture-perfect waterfall for which the park was named.

When he reached the end of the exit ramp, Jack felt compelled to turn right, as if something was drawing him in that direction. He started heading northwest along the narrow road that runs along the Potomac River. It was early January, late at night, in an area with virtually no houses given the green belt that stretched for nearly the next ten miles and extended all the way west to Great Falls Park. With no homes and no street lamps, and no park visitors at this time of night given the season, the area seemed quite desolate. The only light came from the full moon that shone on the river and over the treetops on this nearly cloudless night.

Jack had driven for about three miles along the river, seemingly not knowing why. With no nearby lights for miles and a clear sky, Jack was gazing at the multitude of stars overhead, and thinking about what Galileo had said to him about our destiny, stardust, and our connection with the Universe.

Suddenly, without warning, Jack felt the ground rumbling beneath him. His car began to shudder and vibrate. For a second he thought he would lose control and run off the road, when an almost deafening noise came thundering out of the sky sounding like a hundred trains. To his amazement, a second later he saw a large twin-engine silver and blue aircraft come roaring out of the night sky, plunging toward the cold, moonlit waters of the Potomac River. It almost seemed to Jack like it was all happening in slow motion.

To their credit, the pilots of the aircraft had made a near perfect water landing, but the front of the plane had taken more of the impact as the rear of the aircraft skimmed and bounced across the surface like the skipping of a flat stone thrown from the water's edge.

Jack had slammed on his brakes as the plane rapidly descended, jumping out of his car just as the aircraft slowed its movement like a giant goose landing on the water, now resting in the river. He ran to the water's edge. The slope downward was relatively modest, and the tree line was setback about forty feet. The aircraft looked like the giant carcass of a beached whale, with its wings partially submerged but the main cabin body floating upright in an eerie silence. He would have expected to hear screaming and cries for help.

But all was quiet.

Jack could see that it was a fairly large twin jet engine aircraft, perhaps a 737, that he guessed could probably carry a couple hundred people. As the bright moonlight reflected off the metal skin, Jack could clearly see what had caused the aircraft to drop so precipitously out of the dark. There was a gaping hole in the midsection of the craft that probably measured some five feet high by ten feet long.

Could it have been a bomb? Was it hit by a smaller aircraft? Some sort of electrical or mechanical failure causing an explosion?

But for the moment, what caused the accident didn't really matter. The problem was that the plane, and Jack, were alone in the middle of a remote area—at night. Had others seen the accident? Was the plane on its way to Washington National Airport in D.C. so air traffic controllers would be well aware that the plane went down? Would rescue teams have been notified and be preparing to come and help? Although given where they were, that could take many minutes—precious minutes. With the plane sitting in what had to be at least ten feet of water and a huge hole in its side, it might not be long before it began to sink, trapping all those inside who might have survived the crash.

Jack started to wade into the water, but only got up to his knees before he stopped. The water was frigid, and the current moderately strong. All those people, Jack thought. But he was just one person. Even if he could get out to the plane, some one hundred yards away, how much would he be able to do? Even if he make it on board, what if the plane started to sink? What if there was another explosion?

Jack was afraid. He wanted to help. But he didn't want to die. He pictured Sarah, and the future they so longed to share with one another. Could he just throw that all away in what could be a hopeless cause? He stood there momentarily almost petrified, seemingly unable to move.

Then he remembered the words of some of the noble men and women who had come to visit him, who told him he had special qualities. It all seemed to rush into his mind in a matter of seconds, as if time had stopped. He remembered the recent words of Sir Winston, about heart, strength and courage. He remembered the courage of Peter and the apostles to take up the difficult path Christ had laid out for them. He remembered how even Christ, being fully human, had experienced fear Himself—including fear of an excruciating death. He even remembered the words of the seemingly repentant John Wilkes Booth, who spoke about taking unselfish action to benefit others. Of having trust in God.

Then he thought of Sarah—his beloved Sarah. He felt he couldn't live without her. But he also couldn't live with himself, and be fully true to her, if he didn't take the right, unselfish, action now. If he instead took the cowardly way out.

He looked at the plane, still floating quietly, and he began to move forward into the water toward the aircraft, saying out loud as he took his first step, "I love you, Sarah. Please help me, God!"

But as he began to take a second step toward the plane, he sensed the movement of the water behind him being pushed forward, and the slight sound of waves splashing. He turned his body almost completely around and stared in amazement. Less than ten feet behind him were rows and rows of men, all wearing similar clothes that appeared to be a uniform of some kind, stepping into the water…apparently ready to follow him.

There must have been three hundred of them, all dressed in what Jack thought looked like sailor work clothes. Almost all the men appeared to be anywhere from his age up to their late twenties or so. Then a somewhat older man with graying hair, wearing what appeared to be an officer's khaki uniform with insignias on the shoulders of his jacket, stepped forward. He spoke to Jack in a commanding but calm voice. "Jack, you're not alone. My men and I are here to help you."

Jack froze, trying to comprehend what was happening. It all seemed so surreal. As the officer spoke, Jack realized there were letters embroidered on his cap. He was close enough now for Jack to reach out and touch him. In the

Return to Stardust

bright moonlight, he could read the words clearly. They read, USS *Arizona*.

Upon reading the words, Jack immediately realized who these men were. And why they were here. The few hundred men were just some of the 1,177 naval officers and crew members who perished when their ship was destroyed and sunk to the bottom of Pearl Harbor on that dreadful day of December 7, 1941. Japanese armor-piercing bombs had penetrated the ships deck and detonated a magazine, causing a violent explosion and the ship to sink with many entombed inside. A portion of the ship's wreck still lies at the bottom of Pearl Harbor beneath the USS *Arizona* Memorial, which straddles the ship but does not touch its hull.[1]

With a lump in this throat, Jack said, "Thank you for being here. I'd love to talk with you more about how—and what—brings you here. But there's no time to lose. I don't know what we'll find when we get to the plane."

With that, Jack turned and waded deeper into the water, as the other men followed. It didn't take long before he was over his head and swimming toward the wrecked aircraft. The water was indeed cold, and the current somewhat swift, but Jack was a good swimmer. He approached the large hole in the airplane's mid-section. The bottom of the hole was nearly at water level. With the gently rippling action of the waves, water had already begun to seep into the plane. He pulled his cold and shivering body up and through the hole, being careful not to cut himself on the twisted and jagged metal around the perimeter of the hole.

Luckily, some of the emergency lights in the cabin had remained on after the crash. Jack could see the rows of passengers—quiet in their seats with seat belts fashioned, almost as if they were asleep. Jack could see the cabin was

187

nearly, if not completely, full. He and the men from the *Arizona* would have to move quickly to get everyone out in case the plane began to sink. He started to walk forward through the inch or two of water that already covered the main floor of the cabin.

The *Arizona* crewmen began to climb through the same large hole, extending a hand to their mates to ease their way through the opening. They began to make their way down the aisle, checking on people as they went. The seats that had been adjacent to the hole were gone, with only small metal tracks on the floor remaining. The explosion had undoubtedly ejected and killed those passengers who had been seated there. The others, while unconscious, all appeared to be alive.

No one showed any major injuries, at least to Jack's untrained eyes. Whether it was the impact, the rapid descent, or rapid depressurization of the cabin that caused people to pass out, Jack had no idea. The oxygen masks had not dropped from the overhead as they were supposed to. Maybe the explosion had caused an electrical malfunction. Maybe it was Divine intervention. No matter. They were alive.

Some of the Navy crewmen opened up the other exit doors on the same side of the aircraft to try to move people out as quickly as possible. Groups of men positioned themselves at each door and at the area of the gaping hole. They seemed to work in teams, signaling with hand gestures or giving brief instructions to one another as if their naval training had kicked in.

After unbuckling the passenger seat belts, the men began to lift, carry and pass the unconscious survivors through the openings out to other men floating in the water alongside the aircraft. Sometimes in singles, and sometimes in pairs, the crewman would turn and begin their swim toward shore through the cold, dark waters. Each crewman held each passenger afloat in the standard life saving position using their arms to support the passenger's neck as the unconscious victim floated on their back.

Meanwhile, Jack moved through the forward cabin to check on the pilots. As he passed through the cabin, he couldn't help but observe that the people in their seats were typical of any group of passengers that might be expected on an otherwise normal flight. Men and women, young and old, big and slight. He noticed only a few smaller children buckled in their seats. He was thankful he didn't see any infants, knowing what might have happened to them given the impact of the crash.

As he entered the cockpit, Jack stopped and stared in quiet reflection as he realized from their head wounds and vacant stares that neither of the two pilots had survived the crash. By landing the front of the plane to take the most impact, they had died as heroes to save their passengers and crew. Two Navy men began to move past Jack toward the bodies when he stopped them. "They're dead," he said.

One of the soldiers responded respectfully, with a certain sadness in his eyes, "We leave no man behind, Sir."

Jack nodded with understanding and moved back into the main cabin. He was amazed how quickly the *Arizona* crewmen had been able to move nearly all the passengers and crew out of the plane and into the water, headed for shore. Jack saw a young woman still strapped in her seat belt. He undid it, picked her up, and moved toward the door.

As nearly all of the passengers were out now, Jack jumped in the water while a crewman held her in his grasp at the opening. Jack said, 'I'll take her."

"Okay, Sir," the crewman responded as he lowered the woman into Jack's outstretched arms.

The commanding officer, who had been on board directing many of the men during the rescue, peered out the opening and said, "We'll be right behind you with the last of the passengers, Sir."

As Jack cradled the young woman with his arm under her neck and swam toward shore, he thought: *This girl could be someone else's Sarah. How wonderful it will be when she is reunited with her family and loved ones, rather than to have her life snuffed out so young without realizing who knows how many opportunities and shared joys she might have.*

As he got to shore, Jack saw perhaps as many as 200 passengers and airplane crew laid out on the shore, still unconscious. To the side lay the pilot and co-pilot, with a blanket from the aircraft respectfully spread over each of them. The last few crewmen came ashore behind Jack with the remaining survivors.

Just at that moment the aircraft, which had now taken on a great deal of water, began making an eerie moaning sound and to rotate slightly as it began to sink. The rear end sunk first, seemingly resembling a huge whale breaching the surface. After a few moments, the craft came to rest with part of its nose still sticking out of the water.

Jack could hear sirens in the distance. It had been less than twenty minutes since the plane hit the water. Jack found the commanding officer standing nearby and said, "Thank you so very much, and of course your men, for coming. I would have been of little help without you. You were all—still are—heroes. There's many things I want to ask you, but the rescue vehicles will be here any second."

The officer looked at Jack with an expression of some military formality, but spoke with a tone both warm and friendly. "No, Sir. Thank you. Yours is a special brand of courage."

Dripping wet, and starting to feel chills, Jack stammered back, "It's you and your men that are the courageous ones. You helped save all these people so they could go back to their loved ones, go on with their lives. When for you and your men, your lives were cut short so tragically, and unnecessarily, leaving behind wives, children, mothers, fathers, brothers and sisters. But your memory is still honored by the hundreds of thousands of people who come to see the Arizona Memorial. Your dedication and courage will never be forgotten."

"Thank you for those words Jack. It was an honor to serve with my men...again." The officer then looked at Jack with eyes that felt like they pierced Jack's soul. "But don't you realize, Jack, if you didn't take that first step, we wouldn't be here."

"But *why?*" Jack seemed to plead. "How could *I* bring you here?"

"Two reasons," the officer countered. "Your heart. And your trust in God, Jack."

With those words, the officer saluted Jack, then vanished—just as the lights of several rescue and emergency vehicles approached the scene.

Not wanting to be seen, Jack ran to a wooded area off to the side and hid himself behind a large tree out of view. When he turned to look back at the shore, the passengers and crew of the aircraft on the ground were beginning to stir, though dazed and confused. Meanwhile, the men of the USS *Arizona* were nowhere to be seen. They had disappeared as quickly as they had appeared. As Jack looked up at the moonlight sky, he thought he saw a shooting star pass overhead.

As dozens of rescue workers moved to administer to the survivors, Jack slowly crept back through the woods to his parked car. With all the excitement and rescue workers focused on doing their jobs, no one seemed to take any special notice of his car, the rescue workers probably thinking it belonged to another first responder.

As Jack drove away to make his way back to the interstate and home, the adrenaline was still rushing through his bloodstream. He pumped his fist and yelled out loud—to no one other than himself— "YES!"

He had done the right thing. The unselfish, caring, human thing. Consciously or not, he had also put his faith in God.

Perhaps most importantly, he was alive. Alive to be with his beloved Sarah again, just as all those survivors were alive to go on with their own lives. He remembered the story Sir Winston told him about Doctor Fleming, even if it wasn't fact and was just a parable of sorts. He thought about how saving a life had somehow resulted in another person making a wonderful discovery that would help to save millions from pain or even death.

Maybe one of those survivors from the plane crash would also be destined to do something great. Perhaps discover a cure for cancer. Perhaps invent an alternative fuel source to help save the environment. Maybe become a great leader to bring a semblance of peace to the world. If not themselves, maybe one of their sons or daughters, or grandchildren, many years into the future, who might not otherwise be born.

Jack also recalled the words of Galileo. That you didn't have to become famous, to invent or discover something that would benefit mankind, to be of value. Everyone has something to offer. Whether that's just being a good husband, father, son or daughter, or friend. It all matters.

We are all made from the same stuff—in the image and likeness of God.

Jack quickly came back down to earth a bit from his wandering philosophical thoughts of life, faith, hope—all that. He was still a college freshman at Georgetown who, while having been granted a special gift was, other than that, still a pretty normal person. A guy who liked to tell stories and joke around, play sports, watch movies, be with friends. Most of all, he had a great partner, the love of his life, in Sarah. Jack smiled and said to himself out loud, "Boy, I can't wait to see Sarah. Have I got a story for her!"

CHAPTER 20

Over the next few days, local and national newspapers, television and radio stations were flooded with the story surrounding the downed aircraft. Delta Flight 607 from Chicago to D.C. was being referred to as "Miracle Flight 607" and "the Phantom Rescue." The plane had been near full capacity carrying 209 passengers and crew and was beginning a gradual descent to Washington National Airport on that fateful night. Tragically, ten passengers were ejected and killed from the explosion, the cause of which had yet to be determined. In addition, it was clear from their injuries that the two pilots had been killed instantly upon impact. Miraculously, the other 197 passengers had survived with relatively minor injuries.

However, nobody—nobody—had an explanation of how those passengers swam, or were brought, to shore before the aircraft became almost completely submerged in about twenty feet of water. None of the passengers had any memory or recollection of the crash between the time they passed out following the explosion, to the time they gained consciousness (albeit dazed and confused) on the banks of the Potomac River.

Wild speculation began to abound among the press, commentators, and the general public. Some ventured that the passengers suffered some kind of mass amnesia from the trauma of the crash and swimming in the cold water, helping others who needed it along the way, before collapsing in exhaustion. Others claimed the military had somehow mistakenly fired on the plane and immediately sent in a special force of trained operatives to rescue the passengers, but it was all being hushed up.

Some even conjectured that an alien spacecraft had caused the plane to go down, perhaps by accident. That they then had intervened with technology and powers beyond our understanding, successfully rescuing the stranded passengers—after which they were able to use their extraterrestrial skills to wipe the memories from the minds of the survivors.

As Jack well knew, Sarah was a clever girl, and soon began to wonder after hearing the news reports. She realized, based on the time Jack left her house to start home, and knowing his route, that he could have easily been in the vicinity of the plane crash at or near that very moment. No one seemed to have any kind of rational explanation as to what had actually occurred, and she had firsthand knowledge that parts of Jack's life also had no rational explanation either. Plus, the day after the accident, Jack had called Sarah to say that he got home safe, and that he had something incredible to tell her, but not on the phone.

Sarah had to wait anxiously until she was back on campus with Jack a few days later to hear what others would have deemed impossible. To her, what he would tell her was not only plausible, but almost expected. As Jack took Sarah to a quiet corner on campus, and revealed to her what had actually transpired that night, Sarah sat transfixed on Jack's face. Jack went into great detail about the voice he heard; the gripping plane crash; his own fear; the appearance of the *Arizona* crew members; the cold, strong current; and the hurried rescue. She never doubted a word he said. She knew Jack's character, and she had already been through other incidents with him that defied logic.

Jack was obviously excited when telling his story to Sarah, knowing she would be the only other one who could ever know the truth. Still, there was a lot of sadness in his voice and expression when he spoke of the ten passengers and two pilots that had lost their lives. Sarah grabbed his hand and said, "Of course that's tragic for them and their families, Jack. But think of all the people you saved. Because of you, 197 people went home to their families, to their futures."

Sarah continued while she held Jack's hand. "And I know what you're going to say, none of it would have been possible without the men from the *Arizona*. They certainly are heroes. But they wouldn't have been there if not for you! You did something truly wonderful Jack, with the help of God. And your courage. I'm a lucky girl!" She squeezed his hand tight and gazed deeply into his eyes, expressing the love he already knew and felt.

Jack returned the gaze before saying, "You know. All those people that appeared to me. I think back on them and what they said, and I think they were showing me— offering me—*two* gifts. One was to try to give me the courage that, when the time came, I could do the right thing, even though I was honestly terrified. Terrified of dying. Terrified of losing you. But the second gift they gave me was showing me the path to finding and falling in love with you. So I think I'm actually the lucky one. Not everyone has such amazing opportunities."

Jack paused, kissed her, and then continued. "I was also thinking, now that I've...I don't know...experienced—or realized—those two gifts...maybe my "friends" won't come around to visit me anymore. Maybe I've accomplished what they had in mind. I guess time will tell. Anyway, we've got each other. That's all that really matters now. But it's been one hell of a ride, hey beautiful?"

Despite his words, in his own mind, Jack had some serious doubts that the appearances would stop. And it actually made him feel a little anxious. He thought: *After the plane incident, what could possibly happen to me that could equal or exceed that? And would it end differently?*

He held Sarah's hand tightly. He didn't know why, but he suddenly remembered something Sigmund Freud had said to him. "Live life as if every day will be your last. Because one day, you'll be right."

CHAPTER 21

It had been over four years since the plane crash and Jack's heroic, but anonymous, actions. In that time, Jack and Sarah's life had moved on in a manner more typical of other university students and graduates. They had each graduated magna cum laude from their respective colleges, Sarah with a liberal arts degree in English and literature from Georgetown College, and Jack as a finance major from the McDonough School of Business.

Jack and Sarah had decided well before graduation that they both wanted to remain in the greater D.C. area, which offered a great deal that appealed to both of them. Besides the general quality of life and climate of suburban Virginia, they wanted to maintain their ties to Georgetown as alumni and, as history buffs, found immense enjoyment in what the D.C. area offered.

Among their alumni acquaintances, John Carroll, Jack's roommate, had in fact become his best friend. Jack and Sarah had gone on many double dates with John and "one" of his rather long list of girlfriends. Not that John was some kind of "player" in his dating habits. Nevertheless, he could never seem to go with any particular girl for more than a few to several months before there would be a breakup, for reasons unknown to Jack.

Every once in a while, after a breakup, John would say to Jack, "Someday I hope I meet *my* Sarah, Jack." To which Jack would respond with something like, "I hope so John. Sarah and I only want the best for you."

Sarah had even tried to set John up with an occasional date with one of her Georgetown friends. So far, nothing seemed to click for John, despite over three years of trying.

Meanwhile, Sarah had known for some time that she wanted to be an elementary school teacher. She had been very fortunate to find a position lined up even before graduation with the Sunrise Valley Elementary School in Reston, Virginia.

Jack, on the other hand, was never totally certain what his career path should be, and being a spiritual medium to otherwise invisible dead people wasn't exactly something he cared to advertise. He knew he was good with figures, and had a logical mind for identifying needs and finding solutions, so he decided to go to the Business School and major in finance. His somewhat premature thoughts about international travel or secretive government work no longer had the same appeal to him as he originally thought it might. Instead, after his untold adventures, he was more focused on working for a good and valuable cause, settling down with Sarah, and raising a family.

Jack had done a stint as an intern between his junior and senior year working for the Smithsonian Institution. His boss and coworkers seemed to both like and be impressed by Jack. He was thrilled when they told him a job would be waiting for him in the Finance Department if he wanted it when he graduated. Jack had learned during his internship that the Smithsonian was much, much more than the gothic landmark "castle" museum, the Air and Space Museum, and the Museum of American History. It was actually the world's largest museum, education and research complex, with nineteen museums (most but not all of which were located in D.C.), and the National Zoological Park. The Smithsonian employed over six thousand people and had a budget of close to $1 billion, sixty percent of which was federally funded.

Jack was proud to be a part of such an extensive, complex and worthwhile endeavor—an institution involved in an array of activities, whose primary objective was to display and educate the public on the fascinating history and achievements of the American story.

With both of them gainfully employed, Sarah and Jack got married at the end of summer following graduation from Georgetown. The wedding was held at St. Cecilia's Catholic Church in Lebanon. It was attended by some 120 guests, including the extended families of both the bride and groom, hometown friends, and friends from Georgetown. Sarah's sister Kate was the maid of honor, and Jack's best man was his best friend, John Carrol.

Sarah looked absolutely stunning in her traditional white lace gown. Jack could hardly believe he was so lucky, and so much in love. They spent a wonderful honeymoon week on the Island of Bermuda, basking in the sun and clear waters, riding a two-person moped to places like Hamilton Town and Horseshoe Bay Beach. They also drank their fair share of margaritas and pina coladas at the resort hotel, and draft beers at the Grotto Bay Tavern adjoining the hotel. It was an amazing, exciting, romantic and fun beginning to their life together as husband and wife. Like all young married couples, they felt their new life of sharing was just the beginning of a dream come true. They felt incredibly happy—and blessed.

Up until just before the wedding, Jack had not been visited by any of his "patrons," as he sometimes now liked to call them, since the night of the plane crash. One evening, Jack and Sarah were sitting in the townhouse unit they had purchased just a few weeks earlier in Reston, with a little help on the down payment from their parents. Sarah liked being just a few minutes from her elementary school, and Jack's morning drive to D.C. was only about forty-five minutes with traffic, so they liked the location.

They also liked the planned community nature and amenities that Reston had to offer. One of the first planned communities in the country, Reston included ample open space and recreational facilities, shopping and transit centers, and cultural activities. It was a good place to live and raise and family. Moreover, with a wide range of housing types, they hoped they would be able to trade up over time.

Both were sitting on the couch, being simultaneously playful and serious while trying to put words to paper for their upcoming wedding vows. In addition to promising to love her and protect her, Jack was joking about promising never to drive over sixty mph, or some such nonsense, when he stopped in mid-sentence and stared directly ahead at the plaid colonial chair opposite him.

Sarah looked up at Jack saying, "What's the matter, Jack?"

"I guess you can't see her. Wow, this is the first time that any one of my 'patrons' has visited me twice! It's been a long time, Elizabeth. Sarah, say hello to Elizabeth Barrett Browning."

Elizabeth was seated, with her delicate hands folded in her lap. She was dressed in the same Victorian period clothes she wore when she first appeared to Jack when he just started to court Sarah. She had the same kind and gentle expression and soft facial features that Jack remembered from years earlier.

Sarah was speechless. And then Elizabeth spoke. "Hello Jack. It's nice to see you again too. I know she can't hear me, so please say hello to your fiancée Sarah for me. After all, in a way, she's the main reason I'm here."

Looking a little anxious Jack replied, "What do you mean? I mean I'm certainly glad to see you, but is there something wrong?"

Elizabeth laughed gracefully. "No, not in the least Jack! I didn't mean to startle you. I really only came back to congratulate you on your upcoming wedding, and to wish you both much happiness in your life together. I hope you find the same happiness I had, even though it was a little short-lived, with my dear husband Robert. Just like Sarah feels about you, Robert was, still is, the love of my life."

Jack reached over, and put his hand on Elizabeth's. By the look in each other's eyes and their expression, they both knew what the other was thinking. They were picturing the sculpture of the Browning's *Clasped Hands*.

"Thank you so much for coming and your kind words, Elizabeth. And thank you for your encouraging words years ago that helped give me the push I needed to pursue my dream of being with Sarah in the first place." Jack then joked, "If I knew you were coming, I would have added you to the wedding list!"

Elizabeth laughed with her delicate, feminine demeanor. "Well, that's why I'm here today, and not at your wedding! After all this time, I didn't want to startle you by showing up unannounced at the reception and upsetting the happy day for the two of you."

"Yes, I'll tell Sarah what you said. And thank you." Jack paused. "Do you happen to know if my father Tom may be coming to visit me—I mean, us—as well?"

"I'm sorry Jack, but Tom is not able to come, for reasons I don't know and can't explain. But I do know he watches over the two of you, and wishes you the same happiness I do." Elizabeth smiled. "And he's still looking forward to that grandchild." She winked at Jack, saying, "Best of luck to the both of you. Goodbye, Jack."

Jack lowered his eyes, and Sarah, silent the whole time, knew from Jack's expression that Elizabeth was gone. "I'm sorry, Jack. I meant to say hello, but I was just so surprised, and the visit was so short, and I just didn't know quite what to say."

"That's OK, Sarah. Elizabeth understands. She knows."

Then Jack clasped Sarah's hand, laying his on top of hers repeating, "She knows."

CHAPTER 22

Jack and Sarah had been married barely a year, and Sarah was pregnant. It was something they both wanted. They were both doing well in their jobs, and in fact, Jack had already received a promotion to Vice President of Finance. They had been saving their money to be able to buy a starter house in Reston, and they still had several months to save more money before Sarah gave birth. Sarah had received permission from the school superintendent to be a stay-at-home mom for a year before returning to work. At that point, they figured to be in a good position to buy a house.

The baby girl was born in mid-July, essentially perfect timing for Sarah to finish her current school year and be prepared to start again for a new school year a little over a year later.

Like all parents, they just hoped for a healthy baby, but secretly they both wanted a girl. They got their wish. They decided to name the baby Elizabeth. In many ways, it was an obvious choice to the both of them.

Somewhat to their surprise, Elizabeth was born with red hair. Between Sarah's blond curls and Jack's dark brown mane, who would have thought? In fact, Jack first teased Sarah about how could that happen, before pointing out that their mail carrier had red hair—causing Sarah to give him one of her trademark smirks. But Jack was actually well-aware of a couple female cousins of his who lived in Ireland who had red hair, his mother being the first generation of an Irish immigrant. And what started out as almost orange hair would, in a few years, evolve into a beautiful, soft auburn color.

Elizabeth was baptized at St. Catherine of Siena Catholic Church in Reston, where Sarah and Jack were now members of the congregation. All four of the excited grandparents made the drive to attend, along with Sarah's siblings, as well as a few other extended family members and friends.

Time seemed to go quickly over the next couple of years. They purchased a Cape Cod home on a 15,000-square-foot lot with a small but usable backyard. Between their respective jobs, buying and moving into the new house, fixing it up and painting it to make it to their liking, and raising little Beth (as they liked to call her), life was full and they were happy.

In trying to please the grandparents, like many young couples, Jack and Sarah would typically travel to his parents' house in Midlothian for the Thanksgiving weekend, and spend Christmas with Sarah's parents in Pennsylvania. Spending Christmas in Lebanon also gave Jack and Sarah the excuse to visit Hershey Park with Beth, even though she was probably too young to enjoy it, at least in the beginning.

It was on one of those Thanksgiving visits to Jack's parents' house, when Beth was already three, that Jack noticed his mother appearing to have lost a little weight and looking a little pale. Jack took her aside to ask her how she was feeling.

"I feel fine, Jack, just a little tired now and then. But don't worry. Your father is making me go to the doctor, and I'm sure it's nothing. I'm just a little run down."

It was early January when Bob called Jack. Jack knew immediately from the strain in Bob's voice that something was wrong. "Jack, your mother has been having several tests done over the last several weeks."

"Yes, Dad," Jack replied anxiously. "Mom had told me at Thanksgiving she was planning on going to the doctor. Is she okay?"

Bob painfully replied, "I'm sorry to have to tell you this, Jack, but the doctors are telling us she has pancreatic cancer."

Bob paused there, to let it sink in. He could have tried to put on a brave front, but both he and Jack knew that pancreatic cancer was basically a death sentence. Jack slumped into a chair, saying out loud to himself, "Oh God, no."

Jack asked how his mother was doing, and Bob said as well as could be expected. "She's a strong woman, with a lot of faith. You know that," Bob said, his voice wavering. He told Jack she was resting now, and didn't really want to talk on the phone about it anyway. Jack told Bob he would drive down to see her in a couple days, on Friday. After hanging up the phone, Jack hung his head while tears filled his eyes.

Within six months, Jack's mother was gone. With Bob always by her side, Jack, Sarah and Beth spent as much time with her as possible during those last months. A number of times, especially near the end, Patricia Gray expressed her happiness that she had lived to see Jack grow up, to see him marry his cherished Sarah, and especially to see and hold her beautiful granddaughter Beth. It broke Jack's heart.

At the funeral mass, Jack thought it only appropriate that he give his mother's eulogy. He knew he might have difficulty getting through it, but he wanted to do it—to honor his mother, out of his love for her.

After Communion, Fr. Duffy motioned to Jack to step up to the lectern to speak. Jack slowly walked to the lectern to the right of the altar, holding the paper on which he had written his expression of love. He looked out over the congregation consisting of his mother's and Bob's extended family, Sarah and her parents, and a few dozen friends and coworkers who had come to the service. Jack began to speak in a clear but solemn voice.

"Thank you all for coming today.

"Growing up in my house, first on Hill Street, and later on Spring Street, I was used to seeing several Knick knacks, small paintings, photos, and wall hangings that made it home. Things that meant something personal to my mother. But there were two wall-hangings with sayings on them that I think especially reflect the person my mother was.

"One was a small plaque with the words written on it: 'I shall pass this way but once. Therefore, any good that I can do, or any kindness that I can show, let me do it now. For I shall not pass this way again.'[1]

"The second was an embroidered tapestry in a small frame on which the words told the story of a man who, upon leaving this world to meet his Maker, asked the Lord a question. The man says, 'Lord, as I'm looking down the paths I've trod in life, I see two sets of footprints on the easy paths, where you walked beside me. But down the rocky roads I see only one set of footprints. Tell me Lord, why did you let me walk down those difficult paths alone?'

"The Lord smiled and simply replied, 'My son, I know those were the most difficult paths. And that is why, it was during those times, I carried you.'"

Jack continued. "I think those two messages convey a lot about who my mother was. She was someone totally devoted to fulfilling the needs of her family, whenever and wherever she could help, unselfishly and lovingly. Always providing guidance to me as her son. And accepting of the terrible illness that would take her from us.

"She was also someone of deep faith and devotion to her church, and to Jesus. So when you think about her, remember those traits of patience, faith and devotion." Jack's voice began to crack as he neared the end of his eulogy.

"But what I will remember most about my mother is her smile and her laugh. So remember those as well. I'm sure she's smiling down on us all from heaven right now, and always will be."

With his head bowed, Jack walked slowly back to his seat. There was probably not a dry eye in the church. Sarah grabbed his hand as he sat down in the pew next to her and Beth.

As Jack looked over at his mother's casket resting just a few feet away, his facial expression remained calm when he saw a figure dressed in a white, glimmering robe that extended all the way to the floor. The figure had flowing golden brown hair and a face so startling beautiful, with delicate, almost fairy-like features, he couldn't tell if it was a man or a woman. Most striking, were the two large wings made of what looked like huge white feathers from an immense swan spreading out of the creatures back.

So angels do exist, Jack thought to himself. No one else in the congregation except Jack was aware of the celestial being's presence. The angel rested its hands on the top of the coffin and turned toward Jack with an expression that seemed intended to convey both comfort and hope. Jack returned the gaze with his own expression of understanding and thanks, at which point the angel faded into a beam of light, and vanished.

Shortly thereafter, Jack, Sarah and the congregation followed the casket out of the church and stood silent as it was placed into the hearse to be taken for cremation, as his mother had wished. After receiving the obligatory but heartfelt condolences and expression of sorrow from those attending the funeral, Jack and Sarah made their way to their car. Beth was being taken under the wing of Sarah's parents to their own car. Sarah sat in the front seat with Jack, waiting for Jack to start the engine. Jack stared straight ahead, then leaned over to bury his head in Sarah's shoulder, and wept.

CHAPTER 23

For a several years after his mother's death, life for Jack was relatively typical of most young married couples with a child. Well, almost typical.

Sarah continued working at the elementary school teaching third grade. She loved her job and the children. Beth spent her time in pre-K, then kindergarten and elementary school much the same way other children did who had two working parents. Most of the time Sarah was able to drop Beth off at school, which was only two miles from her own school where she taught. Jack and Sarah had hired a nanny/housekeeper to work a few hours every weekday afternoon to be there when the bus dropped Beth off. Sarah could normally make it home by about 3:30, but often had meetings after class, or lessons or wall displays to prepare for the classroom. As much as Sarah felt a little guilty about not being a stay-at-home mom, the arrangement seemed to be working out well for Beth.

Jack sometimes had to work late at the Smithsonian, and it was usually during those times that he would continue to be visited by what he now began to refer to as his "benefactors." When they weren't working, Jack and Sarah spent as much time as possible together with Beth. It was only natural that, as most parents find, their focus had now shifted from their relationship as a couple, to their relationship and responsibilities as mom and dad. Beth was the new joy in their life, each part of themselves, and the creation of their love for one another.

The love and passion between Jack and Sarah was very much still there, and they were trying to have a baby sister or brother for Beth, but for whatever reason it didn't seem to be happening. While disappointed, they were very grateful and thankful for Beth, and would continue trying. And trying. As Jack would say to Sarah, "trying is half the fun!"

As for Beth, she continued to develop into an inquisitive, beautiful child, taking after her mother, except for her distinctive deep auburn colored hair. In fact, she was beginning to take the same interest in history, of a sort, much like her parents. Perhaps it was the stories usually Sarah, and sometimes Jack, would tell her of who was by far Beth's favorite fictional character.

Sarah would tell her the story of a make-believe man who, while otherwise completely normal just like Dad, had the extraordinary gift of being visited by, and being able to see and hear and talk to, people from the past who had gone on to the afterlife to be with Jesus in heaven. Sarah would describe these characters quite vividly—some famous, some not—and tell Beth of their interaction with this gifted man, whom Sarah called Mr. James Neach. Both Jack and Sarah wanted to share the knowledge of this gift with Beth, realizing some day in the distant future, they might actually decide to tell Beth that the character, James, was in actuality her father, Jack.

Meanwhile, despite the infrequent number of visits Jack had received since the time of the plane crash years earlier, he began to experience an increasing amount of activity at the Smithsonian itself after working there for a few years. Unlike many of his earlier visits, the people who appeared to him now seemed to be interesting but more common folk from all walks of life. But all, somehow connected to the Smithsonian experience. They would normally appear and stand before him in the early evening hours when the museums and exhibits had closed for the day. Jack would be in his private office, now with his name on the door with the title of Director of Finance underneath. It was at this time these figures from the past would suddenly turn up, rather nonchalantly, as if they were expected for an appointment they had previously booked with Jack.

To name just a few, there was the captain of a New Bedford Massachusetts whaling vessel from the 1800s, who would sit and talk with Jack about some of his adventures on the high seas, and the many fascinating foreign, some exotic, ports he had visited over his life. New Bedford could boast not only having the greatest number of vessels along the east coast of the United States in that period, but also having the most voyages of any whaling port.

The bearded captain, with his weather worn face and booming voice rising at times like the stormy sea itself, would talk of strange foreign customs and cultures he'd witnessed. He would bring to life the breathtaking land and seascapes he had seen, not to mention some of the very hazardous experiences he and his crew had faced. It was a dangerous occupation, and the men considered themselves fortunate to get home to their wives and children alive and in one piece after a long voyage.

There was the frontiersman who had accompanied Lewis and Clark on their arduous and incredible two-year adventure of discovery as they marched across the unchartered north continent following President Jefferson's purchase of the Louisiana territory from Napoleon and France in 1803. The purchase consisted of a vast 887,000 acres of land extending from the Mississippi River to the Rocky Mountains. [1]

In addition to exploration, their mission was to establish trade with the Native tribes living there and to reaffirm the sovereignty of the United States in the region. Second perhaps only to the events surrounding the American Revolution, the Louisiana Purchase, by nearly doubling the size of the United States overnight, would have the greatest impact on the development and destiny of the United States of any other single event.

Then there was the Indian chief of the small Choctaw tribe who told Jack about the Indian belief in the wellness of mind, body, spirit and natural environment, and how it is an expression of the proper balance and harmony in the relationship of all things. The chief also spoke to Jack about their struggles during the forced relocation by the United States government known as the Trail of Tears, where many died. How their people had simply been overcome by the loss of their home lands and seemingly endless expansion, and greed, of white settlers. Listening to the chief, Jack remembered his conversation with John Wilkes Booth years earlier and thought to himself that the United States' treatment of Native Americans was perhaps our nation's *second* original sin.

There was the visit by the Union infantryman who had been part of Colonel Joshua Chamberlain's 20th Maine

Regiment and their taking of Little Round Top at the Battle of Gettysburg.[2] Jack had read many stories about how certain seemingly small events, especially in war, can often change the course of history. The Union soldier recounted the story of Little Round Top to Jack, where if his unit had been just a few minutes later in reaching and defending the top of that hill, it would have been controlled by the Confederates.   If that had happened, the Confederates would then have had a commanding position to reign terror down on the Union forces. But by his squad taking the hill first and maintaining it—through a combination of luck and courage, including a dramatic downhill bayonet charge with the men virtually out of ammunition—the Union forces were able to turn back General Lee's Confederate forces at Gettysburg, and essentially turn the tide of the Civil War in favor of the Union.

Occasionally, Jack's visitors would appear to him in his home in Reston. He would discreetly guide them into his study, where he could close and lock the door. Sarah was well aware of what was happening in each instance, and Beth would occasionally overhear her father talking in his study—seemingly to himself. Beth wouldn't question her mother's response when Sarah convincingly explained to her that Dad was simply rehearsing a presentation he would have to make at work in a couple days.

On one such occasion, in another case of "historic chance" as Jack liked to refer to it, a WWII pilot appeared to him. The pilot had been on a reconnaissance mission in the Pacific, when he decided to ignore his dwindling fuel supply and travel a little further than he had been instructed. It was this fateful decision that enabled him to spot a huge armada of Japanese aircraft carriers, destroyers and support ships where no one in U.S. Navy Intelligence had expected them. It allowed the Americans to quickly revise their plans, redirect their forces, and win a decisive victory over Japan at the Battle of Midway—a battle that would change the course of the war in the Pacific and ultimately end in the Allied Victory over the Japanese Empire.[3]

Perhaps the most jarring appearance was one evening at the Smithsonian when a black slave from the pre-Civil War period came to see Jack. He said his name was Moses, but unlike the ancient Biblical leader, this Moses would not experience deliverance until close to his death. He told Jack his story, how his wife and young son had been sold by his owner on the Georgia Plantation he worked to another plantation owner less than 50 miles from his cotton farm. But it might as well have been five thousand miles away. Moses had escaped on one occasion to try to reunite with his family. Tragically, he was captured before he could reach them.

Moses then showed Jack the deep abrasions on his wrists and feet, where he had been shackled with heavy chains. He turned his back to Jack and lowered his shirt to his waist, revealing the deep scars from the violent whipping he had received as punishment, nearly having been beaten to death. While the plantation foreman would remove Moses' shackles from his hands so he could continue to work during the day, Moses would not be free of those shackles on his feet until Emancipation near the end of the Civil War. He was ultimately reunited with his wife and son, some twenty years after they had been separated, only to die a couple years later from his injuries and abuse. Heroically, he had never given up hope.

It was not just men who had appeared to Jack at the Smithsonian and his house these several years, but women as well. Nurses who had braved the ferocity and danger of war to care for the injured, and the dying. Women who had sacrificed much to create orphanages, food missions, shelters for the homeless. Mothers who had emigrated from parts of Western and Eastern Europe and worked long hours in deplorable conditions in garment factories to help feed their families. All of their actions seemed to be done out of a sense of duty, devotion and unselfishness.

At first Jack thought there was a noteworthy difference between these latest visitors and those he had been privileged to talk with prior and up to the plane crash on the Potomac. The earlier visitors seemed to have a common focus in giving Jack direction on things he would face in life. To encourage him to develop and forge in himself some of the ingredients he would need to arouse and rely on to be able to do the right thing when the time came—whether it was courage, unselfishness, or love.

Yet the more he thought about these less heralded men and women, the more he realized that they possessed many of the same dynamic attributes instilled in the more famous historical characters that had appeared to him. They all had shown, at some point in their lives, the fundamental qualities of courage, or perseverance, or unselfishness for others.

Naturally, Sarah was privy to all that was happening to Jack, even though she couldn't see or hear it. Sarah could immediately tell when Jack came home from work if he had had another "incident," just by the tone of his voice and expression on his face when he greeted her. Similarly, she could readily tell when Jack was going into his study for another "consultation," as she called it.

When both Sarah and Jack would tell Beth the stories about the fictional Mr. Neach after dinner or before bedtime, they would try not only to pique her interest in the historical lessons of significance, but of the noble traits of the people they spoke about. (They would be careful to leave out some of the more graphic details of some stories to be age-appropriate for Beth).

As Beth advanced in age and understanding, Jack and Sarah would explain to her that these were not just stories about Americans, but about various peoples and cultures. How different cultures at any point in history were formed in large part by the events and perceptions of the day, by information or the lack of it given the time and circumstances. How it all had a role in directing peoples' thoughts, decisions and actions. But that the very human qualities of courage, unselfishness, perseverance, love…these were not captive of any one particular time or culture, but were all part of the human experience.

At the same time, Jack and Sarah tried to convey to Beth that both American and world history has always been replete with both contradiction and unanimity. On the one hand, inequity, injustice, greed, tragedy, hardship, cowardice, ignorance, ambition, atrocity, indecision, hate, misguided individuals (and even whole populations). While on the other hand, acts of charity, sacrifice, triumph, heroism, firm resolve, great intellectual leaps, joy, prosperity, peace, and love. All part of the human condition and of mankind's journey. Perhaps these contradictions and commonalities were the threads that were interwoven to create the endless tapestry that we call Human History.

They told Beth with frankness and honesty that there were both forces of good and forces of evil in the world. As people of faith, and followers of Jesus Christ and his teachings, it was their role to do good where and when they could, to use their gifts to serve others.

Beth seemed to have a genuine interest and affinity for learning and trying to understand the history and moral lessons her parents provided her. Jack and Sarah hoped to supplement Beth's knowledge from their stories by planning family outings and trips together that could be both fun and informative. As Jack's daughter, Beth pretty much had free reign of the Smithsonian and the three could spend many hours there, more so as tourists, though some of Jack's coworkers wondered if he spent too much time there.

As Beth was now in middle school, the three had ventured to taking trips to places like Gettysburg, viewing the exhibits at the Visitors Center, and taking the self-drive car tour with the audio tape in hand. They stopped at each of the sixteen stations that highlighted some particular aspect of the battle and what had transpired. They looked out over the vast meadows and woodlands of nearly four thousand acres that stood today much as it did those tragic but momentous days in July of 1863. It had been the most crucial but deadly battle of the war, where some 50,000 men were killed, wounded or went missing over three bloody days. Beth was so fascinated by it all that a well-known book about the conflict, *Killer Angels* by Michael Shaara, soon became one of her favorite reads.

They toured Philadelphia to see such historic sites as the Liberty Bell, Independence Hall, the Museum of the American Revolution, Benjamin Franklin's gravesite, and Elfreth's Alley, America's oldest continuously inhabited residential street.

The three spent a few days in Boston walking the two-and-one-half mile Freedom Trail with its sixteen sites of historical significance. Of course, as loving and good-natured parents, Sarah and Jack fully recognized the need and desire to do other interesting kid things as well, like visiting the Franklin Park Zoo, going to a Red Sox game, and dining at the Faneuil Hall Marketplace.

Beth seemed to love her visits to the living-history museum of Colonial Williamsburg, where actors portrayed real life characters of the 18ᵗʰ century among the historic shops, homes gardens and streets spread over 173 acres.[1]

Once again, Beth was just a kid, and Sarah and Jack surely didn't want their family trips together to be solely educational. They were fun-loving and young themselves, and wanted Beth to enjoy the fun times of just being a kid. With that in mind, half their time at Williamsburg was spent at the nearby Busch Gardens amusement park. Beth (not to mention Jack), had a blast riding on the park's many roller coasters of escalating speed and fear, topped off by the many laughs they enjoyed at Virginia's largest water park.

Jack and Sarah knew they would have been remiss if they hadn't taken Beth to Disney World a couple times, once with Sarah's parents in tow. The rides and food were non-stop, but they also spent a considerable amount of time in Epcot's World Showcase. The American Adventure, with its audio-animatronics stage show of American history, was one of their highlights. They also thoroughly enjoyed touring the other country pavilions, including Germany, France, Italy, Canada and others. Eleven pavilions in all, each capturing a brief glimpse into the history and culture of different countries, but whose citizens shared a similar national pride as did the Americans.

Beth was proving to be not only an excellent young historian, but also beginning to exhibit the common-sense attributes of her mother, along with the affable personality traits of her father. She was also turning into a good athlete, having been one of the stars on the elementary school's basketball team. Beth was tall and quick, and had her eyes set on joining the lacrosse team when she got to high school the following year. Not to be outdone on the academic front, it was no surprise to her parents when she won the history medal award upon her eighth-grade graduation.

Beth had become a happy, well-adjusted girl. Nevertheless, what she was perhaps too young to realize or yet experience in her own life: history is crammed with examples of how a single event can change not only the course of history, but of the lives and happiness of those impacted. Where life's contentment and peace of mind can turn on a dime. The happy family was about to experience such an event.

CHAPTER 24

B eth had recently entered her first year at Langley High School in Mclean, Virginia. Jack and Sarah considered themselves fortunate that they lived in a small area of Reston where the school district lines permitted Beth to attend Langley, which was considered one of the higher-ranked public high schools in Virginia. Beth had been attending Langley for about three months now, and she seemed to be thoroughly enjoying her classmates, teachers and experience there.

With things seemingly going well, Jack was a little surprised one evening after he heard Sarah talking to Beth about how she was doing at Langley, if there were any issues or problems. Sarah seemed a little depressed later that evening when she came to bed.

"What's wrong, honey? You seem a little down," Jack asked.

"Oh, nothing" Sarah replied, not convincingly enough for Jack.

"I know you better than that, love. What's the matter?"

"Oh, I guess I'm just feeling sorry for Beth, or partially for myself. I had so hoped we would have given her a sister or brother long before now. But it just hasn't happened. And I'm getting to the age now where the odds are against it."

"I know, Sarah, of course we all want that. But if it doesn't happen, don't you think we're incredibly lucky to have Beth, and each other? She's always brought us nothing but joy."

"I know. Just the same…"

"Listen," Jack said. "Let me tell you something that happened to me last week. I was feeling a little stressed out and depressed about something at work. So, I took a long walk at lunchtime. As I was walking along Independence Avenue, deep in my own thoughts and feeling sorry for myself, I heard a strange sound coming up from behind me. It sounded almost like two or three teenagers riding their skateboards on the fairly busy sidewalk. I turned around with the intent of giving them a dirty look or maybe saying something.

"Instead, I saw a young man with a somewhat straggly beard, probably in his late twenties or so, wearing what looked like an unbuttoned military shirt over a T-shirt. He was on a board that looked like the bottom of a milk crate, on which he had mounted sets of metal wheels at each of the four corners. He was squatted down on his thighs on the board, wearing leather gloves, and pushing himself along the sidewalk using his hands. You see, both of his legs had been amputated just above the knee. That was the way he got around.

"I stepped aside to let him pass. He never made eye contact with me. He wasn't stopping to ask people for money. He seemed to have some destination in mind. Where I don't know.

"My heart went out to him, I felt so bad and helpless. Here I was a second ago feeling sorry for myself about some minor irritation at work, and here was this young man, destined to go through life burdened by his tragic handicap. I felt sorrow, then guilt, then shame. Who knows why God allows so many people to suffer in life. It probably has nothing to do with God at all. It just is, for whatever mysterious reasons we can't possibly fathom.

"We've been very fortunate, Sarah. I couldn't be happier having both you and Beth in my life. We should be thankful and appreciative for what we have. If we somehow are able to have another child, great. If not, we have to accept it and not feel sorry for ourselves, or feel like we've been cheated somehow. By most standards, we're the lucky ones."

After a brief pause, Sarah looked at Jack with a contemplative expression on her face. "I know. You're right, Jack. I should be thankful. So many terrible things happen to other people. Something could happen to us. I'm thankful for what we have, here and now. Hopefully, it's forever."

"I love you, Sarah." Jack grinned. "And if you want to keep trying for that second child, I'm your man!"

Sarah smiled back at Jack. "I love you too, Jack. Let's go for it." Sarah reached over to turn out the light, as they kissed, and Jack took her in his arms.

***

The next morning as he kissed Sarah goodbye, Jack asked if she was feeling any better from last night.

"Yes, Jack. As always, you were very convincing," she said as she gave him a knowing wink.

"Glad I could be of service," he said while hurrying out the front door. "Love you. See you tonight."

A few hours later, shortly before lunch, Dave, one of Jack's coworkers, abruptly walked into Jack's office. Dave and his wife Trish lived in the town adjacent to Reston and had been out with Jack and Sarah on more than one occasion. Looking a little concerned but trying not to act the part, Dave said, "I don't want to alarm you Jack, I'm sure everyone's okay, but I just got a call from Trish. Apparently there's been some kind of incident, a bombing, a shooting, or something, at the school where Sarah works."

Jack froze in his chair and, looking very concerned, said, "*Really?* That's sounds scary. I'd better call Sarah on her cell."

Dave left the office while Jack immediately tried calling Sarah, but after several rings, it went to her voice mail. He thought to himself, if there had been an incident, Sarah was probably very busy with her students and their parents. He placed a call to the Reston Police Department to see what was going on.

Jack got hold of a desk sergeant, who told Jack, yes, there had been a shooting incident at Sunrise Valley and the school was under lockdown. There was nothing more he could tell him at this time.

Starting to feel more anxious, a strained look began to creep over Jack's face. He grabbed his jacket and told Dave, "Tell anyone looking for me I had to leave to drive to Sarah's school to see what's going on and make sure she's okay. Thanks Dave."

It took Jack nearly an hour to get his car out of the garage and make the drive to Reston with traffic at that time of day. As he approached the school, his heart began to race as he gasped at the large number of police and other emergency vehicles outside the school. Jack parked on the side of the road a couple hundred feet away, then walked toward the school building. There was a long line of yellow police tape extending across the entire front entrance to the school, and police were not permitting any civilians to go inside.

One of Sarah's teacher friends that Jack knew, Christine, saw Jack approaching and immediately walked up to Jack. From her red eyes and smeared mascara, she obviously had been crying and was visibly shaken. "Oh Jack, this is so horrible. How could this happen?"

With obvious worry and strain in his voice, Jack said, "What exactly happened Christine? What's going on?"

"I'm sorry, Jack. I assumed you'd heard. Some crazed gunman with a rifle entered the school a couple hours ago, and started shooting in the halls and classrooms. Several people were apparently shot before the custodian, who had access to a gun, confronted the shooter and killed him before the police could arrive. It took only a couple of minutes to be over."

Many of the students were huddled around their teachers and parents in the parking lot, with some parents not having arrived yet. Some students had apparently already been picked up by their parents and taken home.

Jack asked Christine in a subdued voice, "Christine, do you know where Sarah is? I don't see her."

"Sorry, I don't know, Jack. I haven't seen her since the shooting started. Maybe she's still inside the building. You had better ask one of the police officers. I'm sorry."

Jack walked up to one of the police officers standing guard at the yellow tape restricting access and said, "Sir, my name is Jack Moran. My wife, Sarah, is a teacher here, and I don't see her anywhere. Do you have any information? I mean, are some people still being interviewed inside by detectives or something?"

The Reston police officer told Jack to wait there a minute. "I'll see what I can find out from one of the detectives, Sir."

The officer walked about fifty feet toward the entrance and approached what Jack assumed was a detective in plain clothes. He noticed how the man looked over toward Jack as the police officer pointed to him. Jack didn't understand, or like, the expression on his face.

The detective walked over to Jack and said, "Mr. Moran, would you mind coming with me." Jack said nothing and followed him as they walked into the front entrance of the building. As he walked, Jack felt like a haze was descending over him, as if he were in some kind of fog, not knowing what to think.

The detective motioned to Jack to go into the empty administrative office off the main lobby. After they entered the office, the detective shut the door behind them. Jack was beginning to feel sick and extremely anxious, but still said nothing.

"Mr. Moran," the detective started, "My name is Detective Keller. Before the shooter was killed, we estimate he got off some fifteen rounds. Several adults and children were wounded, some seriously, and unfortunately, two teachers and three children were killed. They probably died instantly." Detective Keller paused. "I'm so sorry to have to tell you this, Mr. Moran, but your wife was one of those killed by the gunman."

Jack still said nothing, but immediately felt himself start to tremble. He sank into a chair directly behind where he was standing and lowered his head into his hands.

"I know it's of little or no consolation, Mr. Moran, but we believe your wife was probably shot as she herded her students into a closet, using her body as a shield to separate the shooter from the children. She died saving those children."

Jack leaned forward in the chair with his head in his hands and began to sob. "Oh my God," Jack said out loud. "I can't believe this is happening. My wife Sarah is dead? Why? I don't understand how something like this could happen to her."

Detective Keller put his hand on Jack's shoulder. "I'm so sorry, Mr. Moran. None of these people deserved this. But I need to ask you if you can accompany me down the hall to your wife's classroom so you can identify the body. Whenever you're ready."

Detective Keller moved to the door, opened it, and stepped into the corridor to leave Jack alone for a minute. After a few moments, Jack stood up and walked over to the detective, who could see the deep pain etched in Jack's face.

As Jack walked alongside Detective Keller, he passed a few classrooms. In one, he could see a young woman, huddled over the covered body of what was obviously a child, crying hysterically. Detective Keller motioned Jack to go into the classroom that Jack knew to be Sarah's. Over by the closet, he saw a body covered by a large blanket, with bloodstains on the floor beside it. Forensics had apparently already completed its work for any evidence just prior to Jack's arrival at the scene.

Both men knelt down next to the body, as Detective Keller lifted the blanket so Jack could view. To Jack, Sarah's face looked as beautiful and peaceful as the day he met her. There wasn't a mark on her head or face, except for a bruise on the side of her head where she had apparently hit the floor after being shot.

Jack uttered in an anguished voice, "Oh Sarah. Please. No." He put his arms beneath her shoulders and lifted her into his chest, holding her tightly. He could feel the partially dried blood on her back where the bullet had entered, passing close to her heart. Every bit of him seemed to ache, but mostly he felt like his heart had been torn in two.

Jack thought, why would God allow something like this to happen? We were so happy together. Why didn't his "benefactors" warn him, or prevent this tragedy somehow. Like the people that appeared who help to lift the car off Bob. Or all those men from the *Arizona* that appeared to help him the night of the plane crash?

But anger wouldn't do any good right now. That would come later. All he could feel was his pain and agony for the loss of his beloved Sarah.

He whispered to her as he held her, "I love you, Sarah, with all my heart. I'll never stop loving you. Please don't leave me. And Beth." He paused a moment. "Oh God! How do I tell Beth?"

He looked into her face again, her eyes shut. Never to look into those beautiful bright blue eyes again. Then he bent his head down as he embraced her, and kissed her softly on the lips. The tears streamed down his face, falling lightly onto hers, as if the tears now running down her face were her own.

CHAPTER 25

It had been three weeks since Sarah's death. Jack was at home, having taken a leave of absence from work. Beth had just returned to school the day before, but not the same person she was. Her demeanor now was certainly more subdued than her usual joyful self. She moved a little slower than in her usual energetic manner, as if a weight had been placed upon her shoulders. Even her blue eyes seemed less bright. It would be several months before the old Beth began to emerge again, encouraged by the love, guidance and resolve of friends and family who loved her.

Even if he lived to be one hundred, Jack would never forget the look of anguish on Beth's face when he told her that day she got home from school about what had happened. After weeping in her father's arms for what seemed an eternity—as if time had stopped—Beth had secluded herself in her room for the remainder of the day and the entire next day, to cry and grieve in solitude. At Jack's fatherly urging, she had emerged from her small cocoon a couple of times to sit at the kitchen table with Jack to eat some of the food that friends and neighbors had kindly dropped off. But for the most part, they ate in painful silence.

The funeral for Sarah had been heartbreaking, almost too much for Jack and Beth to bear. Many people had come, and many of them had cried quietly like Jack and Beth had. Bob and many of Jack's extended family had come, as had virtually all of Sarah's immediate and extended family. Sarah's parents were devastated to lose their cherished daughter. Their pain was the unique pain that only a parent who sees their child die before them could ever fathom, with swirling images in their minds of a laughing child growing up into a caring, loving mature woman and mother herself—taken so tragically and unexpectedly.

Many, many friends of Jack and Sarah came, including the parents and all the children in her homeroom class. None of Sarah's students had been seriously injured, at least not physically, in part due to Sarah's sacrifice and bravery. Many of the children were receiving special counseling. Sunrise Elementary School was still closed, and the town of Reston was in mourning for the loss of Sarah, another teacher and the three young children.

Many people told Jack that Sarah died a hero. He understood the unselfishness of her act. That was just part of Sarah's strength, and love for her students. But it did nothing to ease the pain of his loss.

No one could comprehend the senseless and cowardly act of the young, unemployed college dropout, who had a history of emotional and mental illness. People even pitied the parents of the disturbed young man, who had broken into his father's closet to gain access to the rifle he used in the heinous act.

After a few months of grieving, Beth seemed to be adjusting as best as she could under the circumstances. Life continued, as it must. Despite her pain and the memories of her mother, Beth was strong—like her mother—as Jack well knew. Slowly she progressed and began to flourish once again, in school, sports activities, and among her friends. What is more, she had recently met a guy at school she liked.

Beth would often sit with her father in the living room or on the back porch as they browsed through old photos of Beth growing up, of their historic tours like Gettysburg and Williamsburg, and their fun-filled times at Disney World and Busch Gardens. Beth tried her best to be positive for her father's sake, laughing as they recalled some of their favorite times together as a family.

"Look, Dad. There's the photo Mom took of you and I getting on that awesome but terrifying roller coaster at Busch Gardens. We could never convince mom to get on any of them, not with her fear of heights."

"True, except that one time I got her to go with me on Space Mountain in Disney World, convincing her it wouldn't be bad since it was an 'indoor' roller coaster. And then, the entire ride she kept her head down, never looked up, and half the contents from her purse emptied out into the bottom of the car we sat in. 'Never again!' she exclaimed. But we made it up to her when we had dinner at the Italy Pavilion in Epcot, waving those red napkins over our heads and singing along with the waiters and the rest of the diners, everyone smiling and laughing."

Jack would smile and laugh along with Beth reminiscing together, but she could see the pain of loss in his eyes. Jack thought he was doing a good job of covering up, and he loved spending time with Beth. He remembered how kind and understanding his own mother had been to him after Tom's death. He put on a brave front for Beth, to try to give her the happier home life that she deserved.

But Beth was a keen observer of people—much like her parents—and with the unbreakable connection of a daughter to a beloved father, Beth could see Jack was missing a big part of himself, in the form of Sarah. Jack thought he was being a good actor, for Beth's sake. Still, deep inside, Jack was feeling despair.

Despite many invitations, Jack seldom went out with friends on his free weekends, often using the excuse that he needed to drive Beth somewhere, or be home in case she called when she was out. He would call Bob to make sure everything was okay with him, and he was taking care of himself. Jack preferred to be alone, watching some favorite old movies of his and Sarah's or pouring over old photographs when they were dating, their honeymoon in Bermuda, and others from after Beth was born.

On one occasion Jack drove to the National Arboretum, wandering around the lush landscape, lost in thoughts of Sarah. Remembering his time there with Sarah, and of Tom's very special visit to the both of them. He stood in the gazebo, gazing over the flowing waters of the Anacostia River. He remembered a story he read once where the author imagined time was like a flowing river. The author postulated what if you were in a small boat travelling down the river through time. What would stop you from maneuvering the boat to shore, getting out, and walking back along the shore of the river—back through time?

If only he could do that. Go back in time and somehow stop the senseless death of Sarah. Alternatively, if only Tom could have warned him of that tragedy to come many years into the future, so that Jack could somehow prevent it. Yet perhaps Tom didn't know, nor did any of his so-called benefactors. Only God knew—and He didn't warn Jack—or protect his Sarah.

One evening he agreed to meet his old friend John Carrol, at John's insistence. Several years after graduating Georgetown, John had finally met "his Sarah", a physical therapist named Annette whom he met at a rehab center after breaking his leg skiing. He had been happily married for over ten years, and was the proud father of two young boys. John had also stayed in the D.C. area, working for a publishing house downtown.

They met on a Thursday after work at an upscale pub just outside D.C. John tried to cheer Jack up with some favorite old stories of their days at Georgetown, talk about how the Hoyas basketball team was doing, and life with two hyperactive boys. He thought he had done a good job until, walking to their cars, Jack said, "I'm so happy you found the love of your life in Annette, John. Keep her and the boys close, and remember, the time you have together is precious. Treasure it."

Listening to Jack, John was reminded of something Jack had said earlier in the evening. How he wished he could have had one last moment with Sarah before she died, just to remind her how deeply he loved her. How close he would keep her in his heart until they were together again. For all eternity.

They hugged, said their goodbyes to one another, and said they'd get together again soon. Still, as Jack walked away, John could sense the slower gait in Jack's walk and a small hunch in his shoulders.

Jack felt life for him would always continue to be a struggle, one without real hope or passion. He tried to put on a front for most people, but those closest to him could see his inner sadness. People knew him too well for that, and how much he loved and missed his Sarah. At times,

Jack felt like he was in an amusement park House of Mirrors, but instead of seeing all sorts of distorted views of his reflected image, it was his emotions that took on varied forms—anger, rage, anguish, loneliness, grief, pain, disillusionment, emptiness.

In those months, Jack didn't stray too far from the house except occasionally or when necessary. He finally went back to work after about two months. Jack was good at his job and well liked at work, so there was no question that the job would be waiting for him when he was ready to return. He also continued to do all that he could to be a dedicated father to Beth, whether that meant talking to her about school, preparing dinner, picking her up at a friend's house or dropping her and her friends off at the movies. He continued to go to all of her lacrosse games that didn't interfere with work so he could cheer her on.

When he was home alone, Jack would often listen to beautiful, romantic, sometimes solemn music. Listening to a favorite piece of music that reminded him of Sarah, like English composer *Vaughan Williams Symphony No. 5*, especially the third movement titled *Romanza*, he would occasionally begin to cry silently to himself. The movement was perhaps the most beautiful twelve minutes of music he'd ever heard. He would always picture Sarah listening to it sitting next to him. The pain of losing her seemed as vivid to him now as the day she died.

For exercise and to get some fresh air, he would frequently take long walks, or drive to the nearby park for a short hike. One day at work, he left his office at lunchtime to take a walk, alone. Instead of clearing his head, his thoughts seemed one dimensional and continued to weigh down on him. *How could God allow this to happen to my Sarah? I would have preferred it to be me who was taken. Why does he allow such pain and suffering in the world if*

He loves us so much? Don't I have a right to be angry with God? After all, it was my "trust" in Him that helped to save the lives of all those plane passengers' years ago.

As these thoughts raced through his mind, he looked around to discover he had walked around so aimlessly he was in a part of D.C. he was generally unfamiliar with. As he came to a street corner, he noticed a small, but interesting old church across the way that looked to be about a hundred years old.

Jack crossed the street to enter the small church with the intent of saying a short prayer, since he had hardly been to church since Sarah's funeral. Maybe, he thought, it would be a good place for me to say a prayer to Sarah, as he often did by himself, in the silence of his own bedroom.

The inscription carved into the stone header above the two large front wooden doors read, Holy Rosary Church. A small plaque in the foundation wall read Founded 1913. He entered the foyer, dipped a couple fingers into the holy water font, and blessed himself. He walked into the somewhat dimly lit nave of the church and saw that it was completely empty of people. Not unusual, he thought, since it was after lunchtime now, and he had left the business downtown area blocks ago and was now in a more residential neighborhood.

He turned to the left to walk down one of the side aisles, stopping about two-thirds of the way down to sit in a pew made of well-worn dark mahogany. He didn't kneel, but sat there looking toward the crucifix above the altar, and the statues on each side of the altar. One was the Virgin Mary, and the other was Jesus, sitting on a small boulder talking to a handful of children.

He thought about Sarah, how he missed her terribly, and of how and why God could tolerate such pain and suffering in those He created in His own image. He thought about Beth, and how much he needed to be there for her. But part of him sometimes wished, selfishly he knew, that some terrible accident would befall him and he could be with Sarah, perhaps as each other's stardust would somehow float and merge in the expanding universe, forever connected.

Suddenly, out of the corner of his eye, he saw a white light go on just above the door to the confessional booth located off to the left side just a few pews ahead of him. He hadn't really noticed the confessional booth until now. Curiously, a small sign just beside it read in block letters: "CONFESSIONS — TUESDAY AND FRIDAY — 3 to 6 PM."

Jack looked at his watch, a little confused. Not only was it only 1:30 in the afternoon, but today was Thursday. Moreover, there was nobody else in the church at the moment. *I know that light wasn't on when I first sat down in this pew,* he thought.

In most Catholic churches, when confessions were being heard, a red light signaled that someone was in the confessional booth, speaking with the priest or confessor. When the confessional booth was empty and the confessor was available for the next penitent, a white light would illuminate.

Having had the experience of many profound, supernatural incidents in the past, Jack sensed that the light going on above the confessional booth at unscheduled hours in an otherwise empty church, might be a potential precursor to some new counsel being directed toward him.

He stepped out of the pew, opened the door to the confessional booth, and bent down to position himself on the kneeler, closing the door behind him. He could see through the screen grille over the small opening that separated him from the other side of the confessional booth that the adjoining side was dimly lit, and he sensed the silhouette of another person. Jack began to speak the traditional beginning prayer of any confession. "Bless me father, for I have sinned. It has been..." Jack paused, "several years since my last confession."

A calm voice spoke from the other side of the grille. "It's been a long time. What draws you to the confessional today?"

Jack hesitated before responding: "I had something terrible happen in my life recently, and I'm feeling despair. Despair in my life, and doubt about my faith."

The confessor responded, "I know Jack. It's a terrible thing to lose so close a loved one, especially at such a young age. It can test the faith of any man or woman."

At first, Jack was startled by the response. But he had learned not to fear such situations. "How do you know me? And why did this happen? *And who are you?*"

The figure slid the grille to one side to reveal himself to Jack. He was a man of about fifty, wearing a black skullcap and what appeared to be the black robe of a friar. Jack noticed a slight Italian accent.

"Hello, Jack. I didn't mean to startle you." He smiled. "I figured you're a little used to these visitations by now." He continued, saying, "My name is Thomas Aquinas. I'm called a *Doctor of the Church*, but I prefer to think of myself as a simple Dominican friar."

Jack's head and shoulders straightened up as he exclaimed, "*St. Thomas?* Why, we studied some of your writings and theories in my Georgetown Religion class. You're considered to be one of the greatest philosophers and theologians of the Catholic Church. Ever!"

"Thank you, Jack. You flatter me. But you know, all the accolades do nothing for me if I cannot help people like you who are experiencing such pain and doubt…justifiably so. I only hope my words can provide you some comfort."

Jack responded anxiously, perhaps with a touch of bitterness in his tone, almost pleading for an answer. "Well, then we might as well get right to it. I don't understand how a truly loving God can allow such pain, suffering, and senseless death to occur." His voice raised slightly, he asked, "*Why?*"

"I didn't say I can provide concrete answers, or understanding, Jack. Only some comfort, I hope. God is mystery. How can we begin to comprehend Him? Even now, connected with him in the expansive Universe, with all my studies, learning, and meditative thought, I can't begin to comprehend Him. To think I, or anyone, can understand God is not only absurd and unobtainable. To me, it is akin to blasphemy.

"But let me tell you what I *do* think. Some will argue that a God that allows such suffering is a distant, unloving God, detached from those he created. Yet, didn't God so love us that he gave us His only Son to redeem the world through His own agony and death, and show us the light of eternal life through His Resurrection? The suffering of Jesus, as part of the Trinity, is in fact the suffering of God. Jesus suffered not only as human, but also as God Himself. Jesus was not a stranger to our human struggle, but rather, as I wrote centuries ago, 'Jesus was a participant of *our* affliction.' Jesus died a very human death on the cross, for us.[1]

"You see Jack, I believe our own suffering is the suffering of God as well. Jesus Himself said:

I was hungry and you gave me food,
I was thirsty and you gave me drink.
I was a stranger and you invited me in,

I needed clothes and you clothed me,
I was sick and you looked after me
I was in prison and you came to visit me.
Whatever you did for one of the least of these brothers
and sister of mine,
You did for me. [2]

"And by being united with Christ, we are also united with Him in his triumph over sin, suffering and death. With this gift, no one should feel worthless, or hopeless, or given to despair. Christ has shown us the path to definitive and ultimate victory over pain and death. Furthermore, what we experience in this world draws Him closer to us.

"Don't you recall the thoughtful eulogy you gave at your mother's funeral service? In it, you talked about the story of the man walking along the path, and the one set of footprints during the difficult, perhaps painful times of his life. That was where Jesus had carried him. Christ truly makes our suffering His own."

Thomas paused momentarily to gaze at Jack, to try to discern if he was getting through to him. Thomas could feel the intense struggle going on within Jack's heart, his mind—his very soul. Seemingly torn between his pain and anger over Sarah's loss, against his basic beliefs in God, how He had shown Himself to Jack in mysterious ways, and his certainty in the promise of an afterlife, having been the recipient of so many visits from beyond our earthly existence.

Knowing the conflict that was engulfing Jack, Thomas thought it best to continue. "And Jack," he continued, "God doesn't *cause* suffering. Most suffering is the result of the exercise of man's free will, whether it be the pain from war, violent crime inflicted upon innocent people, or inhumane treatments of whole populations. Also, pain caused in our relationships to others—the feelings of anger, loss, the inability to forgive—they are all choices we make. God gave man free choice, but he also gave him tremendous potential to learn, to grow, to evolve—not just physically and intellectually, but also emotionally, and spiritually.

"In fact, I have a theory about Christ's second coming, and when that will be, if you'd like to hear it."

Jack had been kneeling quietly all this time, mesmerized by the words of this pious, humble man of God. However, unaware that Thomas could easily see through the shroud that Jack thought he had surrounded himself with, his intense struggle. "Of course I would. Please go on!" Jack respectfully replied, trying to appear calm. Perhaps to his own surprise, the words of Thomas were beginning to take hold of Jack. His heart began to open once more to the mysteries, power and love of Christ. The burden that he had been carrying around all this time since Sarah's death, while it would always be a part of him, his past feelings of hope, faith, and trust, were slowly being resurrected.

He knew he would see his Sarah again one day. Yet for now, he had time to be with his daughter Beth. Rather than feeling angry and sorry for himself, perhaps he should feel blessed that God had granted him the wondrous gift of two very special people to be an essential, intrinsic part of his life.

Thomas gave an empathetic smile and continued. "Very well, Jack. To be clear, not that God has confided anything to me, you know. That certainly would be beyond presumptuous on my part, don't you think?"

Jack politely nodded in agreement.

"I do too, Jack. Nevertheless, I think, given man's great capacity that God instilled in him, I believe he has the power and ability within himself to eliminate the moral evil from the world that causes so much pain and suffering. If *all* men and women treated each other with love, understanding and respect—and I don't mean just Christians, but all Jews, Muslims, Buddhists, Hindus—all religions and peoples—would we not have the ability to end all war, all crime? To end all poverty in a world filled with both abundant natural resources and man's unceasing industrious nature and intellectual prowess—to produce, to build, to grow, to invent, to find solutions to problems. That would enable man to feed, clothe, and administer to the health and well-being of all God's children.

"It might take tens of thousands, even millions of years, but if and when he reaches that staggering zenith of humanity, God will see how His creatures were able to honor and love each other, and in doing so, honor and love Him. That, Jack, would be the culmination of God's original act of creation that would allow for—be crowned with—the second coming of Christ. Or—" Thomas grinned slightly—"in your present day language...end game!"

Forgetting that Thomas could sense his thoughts, Jack smiled and thought to himself, *You know, this guy is not only an intellectual and spiritual giant, he's actually pretty cool!*

Thomas smiled again. "Why, thank you, Jack. You flatter me again. Before I go on too long, let me finish up here.

"Finally, you might ask, what of *other* pain and suffering not directly the result of moral evil, like illness and disease, physical deformities, premature death. For the sufferer, can it not bring him or her closer to the Jesus who suffered for and suffers with us? For those who would act to relieve and comfort the sufferer, is that not what Jesus instructed us to do? For in doing it for them, are we not

John Kenyon

doing it for Jesus? Doesn't that bring us closer to Him, and to eternal life? As hard as it may be for us to accept or understand, that, I believe, is the redemptive part of human suffering.

Jack's eyes began to fill with water, as he began to feel remorse for his doubts, for his loss of trust in God. At the same time, he began to feel a tremendous burden being lifted from his shoulders, much like the story of Christ carrying the man across the rocky paths in life.

Thomas felt his words were truly having an impact on Jack, and he continued. "But understand, Jack, these are just my thoughts, my opinions. Ultimately, God is mystery, and as much as we try to rationalize Him, He is beyond human comprehension. In the end, He simply wants us to give our love to Him—unequivocally and unquestioningly. That is why Jesus said, when asked what is the greatest commandment? 'Love the Lord your God with all your heart and with all your soul and with all your mind.' [3] Just as Jesus said in the Garden of Gethsemane: 'Father, not my will, but yours be done.' [4] You see, Jack, our understanding is finite, whereas God is infinite. You cannot fit the infinite into the finite. That Jack, is what we call *faith*. Faith, as demonstrated by the centurion who implored Jesus to help him, with perhaps the greatest words of faith ever expressed by man, when he said, 'Lord, I am not worthy to have You come under my roof, but only say the word, and my servant will be healed.' [5]

"I know I've been going on for a long time, but I hope you find some comfort in what I've said to you, Jack. That it gives you the strength to appreciate what you have, and that you are not alone. Of course, it's only natural that you continue to grieve for the loss of Sarah, but I hope that you will have the courage, and the faith, to endeavor on with your life—and Beth's. To take advantage of the gift of life that God has given you. Knowing that someday you will be united with Sarah again."

Jack looked on with a deep respect for this pious, well-spoken friar and priest. "Thank you for your words Father Thomas. And your spiritual counsel. I can see in your words how I can be closer to Christ, and to Sarah, by taking action for those who suffer or are in need in the here and now. Perhaps having experienced tragedy myself, I can have a greater sense of oneness with others who have experienced tragedy. How I can learn to appreciate what God has given me in this life.

"But I have to ask you: Do you think I'll ever see Sarah again? I mean, in my lifetime. That she will come to see me, just as my father Tom visited the both of us many years ago?"

"I don't know the answer to that Jack. Only God knows. And although you may think time is passing slowly not seeing her, remember that when you are joined with her in the eternal light, this time on earth will seem like less than the blink of an eye. Goodbye, Jack. May God bless you and keep you."

With those words, Thomas vanished. Jack slowly rose and stepped out of the confessional. He could see that the church was still empty of parishioners, and that the light above the booth was no longer illuminated.

Before he left the church, he lit a candle and made a small donation in the money receptacle, saying as he did a brief prayer to Sarah to help him and to watch over him and Beth. Perhaps it was his imagination, but as he made his silent prayer, the candle flame seemed to flicker and dance as he watched. He gazed at the brightness of the flame as it glistened, and it reminded him of the sparkle and brightness in Sarah's blue eyes.

CHAPTER 26

It had been a few years since Jack's talk with Thomas Aquinas. He still deeply felt the staggering loss of Sarah, and there was an emptiness in his heart that would never be filled. But his faith had been restored. Even if he could never come close to overcoming his grief, he had taken the words of Thomas to heart and decided he could continue to live his life as the gift God gave him. Also, perhaps more so, to live for Beth—for her happiness and success.

His work at the Smithsonian was still quite demanding, but he gave Beth as much love and attention as he could—not only providing her the essentials of a happy home, but encouraging her in her academic pursuits. He also had continued his role as a proud parent, attending her high school lacrosse games whenever possible.

Since that time, Beth had graduated and moved on to Georgetown University, a dream she had to follow in the footsteps of her mother and father, which Jack shared. Beth had not only been a strong student, winning the high school award for history at her graduation (not unexpected by Jack), but she'd made the regional all-star lacrosse team as well. It was only natural that she was not only playing lacrosse on the Georgetown University Girls' Team, but that she had decided to major in history. (Again, not unexpected by Jack).

Beyond his dedication to work and Beth, Jack tried to do what he could to bring some small happiness to people's lives. He would often participate in his local church's Midnight Run, which delivered needed clothes to homeless people on the streets of D.C. or other nearby towns. He began a Christmas Toys for Children program at work, which with the help of many other employees and the large number of Smithsonian workers participating, became a huge success.

Every other month he, oftentimes with Beth, would drive down to Midlothian to spend an overnight with Bob. His stepfather was beginning to get up there in age, and Jack had convinced him to move into a retirement community that had the advantages of more people, amenities, and services. Bob had been good to Jack, and Jack loved him like a father. He promised himself he would always stay in close contact with Bob and support him in any way he could.

He also wanted both he and Beth to stay close to Sarah's family, not that he would have had a choice with Sarah's parents and the way they delighted in their granddaughter. Jack and Beth would visit them often, or the grandparents, now retired, would drive down to spend time in Reston. (In taking advantage of the plethora of things to do and see in the D.C. area, they were starting to become a bit of history buffs themselves). Every year, of course, Jack and Beth would drive to Lebanon to spend Christmas with the Mack family.

Jack was leading a full and busy life. He exercised at least a few days a week. He would occasionally go out with friends for dinner or drinks when he wasn't working late—so long as it didn't interfere with Beth. He would even play an enjoyable game of golf occasionally with John Carrol and two other old Georgetown buddies who still lived in the area.

But to Beth and others who knew him best, they could see that he would never be the same Jack again—not completely. Yes, he was a good man—personable, friendly, decent and caring—but there was a big part of him missing—Sarah.

Occasionally, after much coaxing from friends or family, he would even go out on a date with either someone he already knew, or someone a well-meaning match-maker thought he might like. To most people, he seemed almost like the old Jack, living proof that time heals all wounds. Jack would always be the same old gentleman, exhibiting his good sense of humor, talkativeness, and intellectual curiosity. Nevertheless, whether it lasted one date or (occasionally) a few, the women would always see that there would never be a real commitment from Jack. No indication that he was willing to take the relationship to the next level—no sign that he would ever see anyone else as a future partner.

It wasn't like he would talk about Sarah, unless he was asked, and then only briefly. It wasn't as if he wore Sarah on his sleeve, so to speak. Nonetheless, his dates could tell soon enough that Sarah was simply part of Jack's DNA. She was integral to his mind, heart and soul, and that would never change. Jack understood that, and not only did he accept it, he embraced it.

He embraced it wholeheartedly, just as he longed to embrace Sarah. He was still a young man in his early forties, in good health, and figured he would probably live for a long time yet. Every day he thought about Sarah coming to visit him, as so many others had. To his utter disappointment, she never came.

He found his and Sarah's wedding anniversary to be especially hard every time it came around. Beth, with her love for her father and her kind heart, would wish Jack "Happy Anniversary" with a kiss on the cheek every September 17. When she did, Jack would always be reminded of Sarah's same bright blue eyes.

CHAPTER 27

B eth was now in her senior year at Georgetown, and doing very well as a student-athlete. Jack and the rest of the family were all extremely proud of her. She was not only gifted, but a kind, strong and independent young woman. While a living reminder of Sarah, she was her own person.

She had recently become engaged to be married to another Georgetown student named James Avery, a finance major just like Jack had been. Jack liked James, who was smart and friendly, unpretentious and down to earth. Most of all, Jack liked him because he treated Beth with the same kindness and respect he had for Sarah. He could readily tell from the ease in their conversation, their laughter, and their body language, that they were very much in love. Secretly, the hope that Beth would meet someone like James was one of the reasons why he insisted she room and board on the Georgetown campus, rather than make the commute every day from Reston. He also thought living on campus was important so Beth could get the full experience of those four years, and be able to concentrate on her studies and extracurricular activities.

It was mid-February and Beth and James would be graduating in a few short months. James had been through several job interviews, and was being actively recruited by a few well-established financial companies in the D.C. area. Meanwhile, after serving a couple summers as an intern with the Smithsonian, Beth had been offered a job to work as an assistant project manager.

Jack was not at all concerned that it might look to some outsiders as a bit of nepotism or at least favoritism on the part of Jack or the Smithsonian. Jack had nothing to do with her hiring, as she was within a totally different part of the organization. Her bosses were so impressed with Beth's knowledge, attitude, and work ethic, that they assured Jack his employment there had absolutely nothing to do with her hiring. Jack was grateful for the somewhat backhanded compliment, as it was another confirmation that Beth's hiring was completely based on merit alone.

One Saturday afternoon, Beth and James had come to visit Jack before heading to a Georgetown basketball game. Jack thought to himself, *Yes, things are coming together nicely for Beth and James.* Jack joked to Beth, "Engaged, soon to be happily married and gainfully employed. What more would make a father prouder and happier after spending all that money on raising his daughter and paying most of her college expenditure?" He was not surprised that Beth gave him a combination cheerful, appreciative, but mockingly chilly look much the way her mother would have given Jack.

Shortly after Beth and James left for the game, Jack walked into the kitchen to whip up something to eat for dinner. He looked around in the refrigerator and pulled out a container of meatballs he had made a couple nights earlier. As he closed the fridge door and turned toward the cabinet to retrieve a package of spaghetti, he was startled to see a young boy sitting in the dim light at the kitchen table. The boy, about nine years old, wore gray britches with suspenders, a working-class wool jacket, and a woolen cap.

Jack froze for a second. (He was always a little startled by the sudden appearance of these visitors, especially since it had been a long time since the last one.)

"Hello, Mr. Moran," the boy said in what sounded like an English accent to Jack, but not cockney. "How are you?"

"Uuhh…hello young man. I'm fine. And who are you, may I ask?"

"My name is Andrew Watson. Originally from Glasgow, Scotland."

"Oh, a Scotsman," Jack replied smiling. "Nice to meet you. What brings you to my kitchen…uuhh…I mean, my house?"

"Well," young Andrew replied, "I guess you haven't been visited by anyone in quite a while. Not since Father Thomas. I'm guessing that might be because you've found your faith again, and your reason for living, so maybe God just didn't feel the need. I'm not sure, Mr. Moran. But He wanted me to see you, in any event, and to tell you a little of my story."

"Please, Andrew. Call me Jack. From your appearance, I'm guessing you'd be quite a bit older than me if you were alive today. Is that accurate?"

"Yes, Jack, that's certainly safe to say. You see, I was born in 1903, in Glasgow, as I said. My parents were Scottish. But when I was very young, we moved to Surrey, England, south of London. My father was a plumber.

"Life was hard for my parents, trying to raise me and two other siblings on meager wages. They both wanted a better life for us. My mother's sister and her family had immigrated to America in 1909, and wrote to us about the better life there. Both she and her daughter were working as domestics and her husband as a carpenter. So, my whole family decided to immigrate to the United States."

Jack was very attentive, but didn't quite understand yet the purpose of the visit. "Please, go on," Jack replied in a kind voice.

Young Andrew continued. "My family was originally supposed to leave England in October, 1911 on the *Philadelphia* passenger liner. But there was a delay because of a coal strike at the time. So, we rebooked on the *Titanic's* maiden voyage to New York City as third-class passengers, and left Southampton, England on April 10, 1912.

"As you well know, four days into the crossing, shortly before midnight on April 15, the ship hit an iceberg. About two-and-one-half hours later, with the bow of the ship rising out of the ocean as she sank, the Titanic split in two and sank. My entire family and I perished. Over 1,500 lives were lost, with only 706 survivors."

"I'm so sorry, Andrew," Jack responded sadly. "That was a tragic, needless accident that by all accounts could have been avoided. It was undoubtedly the worst maritime accident in history."

Young Andrew nodded in acknowledgment and continued. "My parents were so excited about the opportunities that lay ahead for us in America. Tragically, it was never to be. Perhaps the greatest tragedy was that fifty-three of the one hundred nine children on board...under the age of fourteen... sadly died. Fifty-two of those fifty-three were third class passengers. Just like me, and my younger brother and sister, they would never have a chance to experience the better life our parents sought.[1]

"Tragically, many of us should have been saved. There was capacity for 1,178 people in the lifeboats, but many left only partially filled. One boat had as few as twelve people in it, even though it had the capacity for sixty-five. One boat contained sixty-one men and only seven women. What happened to the code of chivalry of women and children first? Among the twenty lifeboats, only two returned after the ship sank to try to rescue survivors in the freezing water. Since death occurred in those temperatures of twenty-eight degrees in a matter of minutes, the lifeboats were only able to save five survivors."

Jack looked at Andrew, pitying him and the others who died, as though it had only happened yesterday rather than nearly a century ago. "I'm so sorry, Andrew, for all those who didn't have to die. Especially for you and the other children, who died so unnecessarily. And prematurely. But, I'm still not sure why you're *here*. Talking with *me!*"

Andrew looked up at Jack, with a sort of comforting expression that went well beyond his years. "It's difficult for me to say exactly, Jack. It has to do with these connections I have to others who have gone on to the afterlife with me, and what I know about your life, and your experiences. But somehow…I'm guided somehow to give you two messages…or thoughts, if you will."

"Messages from whom?" Jack asked.

"Oh, from people that have gone on before you. People like your father Tom, your mother. And Sarah."

Jack, who had remained standing all this time, almost fell forward toward Andrew. His eyes opened wide as if he had been kicked in the stomach. He asked in an almost pleading voice, "*Sarah? You've seen Sarah?*"

"Seen. Felt. I'm not sure how to describe it. You know what some of the others who have visited you have said. We're basically all connected, in some way, in the afterlife. The commonality we share is in knowing God's presence."

Jack asked desperately, "So, can you tell me about Sarah? Does she talk about me? Say anything about me? Why doesn't *she* visit me, no offense, instead of *you*?'

"Of course she thinks about you, Jack, and watches over you. She knows someday you'll be together for eternity. Sarah loves you very deeply. But you also know from the others, it's still a mystery why things happen the way they do, why she hasn't visited you. I don't have any answers for you, Jack. Only the two messages."

Disappointed that Andrew had no direct answers to give him with regards if and when he might see Sarah, Jack asked in a somewhat discouraged tone, "What are the messages then?

"Well, the first is to continue living your life to the fullest. For Beth's sake, for others, and for yourself. Even for Sarah, in a way, to honor and celebrate her memory. You know the expression about your time on earth being precious, a gift from the Divine? Try to live it the way Jesus showed us. And remember, live every day like it could be your last. Because, as someone once said, one day you'll be right!"

Recalling those same words uttered many years ago by Sigmund Freud, Jack replied, "Yes, I understand. It isn't easy without Sarah, but I'm trying." Pausing momentarily, Jack then said, a little dejectedly, "What's the second message?"

"Well, it must have something to do with why I was sent, my personal tragedy. But the second message is, when the time comes, don't be afraid. You'll know the right thing to do."

Jack seemed a little confused. "What does that mean? When what time comes?"

Andrew raised both hands, palms up, and shrugged his shoulders. "I really don't know Jack." Then smiling added, "Hey, I'm just an eight-year-old kid! But my heart tells me you'll know what it is, whenever the time comes. So long, Jack. I know when it's my time as well. So goodbye, and good luck!"

With those parting words, young Andrew was gone. Jack looked down at the meatballs he had placed on the table. But he wasn't hungry anymore. Instead, he made himself a drink, walked into the living room, and pulled out the wedding album photos of Sarah and himself. He whispered out loud, "I know you're watching over me Sarah, and you're always with me in my heart. I love you. And I know someday we *will* be together. For eternity."

CHAPTER 28

Nearly six weeks had passed since young Andrew Watson's visit. Not that Jack wasn't reasonably content with his life (or at least accepting of it), and how things were going before Andrew's visit. But Jack had taken great comfort in what the boy had said about Sarah, reassuring him he would be with her someday. His faith had been fully restored. Beth seemed happy that she would soon be married to James, and things were going well for Jack at the Smithsonian with his renewed focus as of late.

In fact, in a bit of a rarity for Jack, he was planning on meeting Beth and James at Georgetown University's McNeir Auditorium that night for a history lecture by the head of Georgetown's Department of History. The lecture was to be about the Battle of Gettysburg, a topic on which Jack and Beth shared a keen interest.

Jack planned to meet Beth and James at the Auditorium itself for the lecture, which was to start at 7 p.m. He left his office at the Smithsonian about 6:15, intentionally leaving his briefcase behind, to make his way to the L'Enfant Metro Station about a five-minute walk away. From there he would take the Metro to the Rosslyn Station, where he could catch a bus for the three-minute ride to Georgetown. That would enable him to arrive at the lecture shortly before it commenced.

Jack entered the L'Enfant Station at 7 Street, passing under the arched roof entranceway and making his way onto the escalator that would take him to the lower levels. The lower level for the Orange/Blue/Silver line that would take him to Rosslyn Station mirrored the arched roof at the entrance with its overhead concave structure. A center, one island platform separated the two sets of tracks, one going east and other west.

Jack took a position standing a few feet away from the westbound track, when the display monitor indicated his train would be arriving in one minute. The platform was only moderately crowded, with peak traffic usually occurring between 5:30 and 6 or so.

About five feet to his left a young Black woman neatly but casually dressed stood standing next to what appeared to be her son of about seven years old. She was not holding the boy's hand, as she was busy fiddling for something in her pocketbook, as the train approached.

For some reason, seeing the young boy made Jack think of his recent visitor, Andrew. Jack noticed the young boy seemed fascinated as he stared looking up at the intersecting vaulted ceilings and their unique "waffle" architectural design. For a brief moment the two exchanged glances, and Jack smiled, raising his eyes to the ceiling, as if to say, *Pretty cool, huh?* The young boy smiled back, and then bent his head slightly backward to peer at the ceiling once again.

Suddenly, while Jack and the woman's backs were facing the center of the platform, a somewhat short, stocky, disheveled man with a scruffy beard wearing a nylon sport coat came out of nowhere. With a giant push, the man shoved the small boy onto the tracks. As the mother screamed, Jack watched the boy sail through the air and land directly on the rails.

The culprit took off running before anyone realized what was happening, as Jack's eyes focused on the poor boy sprawled against the far side of the track rails. People nearby on the platform who could see what had just happened looked on in horror as the lights from the approaching subway train hurtled in from the tunnel at the other end of the platform.

Similar to Jack's experience with the rapidly descending airplane over the Potomac River those many years ago, time seemed to slow down for Jack. He realized it would only be a matter of seconds until the train would crush the young boy as it rambled into the station at about twenty miles per hour, each passenger-carrying car weighing roughly fifty tons.

Jack knew instantly what he had to do. He knew no one would be there to help him this time. He took one giant step forward and leaped onto the tracks below, twisting his ankle slightly in the process. With the train fast approaching, combined with his now weak ankle, Jack knew instantaneously that he would not have time to pick the boy up, carry him the few steps, and then lift him onto the platform. He also knew there was insufficient space between the track and the sidewall of the tunnel to stand safely alongside the rails out of harm's way from the thundering train.

The child lay sprawled on his stomach, moaning undoubtedly from the hard contact he had made when he landed on the tracks. Jack immediately grabbed the top of the boy's nylon jacket just below the boy's neck with his right hand. With his left hand, he grabbed the back of the boy's waistband and belt. Then, in one strong movement that was something between a shot put and a discus throw, with his legs bent but centered beneath his body, Jack lifted, rotated, and swung the boy as far and as high as he could toward the center platform. Another young man in his late 20s was fortunately standing in the right position at the edge of the platform to see what Jack was doing, and caught the boy to pull him away from the impact of the lunging train.

Jack knew there was no way or time for him to escape the tremendous blow he was about to take from the train that was now only a split second away from colliding with him. The train engineer had slammed on his brakes as soon as he saw the bodies standing on the track in front of him. Sadly, the laws of physics would not allow him to slow the train enough, much less stop it, in time to save Jack. Just as Jack could see the boy's feet clear the path of the deafening train, he felt the raw power of the lead car smash into him head on.

The momentum and mass of the train threw Jack several feet in the air, before falling beneath it as it roared over him. Without his body falling in a perfectly flat position on the tracks, the chassis of the train cars pummeled Jack's body further as it roared over him before the train finally came to a stop.

People on the platform gasped and screamed in horror. Given Jack's position under the train and difficult access, there was nothing they could do. That would be the work of the rescue personnel and paramedics, who arrived within five minutes of the accident.

The engineer opened the train doors in the car above Jack so the rescue workers could lower themselves into the narrow space between the car and the tunnel wall. Jack was in one piece and semi-conscious, but bleeding badly. Worst of all, he had suffered massive trauma to his head from when the train hit him.

The paramedics tried to stop the bleeding and administer some painkillers to Jack, after which the rescue team was able to extract him from under the train. Carefully, they placed him on a lightweight litter, raised him to the train door, and then moved him through the other side of the train to place him on a larger, mobile cot with rollers to transport him to the ambulance.

As the ambulance raced to BridgePoint Hospital Capitol Hill, located about two miles northeast of L'Enfant Station, Jack seemed to be aware of what had happened, despite going in and out of consciousness. He remembered literally tossing the young boy toward the platform as the train barreled down on him, at which point everything seemed to go black. In the ambulance, his mind wandered, first seeing images in his mind of the young Andrew Watson, then of the black slave Moses, who had appeared to him some years earlier. He even thought of the words of the troubled assassin, John Wilkes Booth, about someday maybe being asked to do something totally unselfish, to be a hero.

He awoke in a haze to see bright overhead lights and several people dressed in white and blue hospital garb surrounding him, as he lay flat. He realized he was being administered some type of medication and that he was hooked up to some machine. As his pain began to become more acute, Jack heard a doctor say something about morphine. Then everything went dark.

***

Beth started to become concerned when Jack hadn't arrived by 7:15 for the lecture at Georgetown. She became more worried when she tried calling him a few minutes later on his cell phone and did not get an answer. She was wondering what she should do or who she should call when her phone began to vibrate at 7:35.

She nodded to James, and immediately got out of her seat to exit the lecture hall, answering "Hello" in a soft voice as she walked down the main aisle toward the exit to the lobby.

"Hello, is this Beth Moran?" a woman asked on the other end. When Beth answered it was, the woman said, "Miss Moran, this is Nurse Davis from BridgePoint Hospital. We got your contact information from an ID card in your father's wallet. I'm afraid your father has been in an accident, and you need to come to the hospital immediately. Are you able to do that?"

Beth was momentarily stunned, but responded, "Yes, of course. Is my father alright?"

"He's been seriously injured, Miss Moran. I'm sorry, but I can't say any more until you come in and speak with the doctor. How quickly can you get here?"

Beth did not like the sound of that, but decided not to ask any more questions. She needed to get there as quickly as possible to see for herself. "I can be there in about thirty minutes."

"Okay," the nurse responded. Beth couldn't tell if she sensed fear, concern, or just routine professionalism in the nurse's voice. "Just come directly to the Emergency Room and ask for me, Nurse Davis, Okay?"

"Yes, thank you nurse, I'll be there as quickly as I can. Goodbye." Just as Beth was hanging up, James walked into the lobby and put his hand on her arm. "Is everything alright, Beth? You look anxious."

Beth was trembling slightly and spoke nervously. "My father's been in some kind of accident. The nurse couldn't say much but…I don't know, I feel like it's very serious, James. He's at BridgePoint Hospital. We need to get there right away."

"Oh no," James replied, putting his arms around Beth as she buried her head in his shoulder. "Come on, we can catch a cab a couple blocks from here just off campus."

***

Beth and James arrived at the hospital at 8:10 and went directly to the Emergency Room. The main reception console had four nurses sitting at their respective stations. When Beth identified herself and asked to see Nurse Davis, a middle-aged woman seated to the far right immediately spoke up. "Miss Moran? Hello, I'm Nurse Davis. Can you come with me, please?"

Beth was silent, her mind wandering in fear, thinking about the story her father had told her about going to the hospital with his mother at the time of his own father's car accident. Nurse Davis walked the couple to the elevator and pressed the button to go up. Beth introduced James to Nurse Davis as her fiancée as they waited for the elevator.

"I'm sorry, Miss Moran, but your father is in intensive care and in critical condition. I'm taking you to see Doctor Wallace, who is in charge of your father's care. He can tell you what he knows." Nurse Davis paused a moment, then added. "I just want to tell you from what I've been told, your father did a very brave thing tonight, Miss Moran, and saved the life of a young boy."

"What? I'm sorry," Beth stammered. "How? What happened?"

As they stepped off the elevator, Nurse Davis said, "I'll have to let Doctor Wallace fill you in on the details. Here is his office right here." She pointed to the second door on the right. "I'll find him and let him know you're here. You can have a seat in his office."

"Thank you," Beth said. They both sat down in the two chairs facing the doctor's desk, as James reached over to hold Beth's hand. Neither said anything, too upset to speak.

A minute later, Doctor Wallace walked into his office and introduced himself. While he was trying to be comforting, Beth could immediately tell by his expression that he did not have good news.

Doctor Wallace sat behind his desk and leaned forward with his hands folded in front of him. "Beth," he began, "your father suffered a very serious head injury that, unfortunately, has led to internal hemorrhaging and serious pressure on his brain. On top of that, he's had serious injuries to some of his internal organs and a few broken ribs."

"*Oh my God*," Beth cried, as tears welled in her eyes. "What on earth *happened* to him?"

Doctor Wallace looked into those bright blue eyes, and took a breath. "Beth, your father did a very courageous thing tonight", he said. "A young boy was apparently pushed onto the train tracks at L'Enfant Station while the train was coming into the station. The police are still looking for the man. But your father, according to witnesses, without any thought for his own safety, immediately jumped onto the tracks and somehow literally tossed the boy onto the platform a split second before the train crashed into your father."

Beth and James sat there stunned, not knowing what to say, until Beth moaned sorrowfully, "Oh Dad."

"Your father is a hero, Beth. I'm sorry, but unfortunately, his injuries are so severe, I'm afraid there's nothing we can do to save him. It's almost a miracle that he wasn't killed instantly. He somehow survived. Regrettably, he doesn't have long. The damage is just too great."

Beth began to cry quietly. "Is he conscious? Can I see him, or talk to him?"

Doctor Wallace nodded. "He has been in and out of consciousness. I was just with him, and he's conscious now. He can talk, albeit naturally a little haltingly in his condition. He's also on a lot of medication to ease his pain and to try to slow the swelling in his brain. However, that won't last too long. Frankly, I'm sorry, but he could go at any time. He asked to see only you when you got here. Alone, if that's alright?"

Beth looked toward James, who immediately said, "Of course. Beth, you had better go see him right away. I know how crushed you are, and how much he means to you. But you may not have much time."

Beth nodded, as Doctor Wallace took her by the arm and said, "James, you can wait here. I'll take you to his room, Beth." James squeezed Beth by the arm, saying I love you, without the words. She understood.

Doctor Wallace turned as he got to his office door and said, "I'll be back shortly, James."

"Thank you, Doctor," James replied, while thinking how deeply he was concerned for Beth's emotional state.

The Doctor went into Jack's room first to check on him ahead of Beth as she stood outside the door. Doctor Wallace returned in a moment and said, "He's conscious, Beth, and knows you're here. Remember, he's on a lot of medication, including morphine to ease the pain, so he may not always be coherent. You can see him now." He directed Beth into the room, closed the door behind her, and then turned to go back to his office.

Beth walked into the room slowly, her eyes fixated on her father lying in the hospital bed. He had a large bandage covering the entire top of his head. She could immediately see the bruises and lacerations on the side of his face. His right shoulder was completely wrapped from the top of his shoulder alongside his neck all the way down to his elbow, with a gown covering the remaining part of his upper body that otherwise would have been exposed. As she got closer, she could also see a bandage wrapped around his chest and ribs. As Doctor Wallace said, it was a miracle he was still alive.

Beth walked to a chair positioned alongside the opposite side of the bed, facing the door. She felt like she was going to break apart into fragments. She could barely stand looking at her father this way, and immediately sat down. Jack's eyes were closed when Beth touched his left hand, saying softly, "Dad, it's me. Beth."

Jack opened his eyes and turned his head toward his daughter. At first, he didn't say anything. Then, with some last remnant of his old self he jokingly said, "Beth. For a moment I thought I already died and was looking at an angel!"

Beth began to cry. "Oh, Dad. I'm so sorry. I don't want you to leave me. I love you."

"And I love you, Beth. With all my heart. But nothing is going to stop that now. And I'm so glad you have James now. I can see how much he loves you, and I'm leaving you in good hands." He smiled. "Sorry I won't be able to toast you at your wedding."

"Oh Dad," is all Beth could utter, as the tears rolled down her beautiful but anguished face.

"You remind me so much of your mother, you know?" Jack said proudly, wincing a bit as he tried to smile.

"You know how much I've missed her all these years. I'll be with her now. I know that to be true. In fact, that's what I wanted to talk to you about, why I know that's true. And I hope that will give you comfort."

Beth paused briefly before replying, "I don't know exactly what you mean, Dad."

"Well," Jack replied, pausing a moment, perhaps from a wince of pain despite the medication. "It's an incredible story, Beth. To most, an implausible, if not impossible story. Nevertheless, it's the truth, Beth. Just listen, and try to believe."

Beth had no idea what was coming. She just looked at her dying father, and listened.

Jack continued. "You know all those stories Mom and I would tell you growing up about the man, the fictional character we called Mr. Neach? About how people who had gone on to the afterlife, deceased people, would appear to him, and he would speak with them? And how he was the only one who could see and hear them…that was his ''gift'?

Beth didn't really know where her dad was going with this or what he was going to say. "Yes, of course I remember, Dad. I loved those stories."

"Well," Jack said, looking directly into Beth's eyes. "Not only were those stories true, but I was that man. They actually happened. In truth, *I* am Mr. Neach."

Beth didn't know how to respond. Naturally, her first thought was that between the medication and the swelling in his brain, her father was becoming delusional as he approached the end of his life. Certainly, she didn't want to hurt his feelings or mar their last moments together. He had always been a loving, caring father who, as far as she knew, never lied to her. So Beth simply responded, *"You're Mr. Neach?"*

Jack fought through the increasing pain. "Well, not exactly. Mr. Neach was fictional. I'm obviously real, and those things really happened....*to me!*

"All those stories Mom and I told you about Mr. Neach meeting Simon Peter, Sigmund Freud, Galileo, Elizabeth Barrett Browning and her "lady friends," Winston Churchill, the frontiersman, the sea captain, the others. All of them. Those few times you heard me talking to someone in my office at home with the door locked and Mom told you I was rehearsing for a presentation? I was actually talking to one of my 'visitors' as I called them. I came up with the name Mr. Neach, because the Scottish Gaelic word for *visitor* is *neach-tadhail*, so I just abbreviated it." Jack tried to smile. "Mom and I thought it had a nice ring to it.

"And though it was before you were born, you remember hearing the story about the airplane tragedy when Mom and I were attending Georgetown? How it crashed into the Potomac River, right?"

"Yes," Beth promptly replied, trying to be kind to her father in his final moments. "It's a great unsolved mystery, how all those people were somehow rescued and survived."

"Well," Jack said, "that's probably the most unbelievable story of all I have to tell you. It happened when I was driving home from Mom's parents' house during semester break. It was actually me, and a couple hundred men from the doomed *Arizona* destroyer sunk at Pearl Harbor in 1941. With God's help, we were able to rescue all those people, without anyone knowing. That's the answer to the mystery."

Beth couldn't help but wonder at how well-spoken and coherent her father seemed—despite being pumped full of medication—and delusional. She interrupted Jack, trying to both humor her father, and to keep up with him. "So Mom saw them—these visitors—too?"

Jack began to wince in pain again, and to open and close his eyes more slowly. Beth sensed that the end was near. In a somewhat more labored voice, Jack continued. "Actually, Mom was always aware when they were there with me by my reactions, but she only saw one of my visitors. That was my father Tom.

"We were in our first year at Georgetown, we were in love, and we had just pledged our love and life together, forever, when Tom appeared to us both. Of course, she was stunned at first, but Tom made it clear to her that his appearance would be an exception to my gift, which was meant to be mine alone. But he knew how necessary it was for her to understand it to understand me, and to be willing to be my partner and soulmate for the rest of my life."

Beth could only look on at her dying father and tell herself, that if this is how he wanted her to remember him, it was okay. She could give him that peace of mind in his final moments.

Jack began to struggle more, and his breathing became more labored. "Even the story I told you on that drive up to Grandma and Grandpa's one Christmas, about Mr. Neach meeting with St. Thomas Aquinas. That happened. I wanted you to know what he said, so that you could have the same faith that Mom and I had—have—that we'll all be together one day, in eternity."

Beth smiled at her father, saying, "Yes, Dad. I believe you. I have faith that we'll all be together one day. I love you." She knew he would find comfort in those words. She could cry after he was gone.

Jack squeezed her hand in recognition. "I love you too, dear."

At that moment, Jack turned his head away from Beth, raised his head slightly, and fixed his eyes straight ahead as if he was looking at something standing at the foot of his hospital bed. He let go of Beth's hand and raised his unbandaged arm up slightly, as if trying to reach out to someone. His eyes were fully open, and to Beth it almost looked like they were on fire the way they glimmered.

The expression manifested on his face was one of total joy and amazement. A single tear slowly fell down his cheek on the side Beth was sitting. For Jack, it was not a tear about death or dying, rather it was a wondrous, miraculous tear about life, eternal life, with his beloved Sarah. Still staring up and away, his hand out-stretched, Jack called out one last word. "*Sarah.*"

Jack's hand dropped slowly onto the bed covers. He lowered his head, and closed his eyes for the last time. Beth knew he was gone, and wondered whether he actually did see her mother in that final moment. Maybe he had. Maybe she would never know.

Beth held her father's hand again, looking at his face, and the peaceful expression he had. She thought about how much he had missed her mother. The love they had shared. "Goodbye, Dad. It's the end of your pain. I love you."

Beth lowered her head as she silently wept. She sat like that for a minute or two, when she suddenly saw a shadow spread across the bed where Jack lay, as if someone had stepped between him and the light over the inside of the door to the room. The door that was still closed.

Beth looked up to see a man with a gray beard about five or six inches long, a bit of a ruddy complexion, and close-cropped grayish hair standing on the opposite side of Jack's bed. He had a receding hairline, and somewhat large ears. Beth was struck by the white collar extending outward some three inches or so on each side of his neck and slightly above his somewhat stooped shoulders. He looked like someone from centuries long ago.

The door was still closed and Beth hadn't heard anyone come in. Her jaw dropped, bewildered at how this strangely dressed person just appeared out of nowhere.

The older man smiled kindly down on Beth and said, "Hello Beth. My name is Galileo dei Vincenzo Bonaiuti de' Galelei, but most people just call me Galileo. I'm a good friend of your father's."

Beth just stared, dumbfounded and confused, her mouth partially open. She glanced over to look at her father, whose facial expression might best be described as one of peace— and fulfillment. Slowly, in recognition of what Jack had just shared with her, she now understood what was happening. She realized what her father had told her was true.

Slowly, as if awakening to a new discovery, Beth smiled at the man named Galileo. And she believed.

And the Universe continued to expand.

John Kenyon

THE END
(OF THE BEGINNING)

NOTES

Chapter 3
1.   John 20:29 NLT

Chapter 7
1.   *"Galileo   Galelei,"   Wikipedia,*
     https://en.wikipedia.org/wiki/Galileo_Galilei.

Chapter 9
1.   *"Georgetown   (Washington,   D.C.),"   Wikipedia,*
     https://en.wikipedia.org/wiki/Georgetown_(Washington,_
     D.C.).
2.   "Georgetown   Historic   District,"
     https://www.nps.gov/nr/travel/wash/dc15.htm.
3.   *"Georgetown   University,"   Wikipedia,*
     https://en.wikipedia.org/wiki/Georgetown_University.

Chapter 10
1.   https://www.nps.gov/thingstodo/visit-the-national-mall-
     and-memorial-parks.htm.
2.   *"Smithsonian   Institution,"   Wikipedia,*
     https://en.wikipedia.org/wiki/Smithsonian_Institution.
3.   *"Lincoln   Memorial: Wikipedia,"*
     https://en.wikipedia.org/wiki/Lincoln_Memorial.
4.   *"Gettysburg   Address,"*   Wikipedia,
     https://en.wikipedia.org/wiki/Gettysburg_Address.
5.   *"Abraham   Lincoln's   second   inaugural   address,"*
     Wikipedia,
     https://en.wikipedia.org/wiki/Abraham_Lincoln%27s_seco
     nd_inaugural_address

Chapter 11
1.   *"Georgetown   (Washington,   D.C.),"   Wikipedia,*
     https://en.wikipedia.org/wiki/Georgetown_(Washington,_
     D.C.).

Chapter 13
1. *"Abigail Adams,"* Wikipedia, https://en.wikipedia.org/wiki/Abigail_Adams.
2. *The Wednesday Letters,* by Jason F. Wright, http://www.thewednesdayletters.com/famous_letters.php.
3. *"Alexandra Feodorovna (Alix of Hesse),"* Wikipedia, https://en.wikipedia.org/wiki/Alexandra_Feodorovna_(Alix_of_Hesse).
4. https://www.elephantjournal.com/2016/11/10-iconic-love-letters-for-the-incurable-romantic-in-all-of-us/.
5. https://www.bustle.com/p/11-love-letters-by-famous-authors-to-inspire-your-romantic-insta-captions-with-bae-2968946.
6. *"Elizabeth Barrett Browning,"* Wikipedia, https://en.wikipedia.org/wiki/Elizabeth_Barrett_Browning.
7. *"Clasped Hands of Robert and Elizabeth Barrett Browning,"* Wikipedia, https://en.wikipedia.org/wiki/Clasped_Hands_of_Robert_and_Elizabeth_Barrett_Browning.

Chapter 14
1. *"United States National Arboretum,"* Wikipedia, https://en.wikipedia.org/wiki/United_States_National_Arboretum.

Chapter 17
1. *"United States Capitol,"* Wikipedia, https://en.wikipedia.org/wiki/United_States_Capitol.
2. *https://www.geni.com/blog/7-things-you-may-not-know-about-winston-churchill-387466.html.*
3. *"Winston Churchill,"* Wikipedia, https://en.wikipedia.org/wiki/Winston_Churchill.
4. *https://www.nationalchurchillmuseum.org/churchill-address-to-congress.html#:~:text=Address%20to%20Joint%20Session%20of,of%20both%20branches%20of%20Congress.*
5. *https://winstonchurchill.hillsdale.edu/alexander-fleming-saved-churchill/.*

Chapter 18
1. *"Lebanon,   Pennsylvania,"*   Wikipedia, https://en.wikipedia.org/wiki/Lebanon,_Pennsylvania.
2. *"Hersheypark,"*   *Wikipedia, https://en.wikipedia.org/wiki/Hersheypark.*
3. *"Times   Square   Ball,"*   Wikipedia, https://en.wikipedia.org/wiki/Times_Square_Ball.

Chapter 19
1. *"USS   Arizona   (BB-39),*   Wikipedia, https://en.wikipedia.org/wiki/USS_Arizona_(BB-39).

Chapter 20
1. *"Louisiana   Purchase,"*   Wikipedia, https://en.wikipedia.org/wiki/Louisiana_Purchase.
2. *"Battle   of   Gettysburg,"*   Wikipedia, https://en.wikipedia.org/wiki/Battle_of_Gettysburg.
3. *"Battle   of   Midway,"*   Wikipedia, https://en.wikipedia.org/wiki/Battle_of_Midway.

Chapter 22
1. Etienne de Grellet, Quaker Missionary.

Chapter 23
1. *"Colonial   Williamsburg,"*   Wikipedia, https://en.wikipedia.org/wiki/Colonial_Williamsburg.

Chapter 25
1. *Tomas Aquinas, Human Suffering and the Unchanging God of Love,* Michael J. Doods, O.P., Dominican School of Philosophy and Theology, Berkeley, California (1991)
2. Matthew 25:35-36, 40 (NIV)
3. Matthew 22:37 (NIV)
4. Luke 22:42 (NIV)
5. Matthew 8:8 (NIV)

Chapter 27
1. "Titanic," Wikipedia, https://en.wikipedia.org/wiki/Titanic.

About the Author

John Kenyon has spent most of his career working in the financial services industry in the commercial real estate sector. He lives in New York and has a master's degree in urban planning from Columbia University. He married his beautiful college sweetheart, with whom he shares a love of American history, nature and family. Together they have four children. This is his first novel.

Made in the USA
Coppell, TX
31 August 2021